THE CROOKED ANGEL

Fair warning, Charles Cutter's Michigan-set murder mysteries featuring attorney Burr Lafayette are addictive. The author draws readers into Lafayette's cases with such ease they realize too late that even a writ of habeas corpus will not release them from the book until the last page is turned. Burr is not a criminal lawyer and only occasionally and reluctantly represents accused murderers. In the present case, his ex-girlfriend talks Burr into defending Brian, her sister's husband, who is accused of murdering his first wife. The trial takes place in Petoskey before a cantankerous judge and a prosecutor who hopes a conviction will launch his political career.

Lafayette is sure there is something odd in charging Brian with murder six years after his first wife's death was ruled accidental. His girlfriend, her sister and the accused all have trouble with the truth, and the prosecutor puts winning before the rule of law. The novel boasts a captivating courtroom drama full of striking twists and turns, great repartee, wonderfully odd minor characters, and a stunning denouement played out against the beautifully drawn backdrop of the Little Traverse Bay area.

Burr's law partner calls him, "half a step short of brilliant." The same could be said for this fourth in the series featuring Burr Lafayette, who is not half a step short of being an utterly fascinating character. As always, a Charles Cutter mystery is grand entertainment.

– Tom Powers, *Michigan in Books*

In *The Crooked Angel*, sleuthing attorney Burr Lafayette gets entangled in a dubious murder charge brought six years after the death. When Burr reluctantly takes up the defense at the insistence of a former lover, his motives aren't entirely pure. But what about hers? Burr outflanks a conniving prosecutor and an inept judge, only to realize that someone just might be trying to kill him, too.

With tight dialogue and a light touch, Charles Cutter's latest tale explores manipulation and misdirection, with compelling characters not always who they would seem to be. And as always, the tale is spiced with Burr Lafayette's ironic take on a legal system that seems just a little too cockeyed.

Not one to take the easy path when there's a way to complicate his life, Lafayette proves to be an entertaining champion in this exploration of truth, crime and consequences.

– Ben Beversluis, screenwriter of *From Wilderness to World Class*, and communications consultant

The fourth installment of the series takes the flawed lawyer-hero back to the 1980s, when he defended a man on murder charges despite never having handled a criminal trial.

The book is full of twists and surprises, enough to keep you turning the pages and needing to read just one more chapter.

Like the other Lafayette books, the courtroom scenes sparkle with Burr's often-wry interior commentary. Lawyers and non-lawyers will delight in how the evidence unfolds and how Cutter shades the presentation to create drama and uncertainty.

Cutter has a sharp eye for detail, and *The Crooked Angel*, set mostly in Petoskey, evokes a keen sense of place for that lakeside town and northern Michigan.

– Paul Fletcher, Editor, *Michigan Lawyers Weekly*

THE
CROOKED ANGEL

A BURR LAFAYETTE MYSTERY

Charles Cutter

MISSION POINT PRESS

Published by Mission Point Press
2554 Chandler Rd.
Traverse City, MI 49686
(231) 421-9513

www.MissionPointPress.com

ISBN: 978-1-954786-28-8
Library of Congress Control Number: 2021909884

Manufactured in the United States of America
First Edition/First Printing

Cover design: John Wickham
Interior design and layout: Bob Deck

For
Christi

"If only there were world enough and time enough, lady, this coyness be no crime."

Andrew Marvell
To His Coy Mistress

CHAPTER ONE

Saturday, December 17, 1977

Brian Dunn stood in his shirtsleeves, shivering in the cold. He watched his house from the sidewalk across the street. The snow had started falling again, and it softened the light in the picture window, blurring the edges of the Christmas tree lights, the old-fashioned kind. Big bulbs—red, blue, green, yellow, orange, and white. The kind that didn't blink.

They'd strung the lights, wrapped the garland and hung the ornaments. Brian was on the stool trying to straighten the angel when Claudia decided she didn't like the garland. The fight about the garland had stopped everything, and that's why the angel was crooked. Brian had gone down to the basement. Claudia followed him down, and that's where he'd left her, lying at the bottom of the stairs.

Chad, their sixteen-year-old son, came out of the house sobbing and covered in blood. The next-door neighbor followed him out. She put her arm around his waist and walked him over to her house.

The Christmas tree in the window started to teeter, swaying back and forth. Once, twice, three times. Then it tipped over.

Brian thought the paramedics must have knocked it over with the gurney.

The cop came out and walked to his patrol car. He turned off the flashers, then waved at Brian to come back across the street.

Brian started back just as the coroner came out, the paramedics behind him wheeling the gurney with Claudia inside a body bag.

***

Earlier that day, they'd slipped into the woods on a two-track north of Harbor Springs, just east of Larks Lake Road, near the prison. They weren't supposed to cut their tree until Sunday, but Claudia said she had to do something at church so they'd moved it up a day. Brian had still wanted to go on Sunday, but Claudia had said no. He hoped Saturday would work out.

Brian was just over six feet. He looked like he had been an athlete, but his stomach stuck out beyond his chest. Short, sandy hair, thinning in back, retreating in the front. Gray eyes, broad nose, straight but yellow teeth, square jaw, red face. He was good looking, but the extra pounds had rounded and softened his square features.

It had started snowing when they parked in the clearing where the tree was. He'd had his eye on it all deer season. It was a white pine, about eight feet tall. He'd have to cut about a foot off the bottom to make room for the angel.

The tree was on state land, which made cutting it illegal, except that around here nobody thought very much about cutting your own Christmas tree on state land. Which was, after all, public.

Chad built a fire before they cut the tree. He sharpened sticks to roast marshmallows and melted snow for hot chocolate. Brian spiked his with peppermint schnapps, which Claudia didn't like.

Brian thought she was getting skinnier every day despite the fact that she ate like a horse. The more she ate, the skinnier she got. And the fatter he got. It was almost as if what she lost, he gained. He thought she'd gotten meaner, too. Skinnier and meaner.

Chad said the Christmas tree prayer Brian had made up years ago. *"Great Spirit, the season of darkness is upon us. Our earth is without life. Give us your gift of life through the eternal green of this tree. We accept this gift mindful that, as we take the life of this tree, we take it into our home so that the green of its needles reminds us of past summers and gives us hope for the new life of spring. For your gift of life, we give our thanks. Amen."* Claudia thought the prayer should have been about the birth of Jesus.

After the hot chocolate and marshmallows, Chad smothered the fire with snow. The steam smelled like ashes. Brian threw the tree in the bed of the pickup.

They started back up the two-track. The pickup skidded in and out of the two-track. The tree bounced up and down in the truck bed.

"Brian, slow down," Claudia said. "You'll shake all the needles off before we get home."

Brian had seen her looking at the bouncing tree through the outside mirror. He'd seen the bouncing, too, but hadn't paid any attention to it.

Claudia had been softer when they had met, attractive in a mousy sort of way, with shoulder-length black hair. But now it was salt and pepper, mostly salt. He wished she would color it. She had thin lips and no eyebrows to speak of. She rubbed them when she was anxious, which was most of the time.

"We could have bought a tree in town," she said.

"No, we couldn't," Chad said. "We've always cut our own tree." He sat in the middle, between the two of them. Black hair stuck out underneath his stocking cap. He looked like a taller, leaner version of Brian, except for his hair, which was like his mother's used to be.

By the time they got back, it had stopped snowing. Brian parked in the driveway and hoisted the tree out of the pickup. Chad dragged it across the snow and into the garage through the side door. Brian cut off the bottom foot of the tree and then a foot of branches. Claudia would make a wreath out of them. He pounded the butt end of the trunk into prongs in the bottom of the Christmas tree stand. He stood the tree up and Chad twisted the screws into the trunk. Brian smelled the sweet smell of the sap as it oozed out.

Brian shook the rest of the snow off the tree and carried it into the house. Chad had found the Mitch Miller Christmas album and it scratched away on the record player they used once a year while trimming their tree.

"You're ruining the carpet," Claudia said.

"It's just water."

"No, it's not. There's mud on that tree and on your boots, too."

Brian looked down at his boots and then at his footprints. He started back toward the door.

"Stop. Stop right there," Claudia said. "There's just more mud if you go back. Stand right there and take them off."

Brian's ears turned red and he felt them burn. "Claudia, just how am I supposed to do that?"

"I don't care how, but I will not have my carpet ruined over a Christmas tree."

"For Christ's sake, Claudia, what am I supposed to do?"

"Don't talk like that."

Brian took his boots off and handed them to Chad, who took them to the garage. Chad disappeared into the kitchen and buzzed back in with three glasses of spiced wine on a tray. Each glass had "Merry Christmas" on it in red and green letters. The wine smelled like cinnamon and cloves.

Brian reached for a glass, stumbled. His wine splashed onto the carpet. Chad ran back into the kitchen.

"Don't say a word," Brian said. "Not a word. We'll clean it up."

Chad ran back in with a pan of cold water and a sponge. He soaked up the wine, then rinsed out the carpet. Brian hoped it was clean enough to avoid buying Claudia new carpeting. She left in a huff.

Brian and Chad started decorating the tree by themselves. They wound the lights around the tree. Then Chad strung the faded gold garland all around. Then they hung the ornaments.

Claudia stormed back in. "My God that garland is ugly. Take it off."

"We always put this garland on," Chad said.

"It's so old and faded," she said.

"Let's put the angel on now," Brian said. "Then we're done."

"Take off the garland."

"Claudia, we always put this garland on."

"It's ugly."

"I'll take it off," Chad said.

"Let's just put the angel on and call it good," Brian said.

"Chad, take off the garland."

Brian took the garland off the tree, then he took their Christmas angel out of its box. He climbed on a stool, put the angel on top of the tree and climbed down.

"The angel's crooked," Claudia said.

"I've got an idea," Brian said. "You be the angel this year. I'll shove the tree up your ass, and you can sit up there for two weeks."

Brian opened the door to the basement. He started down the stairs, slamming the door behind him. He ran his hand along the fieldstone wall on his way down, the fieldstones rough to the touch. He stopped and looked at one of the rocks, pink granite with gold flecks.

He sat on a stool at his workbench. He thought he'd be safe down here. Claudia never came down to the basement since he'd moved the washer and dryer to the room off the kitchen.

He saw his deer rifle leaning against the wall, right where he'd left it after Trevor brought it back. He picked it up and laid it on the workbench.

The gun was dirty and had started to rust. The clip was still in it. He thought it was just like Trevor to return a loaded rifle. The clip looked like it was full, but it was spring-loaded, so he couldn't tell for sure. At least the safety was on. He pushed the catch that held the clip in the gun and pulled it out. He racked the bolt to make sure there was no bullet in the chamber.

He wiped off the stock with a towel. Then he worked linseed oil into the stock with his fingers. He spilled some of the oil onto his shirt.

Claudia will give me hell for this.

He poured gun oil on a rag. The smell of the oil reminded him of the electric train his father had given him when he was nine. He ran the rag up and down the barrel, rubbing away the rust.

Chad bent his head down the stairs. "Mom wants you."

"Tell her I'm busy."

"She said she wants you right now."

"Just tell her I'm busy."

Chad left. Brian went back to wiping down the barrel.

Claudia came to the doorway and yelled down the stairs. "Goddamn it, Brian. I said I wanted to talk to you."

"Listen to yourself. You're a bitch, a raving bitch." He started cleaning around the trigger.

"You will not talk to me like that."

"For Christ's sake, Claudia, give it a rest."

"I hate you. You know that, don't you?"

"Leave me alone."

Claudia started down the stairs.

"Don't come down here."

She looked over at him. "What are you doing down here?"

The gun went off. The crash deafened him, and his ears rang. The rifle fell to the floor.

Then he saw Claudia. The bullet had ripped through her side and thrown her against the wall. She lay in a pool of blood at the foot of the stairs. Blood dripped off the fieldstone. She stared at him, her eyes fixed.

CHAPTER TWO

Six Years Later

Burr knew the wind had shifted when one of the shutters on his cabin had started banging. It only talked to him when the wind blew hard from the southwest. He'd never fixed that shutter because that wind brought good news — big waves on Lake St. Clair that blew the ducks off the lake and into the marsh.

An hour before sunrise, they bucked the chop in the Johnson River, the decoys rolling around the bottom of the boat. Burr slowed down and shined his light on the bank until he found a break in the cattails that marked the entrance to Walpole Marsh. He turned off his light, beached the boat, pulled it over the dike and motored to Holiday Pond.

It started to snow, a fine, light snow, but the wind blew hard, and the snow stung Burr's face. Clouds covered up what was left of the moonlight, but he could see orange off to the east. This would be a day when it never really got light. A gray December day.

He dropped Victor and Zeke, his aging yellow lab, off at the blind, set the decoys, then hid the boat in the cattails.

Burr Lafayette was in his late forties. He'd duck hunted since he was twelve. His first hunt had been with Victor. At one time, Burr had been six feet tall. He was still lean. He had sky blue eyes, a hawk nose, strong jaw and straight white teeth. His hair, the color of an acorn, was thinning just a bit in back. He had a few grays, but he pulled them out as soon as they came in.

He slipped over the side of the boat and slogged back to the blind, his waders sinking in the muddy bottom, the rotten-egg sulfur smell blowing downwind. He climbed into the stake blind and sat in a rusty folding chair, Victor on one side, Zeke on the other.

Burr reached into his bag and handed Victor a pack of Players, honoring a chief with a gift of tobacco. Victor Haymarsh was sixty-five and looked it. Short, stocky, leathery. A black ponytail streaked with gray.

Victor handed Burr a cigarette. Duck season ended in a week and so would his smoking.

It was almost light. Three ducks buzzed the pond. Zeke quivered. Burr looked down, hiding his face, and called. He turned his head and tried to see out the corner of his eye, careful not to spook them. Two mallards and a black duck. They circled downwind. He called again. The ducks fought their way upwind and circled the decoys. Burr called softly. The ducks cupped their wings, rocking back and forth, spilling the wind from their wings.

"Mark," he said under his breath. He stood and swung the shotgun through the lead duck, a drake mallard. It splashed in the pond. The black duck sailed into the cattails after he shot it.

"Zeke, fetch."

The dog launched himself into the pond and retrieved the mallard. Burr gave Zeke a line and sent him into the cattails. He and Victor smoked another cigarette.

A marsh hawk flew low, flat circles where the duck had gone down.

"If Zeke doesn't find it, that hawk will," Victor said.

"He'll find it."

Detroit was across Lake St. Clair, just twenty miles to the southwest. Here though, in Ontario, a ferry ride across the St. Clair River, it was a different world. Not really Canada but Walpole Island, the largest freshwater marsh on the Great Lakes. The unceded land of the First Nation, the Council of Three Fires — the Ojibwe, the Odawa, and the Pottawatomie.

Zeke swam out of the cattails with the black duck in his mouth.

***

Zeke's head jerked up. Burr looked across the pond and saw Suzanne in his boat, poling over to the blind.

"That one, she's a beauty," Victor said.

"Damn it all."

She hid the boat and climbed into the blind. Her parka and her waders hid her curves, but Burr remembered all of them. She was just shy of six feet, a head taller than Victor.

Victor nodded at her and left.

Burr watched him slog through the marsh to his boat. Victor hitched himself into his boat, stiff-legged, and left.

His knee must be bothering him again.

"Why did he leave?" Suzanne said.

"Because you came."

"I didn't mean to chase him away."

Suzanne had her hair in a ponytail, a little shorter than Victor's, but very black. Green eyes and pouty lips.

Perfectly lovely.

"How did you find us?"

"It's too rough to get out to the lake." She sat in Victor's chair, loaded her over-under, locked the barrels into the stock and checked the safety.

Burr lit a cigarette. Suzanne took it out of his mouth and smoked it. He lit another.

"Don't you want to know why I'm here," Suzanne said.

"No."

"There's been a terrible injustice."

Burr ignored her.

"A man has been arrested for murder."

I don't want to know anything about this.

"There was an accident in Petoskey six years ago. And now he's been arrested for murder and hauled off to jail."

"An accident?"

"The police broke into his house in Grosse Pointe and hauled him off to jail."

"I thought you said Petoskey."

"The accident happened in Petoskey, but now he lives in Grosse Pointe."

"I'm not a criminal lawyer."

"You're a trial lawyer. You know how to do it."

"Not anymore, and I'm not qualified to do this."

"You are perfectly qualified."

Burr looked over the tops of the cattails. Some of the tops had gone to seed. The wind blew them off and it looked like snow.

"You practically grew up in Petoskey."

"Summers only. And it was Harbor Springs."

"As a favor to me," Suzanne said.

"I'm all out of favors."

***

Suzanne had walked into his life four years ago. He'd been looking out the windows of his office but not really looking at much of anything. Her scent reached him before he knew she was there. Rose. It had been rose, but smoky underneath.

He turned and saw her framed in the doorway. Striking. Not beautiful. Maybe thirty. Tall, narrow waist, long legs. A jet-black ponytail and pouty, wine-red lips. She had green eyes. The iris of her right eye had gold flecks. Not beautiful, maybe not even pretty, but she took his breath away.

She'd arrived unannounced, the way she always arrived. A copywriter for a big Detroit ad agency. She'd been sent from New York to Detroit to work on a car account, and she hated Detroit. Suzanne had written the copy that had gotten the agency sued, so they hired Fisher and Allen. Burr ran the litigation practice from the 36th floor of the Renaissance Center in downtown Detroit.

She stuck her hand out. "Suzanne Fairchild."

Burr lost his place. Speechless, which, for Burr, was nothing if not unusual. "Are you Mr. Lafayette?"

"Yes. Yes, I am."

"The agency said you need to talk to me."

"Please. Have a seat." She started to sit at one of the side chairs facing his desk.

"No, not there. Please, on the couch." He pointed to a leather couch fronted by a glass coffee table and flanked by a matching chair.

"Are you all right, Mr. Lafayette?"

Burr absolutely was not all right. He couldn't concentrate. His partners protested duck season as it was, but Suzanne Fairchild would be taking things too far. And then there was Grace.

***

Suzanne knocked down a drake mallard in the cattails. Burr gave Zeke a line and sent him.

"He's a great dog, even at nine. But I'd never name my only son after a dog," Suzanne said.

"You don't have a son, and he's not nine. He's eight."

Zeke-the-dog splayed his front legs on the floor of the blind, his back legs still in the ooze. He presented the duck to Burr.

"There is no greater honor than to be Zeke's namesake. Besides, Zeke-the-boy likes it."

"What a way to go through life. Zeke-the-boy because there already is a Zeke-the-dog."

"Suzanne, I can't help you. I'm not a criminal lawyer. I don't do criminal work, and I don't know anything about criminal law."

"Please."

"Jacob and Eve wouldn't hear of it."

"He's going to be charged with murder. By now, he probably has been. His wife is hysterical."

"He has a wife? Does he have a name?"

"Yes, he has a wife. And she needs someone to help her." Suzanne reached into Burr's coat and took out a cigarette. She pulled her parka over her head and lit the cigarette out of the wind.

***

His Jeep skidded on the way back to the ferry, fishtailing on an icy spot. A Grand Wagoneer, blue with fake-wood sides and a rear window that didn't work right. It fogged up with Zeke in the back.

I love this Jeep.

Burr turned along the St. Clair River, Suzanne following in a white Explorer. They drove onto a ten-car ferry with twin diesels and painted-over rust.

There was ice in the river, and they had to wait for it to clear. When the ferry finally left for Algonac, Suzanne climbed in beside him. The windows had fogged up. Suzanne rubbed a porthole on the windshield and looked out.

"We're only half an hour from Grosse Pointe. Just help me get the bail posted. That's all."

"Can't do it, Suzanne."

"Please, Burr."

"Hire a real criminal lawyer. Or get a public defender."

"His wife is scared to death. She hasn't heard from him since Saturday night."

"Almost two days," Burr said.

"Just help me get him out, then you can get back to your esoteric appellate practice."

"I don't have time."

"You can't be that busy if you've got time to hunt on a Monday."

"Who would pay?"

"They would."

"Do they have a name?"

"They'd pay. Over time."

Who is they?

"It's not my scintillating mind you want. It's my fee schedule."

"That's not it at all," Suzanne said. "They have money. Well, some money."

"I don't work for free."

"So it's just about money."

"It's not just the money."

"He's been jerked out of his life and all you can think about is money."

"Why do you care about this so much?"

She got out of the Jeep and slammed the door. Burr watched her in the rearview mirror.

There's something she's not telling me.

The ferry docked at Algonac. After they cleared customs, Suzanne climbed back in the Jeep.

"Please help me. Just this one thing."

"I thought you moved back to Manhattan."

"I did. I wouldn't be here if it weren't for Brian and his wife."

"His name is Brian?"

Suzanne looked away, then nodded.

"Just who is Brian's wife?"

As if I didn't know.

CHAPTER THREE

Burr parked in front of the police station. He stepped around a puddle and opened the door for Suzanne. When they walked inside, Burr heard a woman pleading with the duty officer.

"Where is my husband?"

I knew it would be Lisa.

Burr and Suzanne walked up to the counter. Suzanne put her arm around Lisa, her younger sister.

"You took him Saturday. It's Monday and I haven't heard from him."

Lisa had shoulder length hair, honey blond, and a small, upturned nose. She was short, five-two maybe, and a little plump. Early thirties. She didn't look like Suzanne. She was attractive, pretty, fifteen pounds ago.

"Where have you been?" Lisa said.

"We got here as soon as we could," Suzanne said.

"Here's my lawyer," Lisa said to the cop at the desk. To Burr, "Please help me find my husband."

"I'm not your ..."

Suzanne cut him off. "Where is Brian Dunn?"

"Who are you?" the cop said.

"Co-counsel," Suzanne said.

I'm pretty sure she hasn't gone to law school since she left Detroit.

"Where is he? You can't arrest someone and then lose them for two days," Lisa said. She twirled a strand of her hair.

"Day and a half," the cop said. He shuffled through a pile of papers.

Burr looked around the room. For all the time he'd lived in Grosse Pointe, he'd never been in the Grosse Pointe Park police station.

It looks more like a waiting room in a dentist's office than a police station.

Suzanne bumped him with her hip. "Pay attention."

The cop kept shuffling his papers. Then he picked up the phone, said something Burr couldn't hear and hung up. More shuffling.

A gray-haired cop came in from the bowels of the building carrying a file. "Mr. Dunn is not here," he said.

"Did you let him go?" Lisa said, still twirling her hair.

"We never booked him," the gray-haired cop said.

"You arrested him. Where is he?" Suzanne said.

Burr couldn't see why they needed him. He thought about Zeke in the back of the Jeep and wondered if he was getting cold. Then he thought about Zeke-the-boy, now eight and only a mile or so from here. Maybe he should stop by.

Grace wouldn't like that.

"The chief didn't want a murderer here. The paperwork didn't get filed because it was Sunday. Mostly, though, there was no room," said the cop with the gray hair.

"He didn't murder anyone," Lisa said. "Where is he?" she said again.

"We released him to the Detroit Police," said the gray-haired cop.

***

The three of them rode in silence. Not an awkward silence. A stony silence.

Suzanne had led him on. If she'd come right out and said that it was Lisa's husband who had been arrested, he never would have let it get this far. Lisa had never liked him. She didn't approve because he was almost twenty years older than Suzanne. It had gotten worse when she found out that he'd been married the whole time.

They were on their way to the Fifth Precinct, but none of them knew how to get there. Burr looked in the rearview mirror. The back of the Jeep was fogged up except for the four lines of the rear defroster that still worked. The Jeep smelled like a wet dog, which was fine with Burr.

Grosse Pointe was too proper for a murderer, he thought. That was just like Grosse Pointe. Drunks and druggies, as long as they were residents. No murderers, though.

***

"What do you mean, gone?" Lisa said to yet another duty officer, this one at Detroit's Fifth Precinct. She started to cry.

"Somebody picked him up a couple hours ago," the cop said.

"Who?" Suzanne said.

He read from a file. "Says here ... Emmet County Sheriff." He looked up. "File says he was released to a deputy who said he was taking him to Petoskey."

"You arrested this poor man two days ago. No one has heard from him, and now he's gone," Suzanne said.

"Before my shift," said the cop.

Suzanne jerked the file from him.

"He didn't murder her," Lisa said.

Burr looked over her shoulder. The People of the State of Michigan had charged Brian Dunn with the murder of Claudia Dunn. Open murder. *That could be anything from negligent homicide to first-degree murder.*

"Who's Claudia Dunn?" Burr said.

"Never mind. We have to go to Petoskey," Suzanne said.

***

The snow started at Flint, a light, dry snow. By the time they got to Saginaw, the snow was heavy and the traffic on I-75 had slowed to twenty-five. The windshield wipers couldn't keep up with the snow, and the defroster wasn't working right. Burr wiped off the windshield with his sleeve. The Jeep ground through the right lane in four-wheel drive. The left lane was impassable.

Burr thought they needed him for his four-wheel drive, not his lawyering. Which was fine with him. He'd drop them off in Petoskey and that would be the end of it.

"For the fifth time, Brian didn't murder anyone," Suzanne said from the backseat.

Burr looked at the two of them through his rearview mirror. "Is someone dead or not?"

"Well, yes, it happened," Lisa said. "Brian didn't mean to kill her." She rubbed an eyebrow. "It was an accident."

The Jeep jumped out of the ruts carved in the right lane. Burr jerked the wheel and the Jeep bounced back in.

"Is she or is she not dead?" Burr said.

"She's deceased," Lisa said.

"And did Brian kill her?" Burr said.

"No," Suzanne said.

"It was an accident," Lisa said.

I'm getting tired of twenty questions.

"It was six years ago, and Lisa wasn't there. No one was there except Brian and Claudia. It was an accident. Brian was cleaning his deer rifle in the basement. Claudia came downstairs to talk to him. The gun went off accidentally and killed her. The sheriff thought it was an accident. So did the coroner. No charges were brought."

I guess that's why I never heard anything about it.

The Jeep lurched out of the ruts again. When the wheels grabbed, he eased back in. Ahead, lights flashed at the Standish exit, where state police had shut down the freeway.

"We're going to have to stop for the night," Burr said.

"No, we're not," Suzanne said.

***

The state police closed I-75 Monday night and kept it closed all day Tuesday. Burr, Suzanne, and Lisa had crawled on Old US-23 to the Wayfarer, a long, gray motel left behind when the freeway opened.

Burr left the room arrangements to Suzanne. She took two rooms, which he thought could be promising. He should have known better. Suzanne and Lisa took one room, Burr and Zeke, the other. Fortunately, there was a bar across the street.

***

The freeway reopened the next morning, and the three of them arrived in Petoskey just as Brian was being arraigned. They'd been half a step behind from the start.

Petoskey was on the south side of Little Traverse Bay, about three hundred miles north of Detroit and about thirty-five miles south of the Mackinac Bridge. Harbor Springs, ritzier than Petoskey, was across the bay and where Burr had spent his summers growing up.

The Victorian courthouse was built in the late 1800s just as the loggers finished clear cutting the white pine. The oak-paneled courtroom had seen its share of murders in the logging days, but now the chambers heard mostly divorce and zoning cases as families and land subdivided.

Petoskey, Odawa for "rising sun," was named after an ancient Odawa chief, as was the Petoskey stone, a fossilized crustacean with a pattern like a rising sun.

Burr, Suzanne and Lisa walked into the courtroom just as Brian was being charged. They sat in the back row, the only ones in the courtroom other than the litigants.

Brian sat at the defense table next to a young man in a sincere blue suit.

He must be the public defender.

The judge, a fat, bald man in his sixties, tapped his gavel in the palm of his hand. His shiny brass nameplate read, *Honorable Benjamin R. Gillis.*

The bailiff, a short man with a full head of blond hair, a pleasant but crooked smile and matching crooked teeth, sat off to the right of Gillis. He wore the uniform of the sheriff's department — a dark brown shirt, tan slacks and sidearm. The court reporter, a dowdy, middle-aged woman with the longest fingers Burr had ever seen, sat in front of Gillis.

"Anything else, Mr. Truax," Judge Gillis said.

A tall, gangly man in his mid-fifties stood.

He must be the prosecutor.

His eyes bulged in their sockets and his Adam's apple stuck out like a golf ball. He had a beak for a nose and wore wire-rimmed glasses.

"No, Your Honor."

He doesn't look like a pleasant person.

"Calvin, you better have something here." The judge turned to Brian. "Brian Dunn, stand up."

Brian sat there.

The young man in the sincere blue suit stood.

"Stand up, Mr. Dunn," Gillis said.

Brian rose, legs apart, shoulders back, his stomach hanging over his shirt.

He looks like an athlete gone to seed.

"Brian Dunn, today, December 13, 1983, you are charged with murdering Claudia Dunn on Saturday, December 17, 1977. The charge is open murder. How do you plead?" Judge Gillis said.

Brian mumbled. Burr couldn't make out what he'd said.

Gillis thumped his forehead. He put on a pair of reading glasses and looked through a file on his desk.

"The court notes that the defendant does not respond and determines that he stands mute. Therefore, a plea of not guilty is entered." The judge shuffled through some papers. "The preliminary exam will be February 6, 1984." Gillis banged his gavel. "We are adjourned."

"Your Honor?" said the young man in the blue suit.

"What is it, Mr. Dickson?"

"I'd like to request bail for my client."

"Bail?"

The prosecutor leapt out of his chair. "Your Honor, the defendant has just been charged with murder. There should be no bail."

The public defender shifted his weight from one foot to the other. "It was an accident, and it happened six years ago."

"He's a flight risk," Truax said, his Adam's apple bobbing.

Gillis thumped his forehead again. He looked at Truax over his reading glasses. "I hardly think so. Bail is set at one million dollars. That means you need a hundred thousand to make bail." He slammed down his gavel. "We're adjourned."

***

Burr and Suzanne sat across from Lisa and Brian at a beat-up table in the visitors room on the first floor of the courthouse. It was dreary, with formerly white walls and dingy gray tile. There were no bars on the windows.

Emmet County has a more casual approach to murder than Detroit. Lisa squeezed Brian's hand. "Why didn't you call? We looked all over for you."

"They only gave me one call before, and the line was busy."

"Baby, I'm so sorry. Have you slept at all?"

"Not really."

"You look terrible," Lisa said.

"I feel terrible."

"Burr's going to get you out," Lisa said.

Burr drummed his fingers.

"I have a lawyer," Brian said.

"Burr's going to get the bail reduced," Suzanne said.

Brian looked at Suzanne, then Burr. "I thought you hated Burr."

You could put groceries in the bags under his eyes.

"He's going to get you out of jail," Lisa said.

"When?"

"As soon as he can get in to see the judge."

Burr kept drumming his fingers.

"Would you please stop that," Suzanne said.

Burr looked over at Suzanne and stopped the drumming. "Brian, tell me what happened."

"It was a long time ago. Six, maybe seven years."

"No, not that. I don't care how you killed Claudia. Tell me about your arrest."

CHAPTER FOUR

The wind screamed down Lake St. Clair and blew the Christmas tree off the roof of the Suburban. It somersaulted over the hood and Brian drove over it. Becky screamed from the backseat.

Brian pulled over and got out of the Suburban. The waves crashed against the beach along Lake Shore Drive. It smelled like wet sand and dead fish. He crabbed his way over to the tree, picked it up, shook off the slush and started back to the Suburban. It wasn't quite five o'clock, but all the cars had their lights on, and they all honked at him as they passed.

The tree had blown off just past the Grosse Pointe Yacht Club. Brian expected the Grosse Pointe Shores police to show up any minute. He didn't think they had much else to do.

He jumped when he saw flashing lights, but it was just Lisa, who had turned on the Suburban's emergency flashers.

It had been six years since he'd closed his practice and they'd moved to Grosse Pointe. He still wasn't used to paying for a Christmas tree. Bird's Christmas Tree Farm in Clarkston wasn't the same as cutting your own tree in the woods, no matter what Lisa said. They cut their own tree, but the Scotch pines all grew in rows. Becky liked to ride on the hay wagon, even if it was pulled by a tractor. She liked the cider even though it tasted like a plastic jug. She liked the doughnuts, which Brian thought tasted like cardboard, but this was all she knew.

Brian tied the tree back on the roof and climbed back in the Suburban.

"Nice work on the tree, love," Lisa said.

"I always just threw it in the back of the pickup."

"No one has a pickup in Grosse Pointe."

"Did the tree get hurt, Daddy?"

"No, baby, it's fine."

They splashed through Grosse Pointe Farms, the City of Grosse

Pointe, and were halfway through Grosse Pointe Park, the oldest of the old money, when the tree started to move around again. Brian looked up.

"Watch where you're going," Lisa said.

Grosse Pointe Park, the oldest of the five Grosse Pointe suburbs: five small, old-brick enclaves next to Detroit on the shore of Lake St. Clair. The rich, the very rich, and the somewhat rich lived in the Grosse Pointes, but just inside Grosse Pointe Park there were a few blocks where the not-so-rich lived. They made their living by selling things to the various rich. Ten blocks into Grosse Pointe Park, Brian turned onto a tree-lined, unassuming, dream-come-true street. Not Brian's dream, but someone's.

He pulled into the driveway of their smallish two-story colonial, vintage 1940. The house was about as big as the lot, but that was city life and all they could afford.

***

"No, Daddy. First you have to light the fire. Then you bring in the tree," Becky said. She had Brian's sandy hair and gray eyes. "That's how we always do it."

"How long is always to a five-year-old?" Brian said.

"About five years," Lisa said.

Brian knelt in front of the red brick fireplace and lit the fire. He wished Chad were here, but there wasn't much chance of that.

"Now it's time for the tree," Becky said.

Brian brought the tree in, stuck it in its stand and tightened the set screws against the trunk. The tree leaned to his right, so he slid a paperback under one of the legs of the stand. They strung the lights, wrapped the garland and hung the ornaments. Brian got the angel out of its box.

"We can't put the angel up yet," Becky said. "We have to have our snack first."

"It's got to be just so, doesn't it?" Brian said.

"Just like we always do," Becky said.

Lisa brought out the Christmas cookies and hot chocolate.

"Now we can do the angel," Becky said.

Lisa opened the box that kept the angel safe eleven months a year. She handed it to Becky. In keeping with tradition, Brian bent over and picked up Becky. His back cracked, but no one seemed to notice. Becky stretched to plant the angel on top of the tree. His left leg buckled. Becky teetered. Brian locked his leg and righted them both.

"The angel's crooked, Daddy."

The angel canted off to the side, the top of the tree bent from the collision with the Suburban. Brian put Becky down and handed her the angel. He went to the garage to find the pruning shears.

"I'll get a stool," Lisa said.

He looked out the garage window and saw a shiny Grosse Pointe police car cruise by. He found the shears, went back in the house and climbed on the stool. The shear blades squeaked, rust against rust, as he worked them back and forth.

"Don't cut too much off, Daddy."

Becky picked up the angel.

"Be careful, Brian," Lisa said.

The front door crashed open. Two of Grosse Pointe's finest, pistols drawn, burst through. The first one through had a mustache that hung over his upper lip. The second one was tall and skinny.

Brian teetered on the stool with his shears. His jaw dropped. Becky started to cry.

"What are you doing?" Lisa said.

The cop with the mustache pointed his gun at Brian.

"Are you Brian J. Dunn, 505 Collingwood, Grosse Pointe Park?"

"What?" he said.

"You're under arrest," said the cop with the mustache.

"He's what?" Lisa said.

"Drop those shears and come down, hands up." The cop spit the words through his mustache.

"There must be some mistake," Lisa said.

"No mistake, lady. Not if he's Brian Dunn," said the tall cop.

"Get out of this house this minute," she said.

The cop with the mustache ignored her. "Down off that stool."

Brian lost his balance and stumbled toward the cop with the

mustache, clippers first. The tall cop hit Brian on the head with the barrel of his pistol. Brian fell to his hands and knees.

Becky screamed. The tall cop shoved Brian's face to the floor with his boot, jerked his arms back and snapped a set of handcuffs around his wrists.

Lisa screamed at them, "Get out of here. You have no right to be here."

"We got a warrant for this man," said the cop with the mustache.

"Warrant?" Lisa said. "For what?"

Brian rolled to his side and the tall cop lost his grip. "Don't move or I'll shoot," said the tall cop. He pointed his pistol at Brian.

The cop with the mustache pulled a crumpled paper from his pocket. "Says here, murder. Open murder. That's what it says."

Brian twisted his body and pulled himself in like a turtle. Blood dripped down his forehead. He had no idea why, after all this time, he was being arrested. It was so long ago. He stretched back out and pulled himself to his feet.

"Don't move or I'll shoot," the tall cop said.

Somehow he didn't think the cop would shoot, but then he also thought all of this was over.

"What in God's name are you doing?" Lisa said, screaming at the two cops.

The cop with the mustache grabbed Brian and jerked him through the door. The tall cop pulled him down the sidewalk by the crook in his elbow. Brian skidded along behind him, sideways. Blood dripped down his face. Becky screamed in the doorway.

Lisa ran out of the house with Brian's coat and draped it over his shoulders. Then she ran in front of the cops.

"What are you doing?" she said, screaming again.

"This man is being arrested for murder," said the tall cop. "Get out of the way."

Lisa stood her ground. The procession stopped.

"Madam, all we're doing is fulfilling the obligations of the warrant," said the cop with the mustache.

"You can't just break into a house and take someone," Lisa said.

"When we have a warrant for murder, we execute it with extreme care," said the mustache cop.

"He's bleeding." She ran to Brian and wiped his face with her hands. "You can't do this. It's wrong,"

"She's right," the tall cop said. "You haven't read this guy his rights."

The mustache cop read him his rights. Brian didn't say a word. His coat had fallen off his shoulders and he shivered with fear in the cold. Lisa draped it over his shoulders again. They all started off to the patrol car.

"I'm going with you," she said.

Becky screamed louder. Lisa turned back to the house.

The tall cop ducked Brian's head into the police cruiser.

In just moments, the police car pulled out. Brian craned his head to look behind him. They stopped at the corner of Collingwood and Jefferson. Brian looked back again and thought he saw their Suburban pulling out of the driveway, but he wasn't sure.

The cruiser turned left onto Jefferson. It was only six blocks to the Grosse Pointe Park police station.

When the tall cop got his passenger out of the car, Brian stepped in an icy puddle. The slush ran over the top of one shoe.

They hauled him to the front desk.

"Here he is, Sarge," said the one with the mustache.

"Now we got no room," the sergeant said.

"What?" the tall cop said.

"Just booked the last room," he said.

"Stick him in the drunk tank," said the cop with the mustache.

"I can't stick a murderer in there with drunks while he's wearin' lime green pants with pink whales," the sergeant said. "Two choices: Wayne County or the Fifth Precinct."

"Wayne County's an hour from here," the tall cop said. "Fifth it is."

"I'm a Grosse Pointe resident," Brian said. "I'll stay here."

"The sheriff from up north is coming tomorrow," the sergeant said.

They trundled Brian back to their cruiser and took Jefferson into Detroit. Brian was really getting scared now.

They stayed on Jefferson past Alter Road. Of the buildings that were still standing in the Fifth Precinct, at least half were boarded up.

"I didn't murder anyone," Brian said. "There must be some mistake."

The two cops ignored him.

"You have the wrong guy."

The tall cop looked back at him. "Brian J. Dunn. That's you, right?"

"Yes."

"505 Collingwood, right?" the cop with the mustache said, looking over his shoulder at Brian.

"Let me go."

"So you're Dunn," the cop with the mustache said.

Brian nodded.

"Yeah, you probably are done." The tall cop laughed.

They stopped in front of the Fifth Precinct, now just an outpost. There was nothing left to protect. Bars on everything. Two-story concrete the color of the winter sky. Brian soaked his other foot in a puddle when he got out of the cruiser. "You'll like it here, Mr. Done." The tall cop laughed.

At the front desk, a bored cop close to his pension didn't look up.

"Officer, there's been a terrible mistake," Brian said. "These policemen arrested me, and I haven't done anything."

The old cop peered over his reading glasses.

The cop with the mustache fished the wrinkled document from his pocket and handed it to the old cop.

"Are you Brian R. Dunn?" The old cop dug a little wax out of his ear.

"Yes."

"Says here you're wanted for murder."

"I didn't murder anyone."

"Says here, Claudia Dunn. December 17, 1977. That's a while ago," the old cop said.

"Who's Claudia Dunn?" said the mustache.

"You read him his rights?" old cop said.

"Yep," the tall cop said.

"Who was the blonde? The one who screamed at us," the mustache said. "Your daughter?" Brian stared at the floor.

"Leave him alone," the old cop said. "I'd say he's got enough trouble."

The old cop studied the warrant again. "Doesn't say who she was. But she must have been a relative."

The old cop read the warrant one more time. "Open murder, December 17, 1977."

"There's been a mistake," Brian said. "Please let me call my wife."

"Who'd you say Claudia was?" the tall cop said.

"I have a right to an attorney."

The mustache cop looked at his watch. "Come on, let's go. Our shift's over."

The old cop finished the paperwork and called for a jailer, who unlocked a cell with a bunk, a sink and a toilet with no seat. He took off Brian's handcuffs, shoved him in and slammed the cell door.

CHAPTER FIVE

Burr drummed his fingers again, then looked over at Brian and Lisa. "I'm going to enter an appearance and try to get the bail reduced. That's all." He pushed his chair back, left the visitors room and started down the hall.

Suzanne caught up with him. "First the bail, then we'll get him acquitted." She smiled sweetly at him.

"I'll get Brian out on bail. Then I'm done."

"We can worry about that later," she said.

"No, we won't. You need a criminal lawyer. I'm done after I do this."

"Burr, please."

"I drove you up here because the roads were bad." Burr looked out the window. Wind was blowing hard from the northwest, pushing dark clouds in front of it. The wind leaked through the windows.

I never should have let it get this far.

"If what Lisa said is true, anybody can get Brian off."

"If anybody can get him off, why don't you be the one to do it," Suzanne said.

***

Burr retrieved Zeke from the Jeep and found a conference room for visiting attorneys on the third floor of the courthouse. The radiator at his feet leaked, puddling water on the floor. Burr pressed the palm of his hand on the window and melted the frost away. He looked over the rooftops, north across the bay to Harbor Springs, where he kept his boat. The sky had cleared but the wind was still blowing, piling up waves on the beach. Zeke looked up at him and Burr wondered if the dog had any hard feelings about the duck hunt being cut short.

Suzanne entered without knocking. Somehow she had found a place to change into a black skirt and jacket.

That skirt doesn't do justice to her legs.

She looked down at Zeke. "How'd he get in here?"

"I pretended I was blind."

"You're the big city lawyer who's supposed to get Brian out on bail and you've got a dog up here."

"It's too cold for him to stay in the Jeep."

She flashed her green eyes at him. Her right iris had gold flecks.

I always loved her eyes.

"When was Brian arrested?"

"I don't know." She sat down and crossed her legs. "Where's your tie. We're on in an hour."

"I didn't bring one."

"You can't go before the judge without a tie."

"I don't usually wear one duck hunting."

"I'll go get you one. And a shirt."

Suzanne stood on tiptoes to read the label inside Burr's collar.

Burr was slightly aroused by Suzanne's touch, then felt slightly ridiculous for feeling slightly aroused.

"Are you still a 15-34?"

"What?"

"Shirt."

"Yes," he said. "What day is it?"

"Tuesday."

"When was Brian arrested?"

"Saturday, I think. What difference does it make?"

"He's just now being charged. That's four days. I might be able to get the whole thing dismissed."

Suzanne put her hands on her hips. "Please, Burr. Nothing cute. Just the bail."

"I need a copy of the court rules."

"Please, Burr, nothing cute," she said again. "I'll get you a shirt and tie. You take Zeke back to the car."

She gave Burr a domestic kiss on the cheek and walked out.

***

Their first kiss hadn't been like that at all.

Burr had been on his way to a motion hearing, Suzanne in tow.

There was absolutely no reason for Suzanne to go to the hearing. His motion was perfunctory and would certainly be granted, but it was another chance to be with her and another chance to show off.

He was smitten. He knew it, and he was afraid that Suzanne knew it too. He'd called her in to his office two more times after their first meeting. None of the meetings were necessary. The lawsuit wasn't complicated, and he should have assigned it to an associate.

He made a point of opening the courthouse door for her, partly manners, but mostly so he could look at her. She wore a dark blue suit with a cream blouse, and a slit up the back of her skirt. Her hips swayed courtesy of her black pumps. He couldn't take his eyes off her.

He won the motion hearing, as he knew he would. Suzanne congratulated him.

When they got back to his office, Burr sat on the couch, hoping Suzanne would join him. She walked to the window and leaned against it, her hands pressed against the glass. The light from the window framed her silhouette, long and slim. Burr came up behind her. She didn't move. He put a hand on her hip. She turned to him and he kissed her on the lips.

"I wish you wouldn't have done that."

***

Gillis called them to order. Burr sat next to Brian. Suzanne and Lisa were behind them in the first row of the gallery, Truax was at the prosecutor's table.

Burr stood. "Your Honor, my name is Burr Lafayette. I would like to enter an appearance for the defendant."

"Granted," Gillis said.

"Your Honor, I move that the charges against Mr. Dunn be dismissed."

"This court set the bail at one million dollars based on the nature of the crime and where the defendant resides," the judge said. "There was no protest at the time I set it."

Burr walked up to Gillis. "Your Honor, I'm not asking for the bail to be reduced."

"Why should I reduce it?" Gillis said.

"I'm not asking you to reduce the bail. I'm asking you to dismiss the case."

"What?" Gillis thumped his forehead with the palm of one hand.

"Your Honor, I move to have the case dismissed."

Truax stood. "Your Honor, the defendant has already been charged. Those charges must stand."

Suzanne hissed at him. "What are you doing?"

Burr walked back to his table and picked up the copy of Michigan statutes that he'd found in the courthouse library. He turned to Gillis and opened the book. "Your Honor, according to MCLA 28.51, '*a defendant must be charged within forty-eight hours of his arrest.*'"

"That's exactly what happened," Truax said. His Adam's apple bobbed.

"My client was arrested on Saturday. It's now Wednesday," Burr said.

"Give me that book," Gillis said. Burr handed him the book and walked back to his table. Gillis put on his reading glasses and studied the text.

He has no idea what's going on.

"It's *habeas corpus*, Your Honor," Burr said, still standing.

"It doesn't apply here," the prosecutor said.

"It most certainly does," Burr said.

"Be quiet," Gillis said to Burr. "Calvin?"

"Deputy Brubaker got stuck in the snowstorm on the way back. He made every effort to bring the defendant back in a timely fashion to the jurisdiction from which he fled."

"I wouldn't exactly call moving to Grosse Pointe six years ago fleeing," Burr said.

"Your Honor," Truax said, "there must be a rule of reason applied here. The state did everything reasonable. Beyond reasonable. The deputy said it was very slippery. Then they got snowed in."

The judge looked over his glasses and nodded at Truax. The prosecutor nodded back at him.

Burr took a step toward Gillis. "Your Honor, there is no rule of reason when it comes to *habeas corpus*. This is a Fourth Amendment right. Designed to protect against the tyranny of the state. It is a constitutional right further codified by this statute."

Truax took a step toward Gillis. "Your Honor, it was snowing. There was nothing else we could do."

"There are Wayne County judges on call twenty-four hours a day, seven days a week to protect against this very situation," Burr said.

Gillis took off his glasses and waved them at Burr. "What tyranny?"

"The power of the state, when brought to bear against an individual, is formidable."

"Calvin, come up here a minute." The prosecutor walked up to Gillis. Gillis leaned over his desk and said something to the prosecutor, *sotto voce*.

This may turn out badly.

Suzanne leaned over the rail and hissed at him. "All we need is bail."

"I've got him. They waited too long to charge him."

"No one here even knows what *habeas corpus* is."

"I'm going to get the charges dismissed."

"Counsel, are you ready?" Gillis said.

"Yes, Your Honor," Burr said.

Burr walked up to Gillis and stood next to Truax.

Gillis looked down at Burr's feet. "Young man, as much as I admire your hunting boots, do not, I repeat, do not ever wear them in my courtroom again."

"Yes, Your Honor," Burr said.

"Mr. Truax said he would consent to a bail reduction."

Here we go.

"Your Honor, the state has clearly violated my client's constitutional rights. The charges must be dismissed."

"Don't be stubborn, young man," Gillis said.

"I'll just charge him again," Truax said.

"You do that," Burr said.

"Calvin, are you sure about this?" Gillis said.

Truax's Adam's apple bobbed. He was sweating and Burr smelled Old Spice. "Yes, Your Honor."

Burr turned to Truax. "Why are you doing this?"

"Hush, young man," Gillis said. "Calvin, are you going to release Mr. Dunn?"

"No, Your Honor."

Gillis nodded. "The court rules that the snowstorm made it impossible to charge the defendant any quicker and that the state acted as soon as it could. Motion denied."

He handed the book back to Burr, who opened it, slammed it shut, and walked back to the defense table.

"Counsel, you are still in my courtroom," Gillis said.

"I am aware of that," Burr said, his back to the judge. He threw the book down on his table.

"Counsel, would you like to spend the night next to your client?" Gillis said.

"I would like some justice."

"One more smart remark and you will spend the holidays as a guest of the people of Emmet County." Gillis cleared his throat. "Look at me when I'm speaking to you."

Burr turned to Gillis.

"If that book is from the court's library, I expect you to return it on your way out," Gillis said.

"I'm sure you'd never miss it."

"What did you say?"

Suzanne stood. "Nothing, Your Honor." Suzanne grabbed Burr by the shoulder. "Be quiet. You've done enough damage for one day."

Gillis tapped his glasses. "Mr. Lafayette, your motion to dismiss the charges is denied. Bail will remain at one million dollars. We are dismissed." Gillis banged his gavel and walked out.

"Just the bail, Burr. That's all you were supposed to do," Suzanne said.

"What's going to happen now?" Brian said.

He doesn't know what just happened.

"All we needed was to get the bail reduced. There was no reason to get cute," Suzanne said.

The bailiff came over to the defense table. "Mr. Dunn, please come with me."

"What?" Brian said.

"Come with me. I don't think we'll use the cuffs."

"What?" Brian said.

Lisa took Brian's arm. "We'll try again tomorrow, honey."

"Back to jail?"

"Burr, I can't believe you did this," Suzanne said.

"Come with me, Mr. Dunn," the bailiff said.

Burr looked at Brian. "Brian, I'm sorry. The law is clearly on our side. It's clear. It's not gray at all."

Brian shuffled off with the bailiff, with Lisa still holding his hand. When the three of them were about halfway across the courtroom, Brian stopped. He turned back toward Burr.

"You're fired," he said.

***

Two hours later, Burr walked toward the visitors room, ever so slowly. This was not a meeting he was looking forward to.

I hope Brian has calmed down.

Burr knew he'd been right in that amateur hour of a courtroom. Criminal lawyer or not, Burr knew about *habeas corpus*. Brian hadn't been charged within forty-eight hours of his arrest. It had taken almost four days. He should have been released. Gillis was wrong, but Brian was still in jail.

Maybe I should have gone for just bail.

His ego had gotten the better of him. Again.

I'm going to eat my words and make it right. But Gillis was wrong.

Burr walked into the visitors room. He sat next to Suzanne and across from Lisa and Brian. Hunched over in defeat, Burr thought, Brian was holding Lisa's hand. Burr's eyes fixed on Brian's bald spot.

Burr offered his hand to Brian, who didn't take it.

"You were supposed to get me out on bail," Brian said.

"There's just one thing," Suzanne said.

"What's that?" Brian said.

"Burr can't get you out until you rehire him," she said.

"He's done a great job so far."

"The judge was wrong," Burr said.

"He may be wrong, but I'm still in jail," Brian said, standing. He started around the table toward Burr.

This could get ugly.

Suzanne jumped up and stood between Brian and Burr.

"This is what happened," Brian said.

"It doesn't matter what happened," Burr said.

"What do you mean you don't care what happened?" Lisa said.

"It doesn't matter what happened," Burr said again.

"If it doesn't matter, then why am I in jail?"

Suzanne put her hand on Brian's arm. "What Burr means is that it doesn't matter right now," She looked at Burr. "Isn't that right?"

She can be charming when she wants to.

"None of this makes any sense," Brian said. He walked back to his chair and sat. Suzanne smiled at Burr and sat back down.

"That's right. *The law is a ass.*"

"What?" Brian said.

"Dickens," Burr said.

Suzanne gave Burr the nastiest look he'd ever gotten.

Burr stood. "Your due process was violated. You shouldn't be here."

"I didn't murder Claudia. It was an accident. I want to be home with my family."

"We have to appeal the judge's decision," Burr said.

"Why can't you just get the bail reduced?" Lisa said.

"I'm afraid it's a bit late for that." Burr walked to the window. The wind had picked up and the waves crashed on to the beach.

It's nicer out there than in here.

Burr looked at Brian and Lisa. "Bail isn't the issue. The judge erred."

Lisa jumped to her feet and stood eye-to-eye with Burr, difficult because she was a head shorter. "He erred? He erred? How dare you say that. This isn't the Supreme Court. My husband has been in jail for almost a week. The last time his daughter saw him, the police were dragging him away. He's been charged with murder, and Christmas is in a week."

Suzanne jumped back up, this time standing between Burr and Lisa. "Burr will make it right."

"You totally screwed up the bail hearing. And you have the nerve to say the judge erred." Lisa started to come after Burr but then she sat down and hugged Brian.

"Please," she said, looking up at Burr. "I don't care about your theories. I want my husband home for Christmas." She laid her head on Brian's shoulder and started to cry.

CHAPTER SIX

Back in East Lansing, Burr and Zeke started up the stairs to his law office and living quarters on the top floor of his building. Past the Italian restaurant on the ground floor, past the atrium shops on the second and third floors, only a quarter of them rented. They stopped on the landing of the fourth floor, across from offices, mostly not rented.

"Zeke, I don't trust elevators."

Then past the fifth floor, more offices but no tenants, and up to the sixth floor.

He walked into the reception area, then into his office. He sat at his desk and tap, tap, tapped a Number 2 yellow pencil.

Zeke jumped up on the leather couch on the opposite wall. Burr's partner, Jacob Wertheim, burst in and sat in one of the matching wing-back chairs in front of Burr's desk. Jacob ran a thumb and forefinger along the knife-like crease of his tropical wool charcoal slacks. They went well with his navy-blue blazer, starched white shirt and club tie.

Jacob is natty.

Burr told him what happened with Gillis.

"There's a court rule and reams of case law. Why didn't you cite one?" Jacob said.

"The judge wouldn't let me."

"Why not?"

"He didn't want to hear it. He offered to reduce the bail."

"Why didn't you take it?" Jacob said.

"The judge was wrong."

"The judge was wrong and ... what's his name ..."

"Brian."

"... and Brian is still in jail."

"That's right," Burr said.

"Why didn't you take the bail?"

"We can appeal."

"Appeal? It's almost Christmas."

"You don't celebrate Christmas."

"The Court of Appeals does."

"They'll have to hear this immediately. It's *habeas corpus*."

"I don't think we should go to the Court of Appeals until after Christmas. That's where we earn our living."

If I wait until after Christmas, Lisa will be arrested for murdering me.

Jacob sneezed. He looked behind him at Zeke, who woke for just a moment and barked once. "Damn that dog."

Burr had moved to East Lansing three years ago, after he resigned from Fisher and Allen. Two hundred lawyers strong. Burr was head of the litigation department. Jacob told him not to resign, and maybe he shouldn't have. Maybe he shouldn't have left Grace, either. Jacob, also a partner at Fisher and Allen, had quit, too, though Burr had told him not to. Jacob said he needed a change, so they opened up an appellate practice, Lafayette and Wertheim. State and federal appeals, mostly state. Court of Appeals and Supreme Court, mostly Court of Appeals. Jacob did the research and the writing. Burr did the oral arguments and held the clients' hands.

Jacob reached into his shirt pocket, took out a cigarette and lit it. Then he twirled one of the curls on the side of his head.

His hair is like steel wool.

Jacob was short and wiry, like his hair. Olive skin. Prominent nose, not big. Prominent. Mid-forties. And always dressed to the nines.

Burr smelled the sweet smoke. "Do not smoke a joint in my office."

"It's not a joint. It's a clove cigarette."

"Right."

Zeke barked again.

"Zeke knows a joint when he smells one."

"I got it at Small Planet."

"You can't work stoned."

"It's good for my allergies."

"You're not allergic to dogs," Burr said.

"I'm not allergic to all dogs. Just one dog."

"Put that thing out."

"It helps me relax." Jacob looked at the burning whatever-it-was but didn't put it out. "How much does it pay?"

"Pay?"

"As in money. I am absolutely not working for free."

"We get paid." Burr tapped his pencil. "Just not right away."

Eve McGinty, Burr's longtime, long-suffering legal assistant, came in and sat beside Jacob.

"Put out that joint," she said.

"It's not a joint. It's a clove cigarette. And if it were marijuana, which it's not, it's only a $100 misdemeanor in the City of East Lansing."

Jacob snuffed out the joint in the ashtray on Burr's desk.

He put it out for Eve but not for me.

"You're a forty-five-year-old substance abuser," she said.

"I am a decorated Vietnam veteran. And just how old did you say you were?"

The color rose in Eve's cheeks. She didn't like being the oldest one of their merry little band, and she really didn't like being a year older than Burr, who never let her forget it. She had been his assistant at Fisher and Allen for fifteen years. He had begged her not to quit but she did anyway. She'd divorced well, and she said she wanted a house close to work and a yard with full sun so she could have a perennial garden.

She was five-four, petite, with chin-length brown hair and a mouthful of white teeth. Bright brown eyes that could start a fire, and a wit to match. She had the beginnings of crow's feet around her eyes, which she hated and makeup couldn't quite conceal.

She was classy, and Burr knew she was smarter than he was, which was why he couldn't understand why she still worked for him.

Eve reached for the cold joint in the ashtray, but Jacob grabbed it and put it in his pocket.

"Eve, please. Burr and I have pressing work."

"You two don't have any pressing work. At the moment, you have no work." She tugged at her earring.

She only does that when she's worried about something.

"Burr and I are working on an urgent appeal."

"Why in God's name would the two of you get anywhere near Suzanne after what happened?"

That's why she tugged her ear.

"This isn't about Suzanne," Burr said.

"It might not be now, but it's going to be." Eve looked over at Jacob. "Didn't you think about this? Suzanne is the reason we're in East Lansing."

Jacob squirmed in his chair but didn't say anything.

Burr tapped his pencil, then said, "If anyone ever needed a lawyer, it's Brian Dunn."

Eve glared at him.

***

Zeke snored softly on the couch.

Burr turned around and stared out the window. It was four o'clock and almost dark. The winter solstice was tomorrow. In the winter he got up in the dark and went to bed in the dark. With all the clouds in December, some days it never really got light. Black turned to gray, then back to black. Over and over and over again.

"Zeke, I need to find my lights." Burr walked into the walk-in closet in his office. He'd diagnosed himself with Seasonal Affective Disorder two years ago. By spring, he wouldn't need his light-therapy lights, but he needed them now.

"They're in here somewhere."

The banging noises in the closet brought Eve back in.

"If you're looking for those stupid lights, they're in the basement."

Burr looked out at Eve. "SAD is such a great acronym."

"Please don't take this case."

"Stop tugging at your ear."

Eve didn't say a word, but she topped tugging.

Burr smelled the cedar paneling in his closet. It reminded him of his cabin on Walpole Island.

"I love this closet."

Eve walked over to the closet. "Jacob is doing the research, but I know this is going to end badly."

Burr thought it best not to say anything.

"I know you're ignoring me."

Burr tripped over his old waders. He bent over to see if the hole in them had fixed itself.

Eve peered into the closet. "If you're thinking about fixing something, you should get the elevator fixed."

"I don't take the elevator."

***

Burr looked out from a window booth at Michelangelo's, the restaurant on the ground floor of his building. East Lansing had emptied out when the Michigan State University students went home for Christmas break. With forty thousand fewer people, he could shoot his twelve gauge across Grand River Avenue and not hit anyone.

Buying the Masonic Temple building, circa 1927, had seemed like a good idea at the time. It wasn't a big building, even by East Lansing standards. Six stories, red brick and narrow, very narrow. The renovations, especially the new elevator, which was broken again, had nearly broken him.

As much as he loved pasta, Burr could never eat enough to cover the rent that Scooter, the would-be restaurateur, owed him. Zeke, lying under the table, sucked in a Number 12 angel hair and smacked his lips. Burr ordered another glass of the estate Chianti, which Scooter stocked solely for him.

Scooter came up to his table. "How is it, Mr. Lafayette?"

"Fine, Scooter. It's fine."

"You know there's no dogs allowed, Mr. Lafayette."

"He's a seeing eye dog."

"He may be, but you're not blind."

"I'm also not six months behind on the rent."

Scooter was all WASP, not a drop of Italian in him. He had a pasty complexion and droopy, dirty blond hair. Michelangelo's had great Italian food, but Scooter wasn't a great tenant.

"If you don't pay me, I'll have to evict you."

"If you evict me, how will I pay you?" Scooter scurried away.

Suzanne waltzed in wearing a full-length fox fur coat. Burr knew it well. The snow sparkled on her coat, then melted. She stomped the snow off the black leather boots that disappeared into her coat.

I wonder what takes over where the boots leave off.

"There you are," she said.

"Hello, Suzanne."

She opened her coat before she sat. Blue jeans.

"Disappointed?" she said.

I am disappointed.

"I thought you had to go back to New York."

"I took a leave of absence."

"I see," Burr said, who didn't.

Suzanne and Lisa had grown up in Lake Forest on Chicago's old money North Shore. Her mother walked out when she was fifteen and, but for an occasional birthday card, had disappeared. Her father sent both girls to boarding school and then Vanderbilt. The two sisters were best friends and the only real family either one of them had.

Lisa had worked summers during college at Bay View in Petoskey, a grand collection of Victorian cottages, originally a Methodist retreat. She'd moved to Petoskey after she graduated and ended up as Brian's office manager. Suzanne graduated in English, moved to New York and went to work as a copywriter on a toothpaste account.

The advertising agency transferred her to Detroit to work on a car account that needed a boost. Suzanne said she couldn't decide what she hated more, Detroit or cars. To Burr, Detroit and cars were so mixed up with each other, there was no separating them.

As far as Suzanne was concerned, the only saving grace was that her sister lived in Grosse Pointe.

"How are you going to get Brian out of jail?"

"I'll file the motion and the brief right after the Christmas recess."

"After Christmas."

"The Court of Appeals is on Christmas recess until January third."

"Brian has to be home for Christmas."

"So do I."

"You can do it right now."

"It's almost Christmas, and I'd prefer not to annoy the Court of Appeals."

Scooter appeared with a wine glass for Suzanne. She ordered linguini with red clam sauce.

"You have enough time to get Brian out for Christmas."

"I'm going to pick up my son tomorrow."

"So ... it's all about you."

"Who else would it be about?" Burr swirled his wine, then took a sip.

"Jacob can finish the brief by Christmas Eve," Suzanne said.

"I'm going to pick up Zeke-the-boy tomorrow morning."

"Can't he wait? Just for a little while?"

"Kids don't understand time. Late is like not coming."

"You've made a career of being late," Suzanne said.

"Not for Zeke. We're going sledding. And grouse hunting."

"I'm sure he doesn't want to go grouse hunting."

"How would you know?"

"He likes sledding. He likes Zeke-the-dog. He loves you. I'm sure he doesn't want to go grouse hunting. He's humoring you."

Burr knew that Zeke-the-boy didn't understand wait. Burr was to pick him up tomorrow at three o'clock in Grosse Pointe Woods at the corner of Sunningdale and Wedgewood, a brick Tudor with three fireplaces. He still made the mortgage payment, most of the time.

Zeke always asked why Burr left. Why, if it was so bad being married, did the three of them still have dinner together sometimes. If he didn't love Mom, who did he love?

Burr had borrowed a cabin on the Manistee River near the headwaters. That's where he and the two Zekes were headed for the next four days, for their Christmas. Zeke-the-boy wanted to sled on the big hill next to the cabin. There was a cedar swamp nearby that held grouse when the snow was deep.

"Are you quite done with your reverie?" Suzanne said.

"My what?"

"What you need to do is quit moping and get on with your life."

"I am on with my life."

"It looks to me like you quit life, except for the two Zekes and bird hunting."

"There's sailing."

Suzanne gave him a withering look.

"I have a prominent appellate practice and a large office building."

"You have a beat-up practice with a pothead for a partner and an empty building that smells like spaghetti sauce."

"Spaghetti is one of my three favorite foods."

Suzanne reached across the table and laid her hand on Burr's, then looked at him. "Do this one thing for me. Please."

"Suzanne, that was the most melodramatic thing I've ever seen."

"It was, wasn't it?"

"I liked it."

"I thought you might." She squeezed his hand.

***

The next morning Burr looked out the window of Jacob's office, over the tops of the houses, mostly student rentals with a few fraternity and sorority houses mixed in.

I like my building, but it does smell like spaghetti sauce.

"I told Suzanne we'd get Brian out of jail before Christmas."

"That's only three days," Jacob said, natty in a camel sport coat and navy-blue slacks.

"You know as well as I do that *habeas corpus* issues are heard right away."

"We don't want to upset vacationing appellate judges if we don't have to," Jacob said.

Eve marched in. "Who's we?"

"Jacob and me."

"If the two of you are involved, I'm involved." She tugged at her dangly, gold hoop earring.

"This is a constitutional issue," Burr said.

"Suzanne Fairchild is most certainly not a constitutional issue," Eve said.

"If Burr had asked for bail reduction this wouldn't have happened. He's put himself in a spot." It was Jacob's turn, and he twirled one of his steel wool curls.

"We don't need you as a peacemaker," Eve said.

"Brian needs our help," Burr said.

"What about Zeke?" Eve said.

"I'll take him back early and trade for a couple days between Christmas and New Year's."

***

Burr and the two Zekes sledded while Jacob finished the brief. They didn't hunt grouse. Burr delivered Zeke-the-boy back to the beautiful Grace at noon on the 23rd. He asked Grace if he could have Christmas dinner with the two of them. She said she'd think about it.

CHAPTER SEVEN

Burr tapped his pencil, Jacob next to him, Suzanne and Lisa behind. They were in one of Burr's favorite battlegrounds, the Michigan Court of Appeals on the second floor of the Prudden building in downtown Lansing. The paneling in the courtroom was so old the varnish had turned black.

Burr had just finished his argument, and Truax was just getting started.

"Your Honor, it is altogether fitting and proper that the defendant, Brian R. Dunn, is in jail awaiting trial. He killed his wife. He has admitted as much. He should have been charged with murder six years ago. My predecessor should have done that. In addition ..."

"Stop right there, Mr. Truax," the judge said.

Burr looked up at Chief Judge Miriam Florentine, a petite, attractive, white-haired woman in her sixties. Burr had argued before her many times. She was very smart and took no prisoners.

"Mr. Truax, we are not here to discuss the merits of the case. Frankly, whether or not the defendant is guilty is beyond the purview of this emergency hearing. If, as Emmet County prosecutor, you believe the People of the State of Michigan have reasonable cause to charge the defendant with murder, you may do so. But anything further you may care to say must address the procedural issue before us. Not the underlying issue."

Judge Florentine's reading glasses slipped down her nose. She pushed them back up and looked at Burr.

"As for you, Mr. Lafayette, while I do appreciate the constitutional aspects of your plea ... off the record ..." The court reporter stopped typing in midsentence. "For my entire adult life, I have wrapped Christmas presents on Christmas Eve. On top of that, it's Saturday. I treasure my free time, and I expect what's left of this interruption to be brief. Is that clear?"

"Yes, Your Honor." Burr looked at the other two judges, who both nodded, both equally peeved. The older of the two men looked sleepy, and the younger looked like he wanted to be somewhere else. Neither had missed many meals.

Both of them had intellects that were uncommonly unremarkable. Judge Florentine was the only one of the three who would understand the arguments. The other two, Tweedledum and Tweedledee, invariably went along with Judge Florentine.

Burr stood. "Your Honor, MCLA 28.51 clearly states that a person accused of a crime must be charged within forty-eight hours of his arrest. This is a codification of the Fourth Amendment's constitutional protection known as *habeas corpus.*"

"I am aware of the concept, and if I weren't, you educated me ten minutes ago," she said. Tweedledum and Tweedledee nodded.

"Of course, Your Honor," Burr said. "In fact, the legislature believed this protection so vitally important that it provides for judges to be available on weekends and holidays to ensure compliance with this legislative and constitutional safeguard."

"Mr. Lafayette, as you must undoubtedly be aware, we are here today, on Christmas Eve, because of that very reason."

Truax popped up like toast in a toaster.

"Mr. Truax, do you have something you wish to say?" the chief judge said.

"Your Honor ..." Burr said.

"Sit down, Mr. Lafayette, you interrupted Mr. Truax."

Judge Florentine turned to Truax. The vein on the prosecutor's forehead throbbed.

He looks like a mean-spirited Ichabod Crane.

"Your Honor, the state did everything in its power to arraign the defendant in a timely fashion. Unfortunately, the jail situation and the inclement weather precluded strict compliance with the statute. The state, however, made more than reasonable efforts to ensure statutory compliance, and in any event, charged the defendant less than twenty-four hours after the prescribed time period."

"For the record, it was two days too late," Burr said.

"Whatever," Truax said.

"Stop it. Both of you," Judge Florentine said. She scowled at Burr. "Mr. Lafayette, you of all people should be aware of the deportment required in this court."

"Yes, Your Honor."

Truax took a deep breath and swallowed. His Adam's apple bobbed. "Your Honor, in People v. Hitch, a blizzard, as in this case, prevented the defendant from being charged for a full week. In that case, the court held that a reasonable test should be used in interpreting rights of *habeas corpus*."

Jacob scribbled a note and handed it to Burr, who stood. "Your Honor, the case cited by counsel is from Wyoming and has no bearing on Michigan law." Burr sat back down.

Truax kept going. "Your Honor, in People v. Stocker, the Michigan Court of Appeals held that when a defendant could not be charged in a timely fashion, again because of a snowstorm, a rule of reasonableness should apply."

Jacob whispered in Burr's ear. He stood again. "Your Honor, with all due respect, the case cited by counsel is a Court of Appeals case and not ..."

"Stop right there, Mr. Lafayette. While I appreciate your commentary, it's Mr. Truax's turn. I also remind you that we make good law in the Court of Appeals. Off the record ..." the court reporter stopped typing again, "unless I am mistaken, you make your living here, do you not?"

"Yes, Your Honor," Burr said.

"Then you would be well-advised not to criticize those whose favor you must curry."

"Your Honor, my complete thought was that the legislature enacted this statute subsequent to the Court of Appeals decision. The statute would seem to supersede the prior decision of this court."

"Not at all, Your Honor," Truax said. "Judicial precedent is always useful in interpreting statutes. In fact, there are no cases subsequent to the statute that overrule the reasonableness test. We must, therefore, assume that the legislature intended to codify a constitutional right along with its common law precedents."

Is this the royal "We"?

Burr bent down, spoke with Jacob, then looked back at the judge. "Your Honor," Burr said, "the legislative committee notes directly contradict Mr. Truax. They state that the statute is to have a strict interpretation and that the forty-eight-hour provision is purposely designed to be inflexible. Any arraignment over forty-eight hours is invalid."

"Where did you find that?" Judge Florentine said. Tweedledum and Tweedledee showed some interest.

"We have the legislative hearing records in our law library, Your Honor."

"May I see that please?" she said. Burr handed her the document. "Why wasn't this included in the brief?"

"It's in the footnote, Your Honor," Burr said.

"I see."

"Your Honor, the people have not had access to this material. We request a twenty-four-hour adjournment to review the material and prepare a response."

"Your Honor, the whole purpose of the statute is to prevent citizens from being imprisoned and left to languish in jail without being charged with a crime. It's one of the pillars of our judicial system," Burr said.

"Spare me the rhetoric, counselor," Judge Florentine said. "Approach the bench. Both of you."

Burr and Truax stood before the three judges.

"You are ruining my Christmas, Mr. Lafayette." She took off her glasses and looked down her nose at Burr. "If we grant your motion, what do you suppose will happen?"

"My client will be released immediately."

Truax cleared his throat. "Respectfully, Your Honor, what will happen is, I will immediately ask that a new warrant be issued. The defendant will be charged before he leaves the jail."

The chief judge looked down at Burr.

"I assume you are aware of that."

"What's the point?" Truax said.

"The point is, no quarter asked and none given," Burr said.

"Stop that. Both of you," Judge Florentine said.

"Your Honor, the point is that my client's statutory and constitutional rights have been violated," Burr said.

"No, the point is you should have just asked for a bail reduction without getting cute," Truax said.

"Your Honor, I apologize for the inconvenience. Frankly, I would like my client to be home for Christmas," Burr said.

"I'd like to be home for Christmas myself," Judge Florentine said.

"Your client murdered his wife," Truax said.

"My client killed his wife, but it was an accident. That's not murder."

"It will be when I'm done," Truax said.

"When I'm done, you'll be lucky to have a law license."

"Sit down, both of you," Judge Florentine said. She huddled with Tweedledum and Tweedledee, then, "Gentlemen, we find that the constitutional underpinnings of the statute are of the utmost importance in preserving the individual freedoms of our democracy. We find that the people of the State of Michigan have a duty to charge defendants promptly and that MCLA 28.51 should be strictly interpreted. Therefore, we find that because the defendant was not charged within the prescribed forty-eight-hour period, the charges against him should be dismissed, without prejudice."

The judges filed out.

Suzanne leaned over the railing. "Now what do we do?

"Now we get a true copy of the order and the two of you drive to Petoskey and get Brian out of jail." Burr smiled. "Merry Christmas."

Lisa walked around the table and offered her hand to Burr. "Thank you, Mr. Lafayette. I'm not sure what just happened but thank you."

"You're quite welcome, Mrs. Dunn. Now if you'll excuse me."

"Where are you off to?" said Suzanne.

"I've been invited to Christmas dinner with Zeke-the-boy."

"Don't you think it's a bit odd to have Christmas dinner with the woman you divorced?"

Burr ignored her.

Truax stuffed his papers in his briefcase and rushed out.

"Ladies, you don't have time to drive to Petoskey."

***

Burr drove them to his office as quickly as he could. Becky was typing on Eve's IBM Selectric when they got there and not too excited to see her mother.

She looks like Lisa, but she's about the size of Zeke-the-boy.

Burr knew Truax was trying to get a new warrant issued right away, so he had to get Brian out of jail and spirited away before the new warrant could be served. He had Eve fax the order dismissing the charges to Burr's aunt in Harbor Springs, who got Brian out of jail and took him back to her house. Then Burr sent Suzanne, Lisa, and Becky to fetch Brian and take him to Burr's cabin on Walpole Island for Christmas.

***

Deputy Brubaker, the same deputy who had ferried Brian to Petoskey, arrested Burr in Grace's driveway at 1 p.m. on Christmas Day. He didn't even have time to knock on the door. The tubby deputy had been waiting for him in front of Grace's house, the same house Burr still made payments on.

Burr was charged with harboring a fugitive.

I must have been easier to find than Brian.

"What about my dog?"

"What about him?" Deputy Brubaker said.

"I can't leave him here."

"Bring him with you. If we leave right now, I can be home for Christmas dinner and still get my holiday pay."

Zeke-the-boy ran out to see what was going on. Burr said he had to go with the policeman.

"To arrest somebody?"

"Yes," Burr said.

Deputy Brubaker, full of the Christmas spirit, had been kind enough not to say who was being arrested.

"Can Zeke stay here with me?"

After a short talk with Grace, who liked dogs but not dog hair, and a hand signal from Burr, the two Zekes trotted up the sidewalk and into the house.

A Christmas miracle.

Burr persuaded jolly Deputy Brubaker that he wasn't a risk to flee and followed him in the Jeep for the five-hour drive to the Emmet County Jail.

Deputy Brubaker put Burr in the same cell that Brian had been in, the irony not lost on Burr, the prisoner.

Jacob arrived at ten that evening, festive in a subdued way, wine-colored crew neck sweater, tweed sport coat, and tan corduroys. He'd reached Brian, who said he would drive up to Petoskey and surrender himself on Monday, after the Christmas weekend.

Jacob left for his hotel. Burr fell asleep in his cell.

***

The jailer opened the door to Burr's cell. Five minutes later, Burr, Jacob and Brian sat at the defense table, Truax across the aisle.

Truax smiled at Burr. "I trust you had a pleasant Christmas. Not to mention yesterday. It was a paid holiday. As I'm sure you know."

"Quiet. It was very quiet."

"The accommodations were to your liking, then?"

"A little Spartan, but the price was right."

Jacob hissed at Truax. "Highly illegal. And you know it."

"But highly effective," Truax sneered at Burr.

"It was false arrest. Actionable against you individually, prosecutor. And definitely an ethics violation," Jacob said.

Maybe there's hope.

Judge Gillis entered. The bailiff called them to order. "Gentlemen, I note that Mr. Dunn is present. Do we finally have agreement that he may be properly charged?"

"No, Your Honor," Burr said.

"Why not?" the judge said.

"There is no probable cause that Mr. Dunn murdered his wife."

"There is," Truax said.

"I already decided there is," Gillis said.

"It's not enough," Burr said.

"Listen to me, counselor. I say there is probable cause, so there is. If you don't like it, show up at the preliminary exam. Stand up, Mr. Dunn."

Brian looked at Burr, who nodded. They both stood.

"Brian R. Dunn," Judge Gillis said, "today, December 27, 1983, you are charged with open murder in the death of Claudia Marie Dunn on December 17, 1977. How do you plead?"

"Not guilty, Your Honor," Brian said.

"Enter a plea of not guilty," Gillis said.

"Bail?" Burr said.

"One million dollars," Gillis said.

"That's too high," Burr said.

Gillis waved his gavel at Burr. "Just who do you think you are?"

"Your Honor, I spent Christmas in jail. At your pleasure. Illegally. You can charge Mr. Dunn now, but if the bail is more than one hundred thousand dollars, which means we post ten thousand, I'm going to file an ethics charge against both of you."

Gillis turned his glare from Burr to Truax, whose forehead started to throb. Gillis thumped his forehead. "Bail is set at one hundred thousand dollars. The preliminary exam will be February 6, 1984. We are adjourned." Gillis slammed down his gavel and disappeared out the back of the courtroom.

Burr stopped Truax on his way out of the courtroom. "Could I speak with you for a moment?"

Truax stopped short. "Why?"

"A procedural issue. For the preliminary exam."

Truax shifted from foot to foot. "Like what?"

"Could we talk in your office?"

"You may have one minute."

Burr followed Truax down the hall, then up two flights of stairs.
He must not like elevators either.

Truax opened the door to his office and let Burr in. His walls were filled with awards and diplomas.

I'm sure his high school diploma is up here somewhere.

Truax stood in the doorway. Burr took a step toward Truax, walked into a cloud of Old Spice and backed up.

"This happened six years ago. Why now? What's in this for you?"

"Justice. There is new evidence."

"Come on. After six years there's no good evidence."

"I imagine you'll be turning this over to a trial lawyer now," Truax said.

"I am a trial lawyer."

"In light of the circumstances."

"Circumstances?"

"Since you've been so thoroughly humiliated."

"Humiliated? By whom?" Burr took a step toward Truax.

"I've thrashed you on this."

Burr hit Truax in the face, careful not to break the prosecutor's nose, which he found interesting. Truax fell back into the hallway. "That's for Christmas. I'll see you at the preliminary exam." Burr stepped over the fallen prosecutor on his way out.

CHAPTER EIGHT

Burr tap, tap, tapped his brand-new Number 2 yellow pencil, waiting for the Honorable Benjamin R. Gillis to make his appearance.

Gillis is on the same schedule as every other judge I've been before.

Burr sat next to Brian, who sat next to Jacob. Suzanne, Lisa and Eve behind them in the first row of the gallery. The court reporter, a thin, middle-aged woman with henna-colored hair, sat in front of the judge's raised desk. Truax sat across the aisle from Burr at the prosecutor's table, scowling.

He's still a jerk, but it doesn't look like my right cross did any lasting damage.

It wasn't exactly clear to Burr what he was doing at the preliminary exam. He hadn't been paid, and he still wasn't a criminal lawyer. After Brian had been charged and made bail, Burr had read the autopsy and the transcript of the inquest. He didn't see how Claudia's death could be anything but an accident. He read the transcript of Brian's first arraignment, paying close attention to what had gone on before he, Suzanne and Lisa had arrived. There was new evidence, but it was based on technology, and he'd always been suspicious of technology.

And it had happened so long ago. Brian had gotten on with his life. He'd remarried and had a child. There was no good reason to charge Brian with murder after all this time. He thought Brian was being railroaded. He didn't know why, but there was something going on.

Burr tapped his pencil again. He stopped, looked at it, then broke it in two.

Eve leaned over the railing. "Stop that. We haven't even started." She handed him another pencil.

Burr tapped his new pencil but didn't break it.

At last the bailiff entered. The same bailiff who'd been at the arraignment.

"All rise," he said. It came out *rithe.*

Gillis made his grand entrance and sat. "Thank you, Swede."

The judge looked at Brian. "We are here today for the preliminary examination of Brian R. Dunn to determine if there is enough evidence to bind him over for the murder of his wife, Claudia Dunn." Gillis turned to the prosecutor. "Mr. Truax, you may call your first witness."

Truax called Roland Gustafson, the first policeman to arrive at Brian's house that night. Gustafson was about sixty-five, with oily hair, mostly black, combed straight back, and a red, puffy face. His neck bulged over his collar.

Truax established Gustafson's qualifications, then led the cop through a narrative account of the evening. "Thank you, Officer Gustafson. Just a few more questions." He cleared his throat. "Going back to the beginning, do you recall what Mr. Dunn's first words were when you asked him what occurred at the crime scene?"

"Objection," Burr said. "There is no evidence that a crime was committed."

Gillis looked at Burr. "Mr. Lafayette, as you must be aware, there is no jury present who might be prejudiced by that statement, and I am offended that you might think I would be affected by such a comment."

"Your Honor, I apologize if I offended you. Still, I ask that the prosecutor's statement be stricken from the record."

"Granted," Gillis said. "Proceed, Mr. Truax."

"Yes, Your Honor. Let me rephrase the question. Mr. Gustafson, do you recall Mr. Dunn's first words when you arrived at the, at the, at Mr. and Mrs. Dunn's home on the night of the murder. Strike that," Truax said, turning and smiling ever so slightly at Burr, "on the night in question."

"He said, *I killed her.*"

"He said that?" Truax said.

"Yes," Gustafson said.

"And then what did you do?"

"I went down to the basement and there she was. Dead all right. I should say so."

"Did you examine the body?"

"I did."

"What did you find?"

"Bullet holes," Gustafson said.

"More than one?"

"Yes, sir."

"How many?" Truax said.

"Two." Gustafson raised two fingers on his left hand. He had pink, stubby fingers and a wedding ring that looked like the only way to take it off would be to cut it off.

Gillis leaned over toward Rollie. "Did you say there were two bullet holes?"

Gustafson nodded.

"That hardly seems like an accident." Gillis sat back in his chair. "You many continue, Mr. Truax."

"I have no further questions, Your Honor," Truax said.

Burr leaned over to Brian. "Two bullet holes? How do you shoot somebody accidentally two times?"

"Mr. Lafayette, do you wish to question this witness?" The bald judge peered down over his reading glasses. "If not, I will excuse him."

"Did you shoot her two times?"

"No."

"Mr. Lafayette, are you listening to me?" Gillis said.

"Yes, Your Honor. May I have a moment with my client?"

"No, you may not. When this hearing is over, you may have all the time you want with him."

Burr walked to the witness stand. He pulled down the cuffs of his pinpoint, baby blue oxford shirt which didn't need pulling down. Then he straightened his red tie with the black diamonds which didn't need straightening. He looked down at his oxblood loafers with the tassels. They needed polishing. He lifted the pant legs of his thousand-dollar charcoal suit with the white pinstripe, now a bit threadbare.

At least my socks match.

"Mr. Lafayette."

"Yes, Your Honor?"

"If you feel the need to preen like a peacock, I have a full-length mirror in my chambers."

Burr took a step closer to Gustafson and smiled at him. "Would you like to loosen your collar, Officer Gustafson?"

"I think I will." Gustafson unbuttoned the top button on his shirt. His neck overflowed onto his chest.

"Mr. Gustafson, are you a police officer?"

"Yes." Gustafson said. "Well, no."

"You're not in uniform. Are you a detective?"

"No," Gustafson said.

"But you're a police officer."

"Not anymore. I'm retired."

I knew that.

"Were you the first one to arrive at the house on the night of the accident?"

Truax popped up. "I object. It hasn't been determined that it was an accident."

Touché.

"Your Honor, both the autopsy and the inquest determined that it was an accident."

Gillis sighed. "Listen to me. Both of you. These grammatical niff naws are going to stop right now. You both will refer to this as *the night in question*. Is that clear?"

Truax nodded. Burr rolled his eyes.

"Mr. Lafayette, I'll take that as a *yes*. You may continue."

"Mr. Gustafson, were you the first to arrive on the night of the ... night in question?"

"Yes, I was."

"Mr. Gustafson, how long have you been retired?"

"Five years."

"The accident occurred six years ago. Just before you retired?"

"Mr. Lafayette, do not say *accident,"* Gillis said.

Burr started over. "Mr. Gustafson, did Mrs. Dunn die six years ago, just before you retired?"

"Yes," Gustafson said.

"That's a long time to remember, isn't it?"

"Objection. Calls for an opinion."

"Sustained," Gillis said.

"Mr. Gustafson, how many times had Mrs. Dunn been shot?" Burr said.

"Once," Gustafson said.

"Once," Burr said. "Then why were there two bullet holes?"

"Once where it went in. Once where it went out."

"I see. She had been shot once. Is that right?"

"Yes," Gustafson said.

"Thank you, Mr. Gustafson."

Does Truax think I'm stupid?

"When you arrived, Mr. Dunn let you in. Is that right?"

"Yes," Gustafson said.

"What was he doing?"

Gustafson looked at Truax, who scowled at the retired policeman.

"Officer Gustafson, what was Mr. Dunn doing when he opened the door?"

"Crying," Gustafson said.

"What did you say?" Burr said.

"He was crying."

"And when he did say something, do you recall what he said first?"

"He said, *she's dead, Rollie. The gun went off and she's dead.*"

"Did he say anything else?"

"No, I don't think so."

"Did he say it was an accident?"

Truax stood. "I object, Your Honor. Counsel is putting words in the witness's mouth."

Gillis gave Burr a menacing look. "I told you not to use that word."

"Your Honor, I'm merely asking the witness if my client said it was an accident."

Gillis looked down at Gustafson. "You may answer the question."

"I think so."

"Did he or didn't he?"

"He did," Gustafson said.

"Thank you." Burr looked back at Truax, then turned back to

Gustafson. "So when you arrived, you found Mr. Dunn crying. His first words were, *She's dead*. Then he said, *It was an accident*. Is that right?"

"Yes," Gustafson said.

"Thank you. I have no further questions."

The policeman heaved himself off the witness stand and walked up the aisle between Burr and Truax. Truax scowled at the fat cop, who refused to look in his direction. Gustafson looked at Brian. "I'm sorry, Brian. It was a long time ago."

Truax said, "The people call Lawrence Van Arkel."

Truax had tried to use Gustafson to mislead Gillis. Burr knew it and he was sure Gillis knew it. Van Arkel, though, might be a different story. Burr had read the autopsy, and this guy was no fool. Van Arkel wore a gray suit that didn't quite fit him, a white shirt and a solid black tie. His chest looked like it had sunk to his waist. About sixty. Bags under his eyes. Ears that looked like they were taped flat to his head. Wire-rimmed glasses. Thin lips turned into a perpetual frown.

He looks serious. Sincere and serious. But he is an undertaker.

Truax began by qualifying Van Arkel as an expert. As a licensed physician and mortician. Then he launched into the autopsy.

"Dr. Van Arkel, you were the county coroner at the time of Mrs. Dunn's death. Is that right?" Truax said.

"Yes," Van Arkel said.

"You performed the autopsy on Claudia Dunn. Is that right?"

"Yes."

"And what was the cause of death?" Truax said.

"Gunshot," Van Arkel said.

"Can you elaborate?"

"The bullet entered here." Van Arkel touched his left side at his armpit. "It passed through the left lung, the heart, the right lung, and exited here," he said, touching his right side, just above his hip.

Burr pushed his hair back off his forehead.

That's the end of the two-bullet-hole idiocy.

"What actually killed Mrs. Dunn?" Truax said.

"The bullet, as it passed through the heart and lungs," said the coroner.

"Thank you," Truax said. "Dr. Van Arkel, is it consistent with your findings that Mr. Dunn could have picked up the gun and shot Mrs. Dunn?"

"Yes, I suppose so," Van Arkel said.

"You suppose so," Truax said. "Can you be more definite? Is it consistent with your findings that the gun could have been picked up and fired from the shoulder?"

"Yes, it is," Van Arkel said.

"Objection, Your Honor," Burr said. "That's not what the autopsy says."

"The autopsy does not speak to that issue," Truax said.

Burr was on his feet now. "The autopsy does not say that Brian Dunn picked up the rifle and fired it from his shoulder."

"Your Honor," Truax said, "It also doesn't say he didn't."

"Overruled. I will let the testimony stand."

"Thank you, Your Honor," Truax said. "No further questions."

Burr approached the coroner. He saw the pattern in the coroner's tie. Red with little blue diamonds. The smallest blue diamonds he'd ever seen.

"Dr. Van Arkel," Burr said. "It is doctor, isn't it?"

"Yes," Van Arkel said.

"Thank you. Doctor, when you did the autopsy, did you believe the shooting was accidental?"

"I did," Van Arkel said.

"Was there anything in your examination that caused you to believe that the shooting might have been intentional?"

"No," Van Arkel said.

"Did the police ask you to determine if the shooting was intentional?"

"No."

"But you thought it was accidental?"

"Yes," Van Arkel said.

"Then why did you say that the autopsy was consistent with picking up the gun and firing it?"

"It could have happened that way."

"Your report says the gun went off while lying flat on the workbench," Burr said. "Doesn't it say that?"

"Yes. Yes, it does." Van Arkel was getting a bit flustered, which was just fine with Burr.

"Then why did you testify that the gun could have been picked up and fired." Burr said, not really asking.

67

"I suppose it could have."

"You suppose."

"Objection," Truax said. "Counsel is badgering the witness."

"Overruled. We're not quite at the badgering stage, Mr. Truax."

"It was lying on the workbench. I didn't think Brian picked it up. I suppose he could have picked it up and put it back down. They told me it was an accident. I had no reason to ..."

Burr raised his palm to Van Arkel. "Stop."

"Let the witness finish, Mr. Lafayette," Gillis said.

"I withdraw the question," Burr said.

"Very well," Gillis said.

"Dr. Van Arkel. You are a doctor, correct?"

"Yes," Van Arkel said.

"Do you practice medicine?" Burr said.

"No," Van Arkel said.

"Are you a full-time coroner?"

"No," Van Arkel said. "There's not enough work for a full-time coroner."

"I see," Burr said. "You are employed full time?"

"Yes," Van Arkel said.

"You're an undertaker, aren't you?" Burr said.

"A mortician," Van Arkel said.

"You embalm dead people, sell caskets, and do funerals," Burr said. "Isn't that right?"

"I have my own funeral home."

"Why aren't you a practicing physician?" Burr said.

"Objection, Your Honor. Irrelevant," Truax said.

"Mr. Lafayette, where is this going?" Gillis said.

"Your Honor, I am speaking to the qualifications of the witness."

"Mr. Lafayette, Mr. Truax, approach the bench."

"Your Honor," Burr said. "I'm trying ..."

Gillis waved him off. "Mr. Lafayette. As I said, there is no jury present." Gillis pointed to the jury box. "It's empty. All we're here to do is determine whether or not there is probable cause. I repeat, *probable cause* to determine if a murder has been committed. I will decide that. And as I hope you are aware, the rules of evidence are not as strict as they would be in a trial and, I repeat, probable cause is the standard for binding over for trial. The standard is not beyond a reasonable doubt." The portly judge sighed and folded his hands.

"Your Honor, my point is that this was an accidental shooting," Burr said. "The investigating officer thought so. The coroner, if you want to call him that, thinks so, too."

Gillis peered down at Burr over his reading glasses. "Mr. Lafayette, you thought he was qualified when he agreed with you."

"Your Honor," Burr said.

"Mr. Lafayette, in high school, Dr. Van Arkel played tackle and I played halfback. He blocked for me," Gillis said. "His qualifications are impeccable. Do you have any more questions?"

"No." Burr walked back to the defense table and sat.

Gillis adjourned them for an early lunch.

***

It had snowed about six inches overnight. The wind swirled the snow around their feet. Suzanne cut through the snow in her black boots. Jacob had pulled rubbers over his dress shoes. Burr refused to wear rubbers, which probably had something to do with why his shoes needed polishing.

Burr herded his clients down Lake Street to the Park Garden Café, one of Hemingway's Petoskey haunts. He'd told Eve he'd take to her to lunch here, and he thought today might as well be the day to make good on his promise to a fellow Hemingway fan. The hostess seated them at a window table. Burr looked up at the wood paneling that ran up the walls to the original tin ceiling. The carved wooden bar stuck out from the corner. The place smelled of smoke and stale beer. Burr watched Eve take it all in.

Brian, Lisa and Suzanne sat across from Burr, Jacob and Eve. The waitress, a fortyish blonde with gray roots, walked up to their table.

"What do you think Hemingway would have ordered for lunch?" Eve said.

"I never waited on him."

They all ordered the whitefish sandwich except Jacob, who ordered a grilled cheese on white with the crusts cut off, and Lisa, who said she couldn't possibly eat. Lisa looked across the table at Burr. "You said Truax has one more witness. Then this awful business will be over and we can all go home."

"Assuming Gillis finds there's no probable cause," Jacob said.

Lisa turned to Jacob. "Brian didn't murder anyone."

Jacob cleared his throat. "All Gillis has to do is find that it is more likely than not that a crime was committed. That's what probable cause means. If he believes there was probable cause, Brian will be bound over for trial."

Brian put his hand on Lisa's shoulder. "It was an accident."

Jacob cleared his throat. "At a trial, the jury can only find Brian guilty if they believe beyond a reasonable doubt that the crime was committed. It's a much higher standard at a trial."

"I don't care about your standards," Lisa said. "I want our life back." She looked at Burr again. "Mr. Lafayette, what about you? What do you think?"

"I don't think Truax did much damage this morning. He had to show that Brian killed Claudia, which he did, but he also had to show that Brian did it on purpose, which he didn't."

"There's just one more witness. Then we're done," Lisa said.

"The next witness is the one who turned up the new evidence. We don't know what she's going to say."

That's when the fireworks are going to start.

"We don't? Why don't we?"

"There's no discovery prior to a preliminary examination," Jacob said.

I wish our food would show up.

"Let Brian testify this afternoon. Let him tell what really happened," Lisa said.

Jacob cleared his throat again to speak. "Mrs. Dunn, if, at this point, your husband tells his version ..."

"It's not a version. It's the truth."

"Of course it's the truth," Jacob said. "But Brian will be telling what happened to the judge. With no corroborating witnesses, it's really not that useful in this type of hearing." He cleared his throat one more time.

It's the marijuana.

"Anything Brian says can be used against him in the trial," Jacob said.

Burr looked over at Brian, who looked like he was making a point not to look at anyone.

Why doesn't he say something?

"You two have given up, haven't you?" Lisa looked at Suzanne. "Why did we hire him? You said he knew what he was doing."

"We have to trust Mr. Lafayette," Brian said.

He finally said something.

"He hasn't done a thing for us so far."

Their lunch arrived.

Thank God for small favors.

Burr took a bite of his sandwich. He chewed it slowly. Lisa stared at him while he ate.

I wish she would have ordered something.

He ate more of his sandwich and some fries. Then he started on his coleslaw. Lisa kept staring at him.

I give up.

"Lisa, if I put Brian on and he says the wrong thing or if Truax twists it around, it will hurt us later. And if I put Brian on and he has to take the Fifth Amendment when Truax questions him, that hurts, too."

"Then what are you going to do?" Lisa said, on the edge of hysterical.

"I'm going to listen." Burr took another bite of his sandwich.

CHAPTER NINE

After a miserable lunch with great food at a great place, Burr led the way back to the courthouse. Truax called Ellen Gannon, a prim woman in her late thirties. She had on a blue blazer, a knee-length gray skirt, a white blouse with a Peter Pan collar and sensible black pumps. She had a fair complexion, complete with a button nose, brown hair with auburn highlights in a pageboy cut. Perhaps the most fetching pageboy Burr had ever seen.

Swede, the bailiff, swore her in.

She sat and tugged her skirt down to her knees. She crossed her legs, then rocked one leg back and forth. Her heel slipped out of her shoe.

There's something about this Ellen Gannon.

"Ms. Gannon," Truax said, "you work in the criminal laboratory division for the Michigan State Police. Is that correct?"

"Yes, sir," she said.

"What is your educational background?"

"I have a Ph.D. in applied physics," she said.

"So it's Dr. Gannon."

She nodded.

Truax already knew that.

"Do you have a specialty?"

"Laser technology."

"And how does that relate to this case?"

"I studied the path of the bullet that killed the deceased," she said.

"Just a moment, Mr. Truax." The judge took off his reading glasses, looked through them and handed them over the edge of the desk. The court reporter reached up and took the glasses with her long, thin fingers, like a piano player's. Miss Long Fingers looked through the glasses, breathed on each lens front and back, then rubbed them on the hem of her skirt. She passed them up to Gillis, who took them in his plump fingers. The whole performance lasted barely a minute, a ritual they must have performed hundreds of times.

"As I was about to say, in the interest of time, you might ask the witness to tell us what she did in a narrative fashion."

"Your Honor?"

"No more twenty questions."

Truax nodded. "Dr. Gannon, would you please tell the court what you did and what you found. In a narrative fashion."

Burr leaned toward the fetching Ellen Gannon. This was the witness with the new evidence that got Brian indicted. Evidence that Gillis took on the word of Truax.

Now we'll see what Truax has.

"The state police – me, actually – in conjunction with the Physics Department at Michigan State University, developed a new technology to determine the path of a projectile. In layman's terms, a bullet."

Burr raised his eyebrows, surprised she hadn't said *layperson.*

"Actually, I work backwards. Because the bullet passed through the deceased's body, I found where it struck the basement wall. Then I studied the coroner's report to determine where the bullet entered and exited the body."

"And what did you find?" Truax said.

"I found that the bullet entered the deceased about four inches below her left shoulder. It pierced her heart and lungs, then exited her right side three and a half inches above her hip. From there it stuck in the basement wall, approximately thirty inches above the floor."

"Dr. Gannon, please tell us the significance of determining the path of the bullet," Truax said.

"Based on the bullet's trajectory, I can, with the use of a laser, determine where the gun was fired from and at what angle it was pointed."

Burr stood. "Objection, Your Honor. The witness stated the gun was fired. The inquest determined that the gun went off accidentally. Firing connotes a purposeful activity."

"Mr. Lafayette, the shooting was purposeful," Gannon said, bobbing her foot.

"Dr. Gannon, while I take heart at your opinion, please do not respond to defense counsel's question," Gillis said. He turned to Truax. "Counselor, I'm sure you have a response."

"Yes, Your Honor," Truax said. "The witness is expressing her opinion based on her scientific analysis of the evidence. I don't agree with Mr. Lafayette that the inquest found the shooting to be an accident. But that, Your Honor, is the very reason we're here today. To show that the shooting was not an accident. In fact, Your Honor, if I may proceed ... I will demonstrate the factual nature of the witness's statement."

"Mr. Truax," Gillis said, "you may proceed, but may I remind you, too, that there is no jury present." He swept his arm — the black robe sweeping behind his arm in a grand gesture — past the empty jury box. "Spare me the theatrics."

"Yes, Your Honor." Truax walked back to the prosecution table and picked up a thick-bound report. He opened it to a paper-clipped page and returned to the witness stand. Gannon stopped bobbing her foot.

"Dr. Gannon, I have here the report issued following the inquest. On Page 41, the following was found to have occurred: *On the night of December 17, 1977, while Brian Dunn was cleaning his deer rifle on his workbench in the basement of his home, the rifle went off and the bullet struck and killed his wife*. Ms. Gannon, what is your opinion of that finding of fact?"

"That statement is factually incorrect."

"Objection," Burr said. "That statement is exactly what was in the report."

The vein on Truax's forehead started to throb. Burr didn't know where this was going, but he wanted to rattle Truax. Fortunately, Gillis didn't seem too impressed with this laser hocus-pocus. Maybe he could distract Gillis enough to muddle the testimony.

"Let me rephrase the question. Do you believe that the findings of the inquest are factually correct?"

"I do not," Gannon said.

"Objection," Burr said.

"I get the point, Mr. Lafayette, but overruled," Gillis said. "Proceed, Mr. Truax."

"Ms. Gannon, what did your research show?" Truax said.

Here it comes.

"The workbench in question is forty-two inches high. If the rifle went off while being cleaned on the workbench, the bullet's path would be parallel to the floor. That is, the bullet would enter and exit the body at a height of forty-two inches and then strike the wall at forty-two inches."

"And what happened in this case?" Truax said.

"The bullet had a downward trajectory. The path went from high to low," Gannon said.

Burr stood. "I object, Your Honor. This line of questioning, while somewhat interesting, does not prove, does not even hint at, anything suggesting a crime. Let alone murder."

The judge took off his glasses again, looked through them and passed them back to Miss Long Fingers.

They can't possibly need cleaning already.

"Mr. Truax, I don't find this even somewhat interesting. Do you have a point to make?"

Truax turned red. "Your Honor, I apologize for the lengthy testimony, but it's necessary to supply a foundation for the factual conclusions of the witness. If I may have just a few more minutes, it will become obvious that a murder was, indeed, committed."

"I wait with bated breath." Miss Long Fingers passed up his glasses. Gillis put them back on and thumped his forehead.

"Dr. Gannon, please tell us once more what you found, in layman's terms."

I haven't rattled him at all.

The comely witness smoothed her skirt. "Backing up a bit, I was able to establish the path of the bullet because I knew where it struck the wall, where it exited the deceased and where it entered the deceased.

"And how did you know this?" Truax said.

"Because I knew the height of the deceased and where she was standing in the basement."

"And how did you know this?" Truax said.

"From the coroner's report and from a physical examination of the basement. I then set up my laser and determined the bullet's path.

From there I was able to determine the location of the rifle when it was fired."

"Objection," Burr said.

"Overruled," Gillis said.

Burr stood again. "Your Honor, you don't know what my objection is."

"That's right," Gillis said. "Continue, Mr. Truax."

Truax nodded at the judge. "And what did you find?"

"I found that the rifle could not have gone off from the workbench. The angle determined by the laser makes that impossible."

"How, then, do you believe the gun was fired," Truax said. "Strike that. Discharged."

"According to the path of the bullet, there is only one way for the entry and exit wounds to occur the way they did and for the bullet to strike the wall the way it did."

"And how would that be?"

"The defendant would have to raise the rifle to his shoulder, aim it, and pull the trigger," she said.

Brian wrung his hands. Burr leaned behind Brian. "Jacob, are you following this?"

"Yes. Are you?"

"I am now." Burr believed the Earth was round, but he didn't trust science any more than he trusted elevators. He turned to Brian. "Did you pick up the gun and shoot her?"

"No."

Burr stood. "I object, Your Honor. This is speculation. Total speculation. Based on unfounded technology."

"Your Honor, before you rule, may I demonstrate what the witness has said?"

"I will allow anything that will further the cause of clarity."

Truax walked back to his table, reached underneath it and produced a wooden rifle. He introduced the facsimile of a deer rifle into evidence, over Burr's objection. Truax then walked over to the witness box with the pretend rifle.

"Ms. Gannon, assume the railing is the workbench and place the gun the way the inquest reported the position of the gun."

She took the toy from Truax and placed it flat on the railing.

"Is this how your findings show that the gun went off?"

"No," she said.

"Please show us how, according to your study, the gun was discharged."

Gannon uncrossed her legs and stood. She picked up the toy gun.

She's enjoying herself.

"The only way it could have happened was like this." She picked up the prop and raised it to her shoulder. "There's only one way to explain the path of the bullet." She pointed the gun at Burr.

"Bang," she said.

Burr jumped in his seat.

"I have no further questions, Your Honor." Truax turned to Burr, smiled at him, then walked back to his table.

Damn it all.

Burr approached the witness stand. "Ms. Gannon ..."

"It's Doctor," Dr. Gannon said.

Of course, it is.

Burr smiled at her.

"Dr. Gannon, you testified that you determined the trajectory of the bullet by a connect-the-dot method. Is that right?"

"Objection," Truax said. "Defense counsel is ridiculing proven technology."

"Sustained," Gillis said.

"Ms. Gannon, excuse me, Dr. Gannon. Assuming that this technology is scientifically sound, and I, for one, have always been suspicious of the foundations underlying the laws of physics ..."

"Objection," Truax said.

"Please don't prattle, Mr. Lafayette," Gillis said.

"Assuming your straight-line theory, couldn't a bullet strike a bone, be deflected and go off in another direction?"

"I suppose it could," she said.

Burr thought the prim Dr. Gannon might be a bit put off.

"So ... if the bullet hit a bone, it could change the path of the bullet?"

"I suppose that might be possible."

"Dr. Gannon, please don't be coy. Could the course of a bullet be changed if it struck a bone?"

"It could, but it didn't," she said.

"And why is that?"

"At such close range, the force of a 30:06 rifle is so strong, the path of the bullet wouldn't be changed if it struck a bone."

"But it could happen," Burr said.

"It could, but it didn't. Not here."

"Dr. Gannon, your findings were made by your knowledge of the location of the wounds and the location of the bullet in the basement wall. Is that right?"

"Yes." She started to bob her foot again.

"And how did you obtain this information?" Burr said.

"From the coroner's report."

"The undertaker?" Burr said.

"Objection," Truax said.

"Stop it, you two," Gillis said.

"Any other sources?" Burr said.

"The inquest."

"And did either of those reports, particularly the coroner's report, mention whether or not the bullet had struck a bone?"

"I don't remember."

"I see." Burr paced back and forth in front of the jury box. Then he stopped. "Let me refresh your memory. The coroner's report does not mention whether or not the bullet struck a bone. It's silent on the matter."

Dr. Gannon, too, was silent on the matter.

"Did these two documents contain all of the information necessary for your findings?" Burr said. Ellen Gannon's eyes darted to Truax, then back to Burr.

"Dr. Gannon, to determine the angle of the bullet, wouldn't you have to know the height of the deceased? Yes, of course you would." Burr put his hands in his pockets. "I don't recall the height of the deceased mentioned anywhere in either report."

"I'm sure it's in there," she said.

Burr put his hands on the railing of the witness stand and leaned toward her. "I assure you, it's not."

"Objection, Your Honor," Truax said. "This is irrelevant."

Gillis peered over his glasses again. "Mr. Lafayette, where is this going?"

"Your Honor, the prosecution's theory is based on establishing the trajectory of the bullet. To do that, they have to know the victim's height. I believe it is eminently relevant to learn how the witness determined the height of the deceased or if, in fact, she ever knew it."

Gillis sighed. "Continue, Mr. Lafayette."

"Ms. Gannon, how did you determine the deceased's height?"

"I don't remember," she said.

"Surely something this critical ..."

She interrupted him. "I know, yes, now I remember. I got it from her driver's license."

"Thank you," Burr said, who wasn't at all thankful. "And what about her shoes?"

"Her shoes?"

"Yes, her shoes. Most people wear shoes, especially in the winter."

"Oh, yes. Her shoes." She smiled at him and bobbed her foot. "I added an inch."

"An inch. Why an inch?" he said.

"Because that's the average heel height.

"But if she were wearing dress shoes." Burr looked down at his shoes. "Say ... pumps. Sensible pumps like yours. That's a two-inch heel you have, isn't it?" Gannon stopped in mid-bob.

"Yes, but she wasn't," Gannon said.

"How do you know that?"

"Because she'd just come in from cutting a Christmas tree."

"What if she took her boots off when she came in. Then she'd just be in her stocking feet."

"Objection," Truax said.

"Please get to the point, Mr. Lafayette," Gillis said.

"Your Honor, the point is, my client is accused of murder. And the prosecution has based its entire case on this voodoo science. And this voodoo science is worthless if the underlying data is shoddy. And I submit that the data is shoddy. And one more thing. How do we know that the information on the deceased's driver's license is valid? It's my understanding that we all shrink over time. We get shorter as gravity pulls us down. For instance, I report my height as six feet. Indeed, once I was. I know I'm not that height now, but I've never changed my height on my driver's license."

"Then you're lying," Truax said.

"Judge Gillis, how about you?" Burr said.

The judge jumped in his seat. "Who, me? It doesn't matter what I say my height is."

"Your Honor," Burr said, "My point is that the prosecution, in trying to establish probable cause, is relying on precise scientific measurements. Yet it is not clear that their data is at all precise. They don't have any firsthand evidence. It's all secondhand. Hearsay. Admissible hearsay but no firsthand knowledge. They haven't examined the body. They haven't visited the site of the accident."

"That's not true," Gannon said. "I did visit it."

"Even the location of the bullet is the result of reading a report," Burr said.

"No, that's not true. I was there."

Burr spun toward Gannon. "What did you say?"

"I said I was there, in the basement. I measured where the bullet hit the wall."

"You were in the house?"

"Yes," she said.

"How did you get in?" Burr said.

"The realtor gave me the key."

"The realtor," Burr said.

"Yes."

"Were you interested in buying the house?"

"No," she said.

"I take it you weren't going to lease it, either."

"No," she said.

"So ... you entered the house for the purpose of finding information for your study."

"That's right," Gannon said.

"Who suggested you do this?"

"Mr. Truax," she said.

"I see." Burr turned to Gillis. "Your Honor, my client was illegally arrested in Grosse Pointe. Now it appears that his home has been illegally searched. Is the prosecution required to abide by the Constitution?"

Burr thought he had something. All this fumbling around and now he tripped over this. He had lit up Truax, who showed every sign of exploding — throbbing forehead, gulping Adam's apple, crimson face.

It was the prosecutor's turn to stand. "The house was for sale. It's been for sale for six years. The house was available for the public to enter. Ms. Gannon gained access legally."

Burr stepped toward Judge Gillis. "Your Honor, I move that the testimony of this witness be stricken."

"I'll do nothing of the kind," Gillis said. "Mr. Lafayette, I am tired of your procedural shenanigans. I am going to allow Ms. Gannon's testimony. If you don't like it, you may take exception to my ruling and appeal it."

"Does the protection of the Bill of Rights extend this far north?" Burr said.

Truax popped up. "Objection, Your Honor."

"Quiet! Both of you," Gillis roared. "This is a preliminary exam, and I intend to be done with it." Gillis tore off his glasses and whipped them at a visibly shaken Miss Long Fingers. He rubbed his eyes. "If the defense has no witnesses, we'll take a ten-minute recess and then I will hear closing arguments. My glasses, please," he said. Gillis placed them on the bridge of his nose, gaveled his gavel and stomped out.

***

Burr didn't believe Truax's closing argument had gone particularly well. He had a dead wife and an expert witness who said that the rifle couldn't have been lying flat on the workbench when it went off. The gun had to have been shouldered, aimed, and fired. Gillis seemed attentive until the radiator, the old steam kind, started to hiss, which seemed to agitate the judge. Truax, sensing this, had charged through the conclusion of his argument.

For his part, Burr was sure that keeping Brian off the witness stand had been the right thing to do. Truax would have torn Brian to shreds.

Burr had done his best to discredit Gannon's laser study and to batter Truax and his methods. He thought the judge sufficiently unimpressed with Truax, and he intended to finish off the overzealous prosecutor right now.

Burr paced back and forth, then stopped in front of the judge.

"Your Honor, if, just for the sake of argument, we assume that the prosecution obtained its evidence legally and that the findings of the laser study are accurate, then I submit the evidence is still not sufficient to bind Mr. Dunn over for trial. Even if we assume that Mr. Dunn picked up the rifle, there is still something missing."

Burr swept his hair back behind his ears and pulled his cuffs down past the sleeves of his jacket. He turned to Truax. "We have here a killing, a tragic killing. But murder? No. It was an accident just the way Mr. Dunn's statement at the inquest said it happened, the way the investigating officer determined, the way the coroner said it happened, and the way the inquest determined that it happened."

"What about motive? The prosecution doesn't even mention motive. In the state of Michigan, there is no murder without motive." Burr turned and pointed at Truax. "You have done nothing, nothing whatsoever, to show any type of motive. All you have done is continually trample the rights of my client over a tragic accident that happened six years ago."

"Do not attack Mr. Truax," Gillis said.

Burr turned back to Gillis and nodded. "Your Honor, if the prosecution claims, as it must, that there must be a motive because the gun was shouldered, and therefore the shooting was intentional, I object. Mr. Dunn could have picked up the gun and looked down the barrel while he cleaned it, and it went off. It was an accident. That's a reasonable explanation even if you believe everything the prosecution alleges. And that's not murder."

He paced in front of the judge again, then stopped in front of the witness stand. "Your Honor, without a motive, the prosecution has nothing more than a shadowy line of reasoning built on questionable scientific principles questionably applied." He pointed at Truax. "If the prosecution cannot demonstrate a reason why Mr. Dunn killed his wife of almost twenty years, then I submit there is no likelihood, no probable cause that a crime was committed. Even with the lower legal threshold for determining whether Mr. Dunn should stand trial, the prosecution has simply not met the threshold for murder." Burr felt his shirt clinging to his back. "If there's no motive, there's no murder."

Gillis cocked his head like Zeke-the-dog did when he didn't understand. "Mr. Truax?"

"The people believe the facts speak for themselves," Truax said.

"Anything else, Mr. Lafayette?" Gillis said.

"Your Honor," Burr said, still standing, "The defense repeats its objection to the laser evidence and to the illegal entry into Mr. Dunn's house."

"This is an evidentiary hearing, and the court intends to take notice of all potential evidence."

"Your Honor, the defense ..."

"Mr. Lafayette, please approach the bench."

Burr stood in front of Gillis. "Mr. Lafayette, I will note this objection as I have noted your nineteen prior objections. This is my goddamn courtroom, and I will do as I see fit. I'm allowing the testimony and if you don't like it you may appeal." Gillis took off his glasses. "Is that clear?"

That won't work this time.

"Yes, Your Honor."

Gillis looked at the empty gallery. "The court finds that the state has presented sufficient evidence to conclude that probable cause exists that the defendant, Brian R. Dunn, did murder Claudia Dunn on December 17, 1977. Therefore, the district court hereby remands this case over to the circuit court for the County of Emmet, where Mr. Dunn will be tried for murder. Bail will remain at one hundred thousand dollars. The defendant is further ordered to remain in Emmet County until after the conclusion of the trial." Gillis raised his gavel.

"Your Honor," Burr said, standing.

"What is it this time?"

"Your Honor, Mr. Dunn has a home and a business in Grosse Pointe. I respectfully ask that he be permitted to return to Wayne County."

"Mr. Lafayette, the court notes that, based on Mr. Dunn's recent behavior, he could be considered a flight risk. The court further notes that the defendant still has a home here in Emmet County. My order stands. We are adjourned." Gillis crashed his gavel and stormed out.

CHAPTER TEN

Burr chewed the olive, slowly. It had been marinating nicely, along with the other three, in his very dry, very dirty Bombay Sapphire gin martini on the rocks. He sat at the bar of the Resorter, the restaurant on the first floor of the Harbour Inn.

The 'u' is an affectation.

The Harbour Inn rested comfortably on the beach of Little Traverse Bay, just outside Harbor Springs, on the way to Petoskey. The Resorter was one of Northern Michigan's finest and priciest restaurants. It was 5:30 in the afternoon, perfectly dark outside and not much lighter inside. A perfect place to stew about the day's courtroom debacle.

Stewart, the innkeeper, one of Burr's oldest and most difficult friends, sat down next to him. Burr, in light of his cash position, had taken a room at the Harbour Inn, knowing that Stewart wouldn't charge him.

"I'll have what he's having, but hold all the olive paraphernalia," Stewart said to the bartender. He looked at Burr. "I see she's back."

"It's business." Burr took a large swallow of his martini.

"Monkey business."

"This time, it is business," Burr said, but he did quite like seeing Suzanne again, even if it was at arm's length, at least so far.

"Business plus sex."

"Not this time."

"Not yet." Stewart had dark hair, a nose that looked a lot like a dill pickle, and a mustache that started inside his nose. He wore his blue blazer with the family crest on the breast pocket. He studied his martini and took a sip. "As you know, there are no dogs allowed."

"Zeke has been a guest here before," Burr said.

"We have to protect our four-star rating." Stewart always let Zeke stay at the inn, but he always complained about it.

Stewart's great-grandfather had built an elegant four-story, wood frame hotel at the turn of the century, when the two-hundred-foot passenger liners steamed in from Chicago and Detroit to the deep-water port at Harbor Springs. The resorters, as Stewart still called them, came for the cool, pollen-free air of Northern Michigan, the clear blue water of Little Traverse Bay, and the artesian springs.

Burr thought the elegance had slipped to genteel shabbiness.

"I say we adjourn to the dining room and have the veal morel." Stewart, all six-and-a-half feet of him, stood and looked down at Burr. A rough-hewn walking stick with a big nose. "I suppose you'll be wanting to stay here for the trial."

"I thought I'd live on the boat, at least for the summer."

Stewart thudded to his chair. "On *Kismet*?"

Burr traded the use of his *Kismet* for a room at the inn, complete with food and drink. In turn, Stewart sailed the boat when Burr wasn't there, which was most of the time. Apparently, a little more Burr presence would cramp Stewart's yachting style.

"Married women don't like boats," Stewart said.

"I don't have a wife."

"It's something about marriage. Girlfriends always love boats. But you marry them and, all of a sudden, poof, they hate boats." Stewart touched the fingertips of his left hand with those of his right, and, at the poof, he flashed them apart like a magician. "Poof," he poofed again.

"Suzanne likes the boat," Burr said.

"That's because you're not married," Stewart said in his irritating faux English innkeeper accent. "My wife doesn't like boats. She just doesn't like them anymore, and she was brought up on Long Island Sound."

Stewart led him into the dining room — a great high-ceilinged room with wall-to-wall windows on the bay side — to a table just off the fireplace, a floor-to-ceiling fieldstone built from the rocks left here millions of years ago by the retreating glacier.

"We'll start with the whitefish pâté," Stewart said to the waiter. "Now, as I was saying, married women do not like boats, particularly sailboats and, to reiterate, neither my wife nor your former wife for that matter, liked *Kismet* after we married them."

"Grace didn't like the boat."

"And if you were to marry Suzanne, she won't like the boat, even though she likes it now." Stewart picked up his cocktail napkin and started to fold it.

"While I agree with your theory generally, Suzanne would be an exception, but your theory is never going to be put to the test."

"We'll see about that." Stewart dropped the cocktail napkin, folded into the shape of a boat, in Burr's martini. It floated for a moment, then sank.

***

A week later, Burr lay on his navy-blue couch in his office in East Lansing. Zeke lay on the oriental rug in front of the couch, put off at being put off the couch. Burr stretched his toes and brushed against the far arm of the couch. It was long enough for him to take a nap fully stretched out, which was the only reason he'd bought it. He yawned and fell asleep.

It was dark when he woke up, Jacob and Eve gone for the day. No one had come in while he slept. The phone hadn't rung.

"Zeke, old friend, this isn't exactly a thriving practice."

Burr looked across the room. A man was sitting in the dark at his desk, his back to Burr. A silhouette in the shadows. He stood, looked out the window, then turned to Burr.

"My god, Brian, what are you doing here?" These unannounced visitors were too much. First, Suzanne at Walpole Marsh. Now, Brian. Burr walked to his desk and sat in one of the side chairs. Zeke looked over at Brian, barked once, then put his head back down.

You're not much of a watchdog.

"What are you doing here?"

"I was a dentist for twenty years. I coached baseball at the high school. I liked being a dentist. I liked coaching. I liked deer hunting. I love my son. I loved coaching baseball, and I was good at it."

"You have a son?"

"He's in the navy. Chad blamed me for Claudia's death." Brian looked away then back at Burr. "I fell in love with Lisa and we got married. My practice fell apart. We moved to Grosse Pointe, and I bought a practice from a dentist who wanted to retire, but it didn't work out. I took what was left of my savings and Lisa and I opened a greeting card store. Lisa's Cards and Candles. It's on the hill."

Burr nodded.

"Now I sell greeting cards, knickknacks, and perfumed candles. The cards are okay but, my God, the smell of those damn candles.

"We have a little girl. She's five, and I'm fifty. I killed my first wife. It was an accident that I'll never get over. I don't know when I'm going to see my son again." Brian tapped one of Burr's yellow pencils. "I lost my life once. I'm not going to lose it again."

"You'll go back to jail if you don't go back to Petoskey," Burr said.

"What do you mean?"

"We went over this. You can't leave Emmet County."

"I have to run my business."

Burr walked around to his desk chair. He took the pencil from Brian. "You go sit there." He pointed at one of the side chairs. Brian moved and sat across from Burr.

That's better.

"I guess it's time to hear what happened that day, Brian." Burr looked past Brian at the Christmas tree in the reception area.

I should have taken it down a month ago.

***

Burr waited for Suzanne on the front porch of Brian's house in Petoskey. It was on Waukazoo in an old neighborhood just off Mitchell, not far from downtown. The two-story Victorian sat in the middle of the block, surrounded by Victorians of the same vintage, each with its own gingerbread trim. Brian's house was white, trimmed in blue with a baby blue beadboard ceiling on the porch.

It's a fine house, but not a good place to murder your wife.

Burr had spent the past two months working on cases that actually paid and thought that he just might have enough money to get by until the trial was over.

He shivered in his Barbour coat, the dark green, almost black waxed-cotton jacket that smelled like an old-fashioned canvas tent and reminded him of grouse hunting.

I love this coat.

It was April, spring in Detroit, mostly spring in East Lansing, but just a rumor here. The trees were bare, there were piles of snow everywhere and Little Traverse Bay was still frozen. He'd slipped on a patch of ice on his way up the sidewalk but caught himself before he fell.

He shivered again.

I should have known she'd be late.

Suzanne roared into the driveway twenty minutes later. Burr opened her door. She got out but didn't say a word, which wasn't surprising because she'd told Burr she didn't want to have anything to do with seeing where Claudia had been killed.

Burr didn't either, but he was damned if he was going to do this by himself.

Suzanne unlocked the side door to the garage and went in.

This must be the way Brian brought in the Christmas tree.

He followed her into the garage, then through the back door into a mudroom. It was warmer inside but not by much. Burr thought that the furnace was on, but only enough to keep the pipes from freezing.

There was a step up to the kitchen and steps down to the basement. Burr slipped and started to fall down the stairs, but Suzanne grabbed him.

"You could have killed yourself."

At least she's talking.

"Be careful."

Burr steadied himself and put his arms around her.

"Not here," she said.

He pulled her a little closer and remembered her small waist.

"Of all places, not here."

He'd been feeling slightly amorous ever since she'd suddenly re-entered his life. Burr had kept his distance, partly because of the way it had ended between them, and partly because he wasn't sure it was a good idea to relight the fire, but mostly because Suzanne had given him no sign that her interest was in anything other than his lawyering.

He started down the stairs again, one hand on the railing, the other on the fieldstone wall. The stones had white, gray and pink tones, gold flecks and were rough to the touch.

When he reached the basement, he looked around, then made his way over to Brian's workbench. His tools still hung on the pegboard. There was a small room off to his left, with just a hint of daylight filtering through the cobwebs. Standing at the workbench, he looked back at Suzanne halfway down the stairs.

"This must be where he shot her."

"Where she was killed," Suzanne said.

"That's what I meant."

Burr found a broom against the wall and pointed it, handle first, toward the spot where Brian said Claudia had been standing.

"Go stand there," Burr said.

"I will not," Suzanne said.

"I need to understand what happened. That's why we're here. That must be where it happened. Right about there. Go stand there so I can line it up."

"I will not," she said again.

"I need to see what happened. From where the gun went off."

"It's bad luck," Suzanne said.

"What is?"

"To stand where someone died. In their shadow."

Burr walked to the landing. The floor didn't look any different here than anywhere else. The fieldstones didn't look any different, either. He felt the wall. Here, maybe here, a chip out of this stone. But the stonemason could have done it. He couldn't see any blood on any of the fieldstones or on the floor.

"All right then, you go over to the workbench and be Brian."

"No," she said.

"Suzanne, I need to see how it happened."

"Why?"

"Truax has a laser and we've got a broom. Go over there and point it at me."

Suzanne backed up the stairs, a step at a time, then turned and ran out of the house. The door slammed behind her.

Damn it all.

He walked back to the workbench and laid the broom on it, pointing it toward the wall. If the gun had gone off on the bench while Brian was cleaning it, the bullet would have struck Claudia at the height of the workbench, below Brian's chest but higher on Claudia, who was only five-foot-four. It could have happened the way Brian said. But the laser lady said the bullet struck Claudia below her shoulder and exited on a downward trajectory.

Maybe Gannon was right. But it was possible that Brian could have picked up the gun and it could still have been an accident. Just the way Burr had argued in the preliminary exam.

He picked up the broom and aimed it again. He swung it around, banging it on a pair of cross-country skis leaning against the wall. Old wooden skis with the cable bindings. They crashed to the floor. The basement was full, as if someone still lived there, like Brian had never moved out. Brian had his screwdrivers on the pegboard, lined up in a row, little to big. All with red handles. He reached underneath the workbench and pulled on the handle of a paint roller. He tried to lift it out of the roller pan, but it stuck. He jerked on it, but the pan was stuck to the floor. He yanked with both hands and the pan let go of the floor. He hoisted the roller, still stuck in the pan, to the workbench. In the blue of the fluorescent light, the battleship gray paint looked like putty. He pushed his finger in it and the smell of paint — sweet, thick, oil-based paint — oozed up at him.

He walked back over to the stairs. The light faded at the wall, but now, in front of him, he thought he could see the uneven edges where the roller had stopped rolling on the basement floor. He crouched down and ran his fingertips along the edge of the roller marks and felt the ridge where the paint ended.

This must be where Claudia fell.

He had no way of knowing when it was painted — right after Claudia died or later, when Brian put the house up for sale. Who wouldn't want to wash the blood away and paint over it? He couldn't see any blood on the wall. Maybe it had been scrubbed off the fieldstones.

But Claudia must have been shot right here, right where he crouched. He stood and looked over at the workbench.

"Bang," he said. He crumpled to the floor, on the fresh paint. He lay there, shot by his own word. "Bang," he said again, sprawling on the floor.

"Bang yourself," said a voice.

Burr jumped to his feet and saw a pair of legs on the stairs, legs in black tights that disappeared into a camel coat. A woman pointed a semi-automatic at him. She took two steps down the stairs, the pistol still pointing at him.

"What are you doing here?" she said.

"I could ask you the same thing."

"You could, but I'm the one with the gun."

Good point. A nine-millimeter.

She took two steps down the stairs and waved the gun at the workbench, then back at him. "It looks like all you've got is that broom on the workbench."

"I don't really need a gun to sell houses, but you never know who you might run into in this business." She smiled at him. "But you don't look very menacing."

Maybe I'm not going to be the second person shot in this basement.

"She died right there, right where you're standing. They couldn't get the blood off the floor so I painted it. I can't rent out a house with blood on the floor, much less sell it."

She came the rest of the way down the stairs. Burr retreated to the workbench.

She was about forty-five, tall, thin, a pointed nose, very white teeth and coral lipstick. She had shoulder length brown hair with blond highlights.

She's nicely put together.

"Do you have a name?" she said.

"Yes," he said. "Yes, I do."

"I suppose there's a good reason you broke into my listing."

"Your listing?"

"I'm the realtor. Have we met?"

"I wouldn't forget someone like you, especially if you're in the habit of introducing yourself with a pistol. Would you mind putting it away?"

"You can't be too careful, and this house is famous. More like infamous. It's priced to sell. I can have everything out in a jiffy. Or you could take it with the furniture."

She put the pistol in her black shoulder bag.

That thing could hold two days' worth of clothes.

"What happened?" Burr said.

"I thought you knew. What with the bang and all." She bit her cheek. "You mean you don't know?"

"I saw the sign outside and the door was open."

"The door was definitely not open." She twirled a strand of hair around her trigger finger. "You really don't know?" she asked again. The real-estate agent glanced down at the floor where Claudia had been shot. Then she brightened. "The house was owned by an elderly woman. She had a heart attack and died over there." She pointed to where Burr had been lying on the floor.

"What about the blood?"

"The blood?" she said.

"I didn't know there was blood with a heart attack."

"The blood. Oh, the blood. Well, she fell and hit her head. And the blood wouldn't come off. People don't like blood on the floor. Or a house where someone died. So I painted over it." She smiled sweetly at him.

"How long has it been for sale?"

"Not too long."

Burr turned around. "What's that room over there? The one with just a bit of light."

"That's the old coal room. The light must be from the coal chute. I'm sure it's boarded up. Or at least it's supposed to be."

"What about all this stuff?"

"It belongs to the owner."

"I thought you said it belonged to an elderly woman."

"The man who owns it now is her son. He inherited it."

She doesn't miss a beat.

"He can't afford two house payments. The furniture upstairs is included if you like. It's a beautiful old house. Turn of the century Victorian." She started up the stairs. Burr followed her. At the top of the stairs, she looked over her shoulder. "It's a nice basement. Stone walls, the fieldstone from right around here. Very cool in the summer. Not damp at all. It breathes. Come upstairs and I'll give you a tour."

She led him through the mudroom and into the kitchen, ten-foot ceilings with hardwood moldings, windows facing east. Under foot, the linoleum felt like long swells on the lake, wavy and uneven. Straight-back spindle chairs around a maple table. What he took for a bathroom turned out to be the laundry room. The bare lightbulb had a pull string.

Burr followed her through a butler's door. "This is the dining room." She walked through an arch. "This is the parlor. That's what they called it then." She walked to a set of casement windows and sat. "Isn't this bay window grand." She pointed through another arch. "And there's the living room." She took him back to the front of the house.

"This is where we should have started." An oak staircase ran up from the foyer. "You'll want to see the upstairs." She started up the stairs. "Four bedrooms, small ones, and a bath. One bath. That's a problem, I know, but you could make the laundry room off the kitchen into a half bath and move the laundry downstairs. And the furniture is included if you like. I already said that, didn't I?" She looked down at Burr from the top of the stairs. "Are you listening to me?"

"Not really," Burr said.

"I didn't think so. My name's Kaye. Kaye Collins. And you are?"

"Burr Lafayette."

"What do you do?"

"I'm a lawyer."

"Good. Are you're looking for a summer home?"

"Not really."

"You're moving up here?"

"No."

"What then?" she said, irritated.

"I'm Brian Dunn's lawyer."

"Why didn't you tell me? I knew it ... that you knew. What with the bang, bang and all." She sat down on the top step. "Don't look up my skirt."

"I did want a tour."

"You got one. Now get out."

"How long have you had this listing?"

"I should have asked what you wanted at the beginning. I always do that." She blinked, then pulled an eyelash out of her eye. "The way you looked at me. I was being vain. That doesn't explain how you got in here in the first place." She stood up and stared down at him. "The thought of actually selling this damn place got me going. It was stupid of me. Even if you are Brian's lawyer. Let's just forget about this silly tour, shall we, Mr. Peepers?" She started down the stairs.

"I'm sorry, Ms. Collins. I thought you knew."

"You did not."

"Really. I did," Burr said in his most I'm-sorry-I-threw-the-baseball-through-the-window voice.

"You did not. Are you here to pull the listing? Brian doesn't need a lawyer for that. You can have it back. I can't sell it anyway."

"I represent Brian on the murder charge."

"You look too prosperous to be a criminal lawyer." She came all the way down the stairs and looked him in the eye. "Unless you're a drug lawyer."

There's got to be more money in drugs than this.

"I think it's a crime. I really do."

"That's what the prosecutor thinks," Burr said.

"It's a crime that Brian was arrested. After all this time. It must have been an accident."

If I got her on the jury, at least I'd have one vote to acquit.

She walked back into the parlor and sat on the upholstered cushions in the bay window, orange and red flowers on a faded yellow background.

"Do you have any idea why the prosecutor would do this?" Burr said.

"No. Not really. He's a law and order guy, though. Very conservative."

"Do you know him?"

"A little. Just to say *hello*. He's got a decent reputation. I think he's smart. Tough on crime."

Burr walked up to her but made a point of not sitting. "There's something that isn't right about this."

"I sell a lot of houses, but no one wants this one."

Burr nodded.

"Mostly in Harbor Springs. To the Grosse Pointers or the Bloomfield crowd. Some Chicago, St. Louis, Indianapolis. Ohio, too. This is my only listing in Petoskey. It's a favor to Brian. He taught my son how to play baseball. But nobody wants this house. A murder. Not a murder but a ..." Kaye's mouth hung open and sunlight played on a gold crown molar.

"An accident," he said.

"That's right. Who wants to live in a house where someone died? Even if it was an accident. Nobody will buy this house. The realtors here won't touch it. Anyway, no one wants it, and I was hoping you didn't know the story."

Burr smiled at her.

"I would have told you."

I'm sure you would.

"What about Brian and Lisa?"

"He married her and they left. Six months after Claudia died. Just like that." She snapped her fingers. "That turned some heads, but they seemed really happy. They moved to Grosse Pointe. I lived in Bloomfield Hills before I moved up here and divorced Maury." She bit her cheek again. "Actually, it was the other way around."

"I beg your pardon."

"Maury. First I divorced him. Then I moved up here."

"I see," Burr said, but didn't. "But Brian and Lisa could have stayed here."

"I suppose, but it was pretty ugly." She looked at a piece of the wallpaper next to the bay window. It had come unglued and flipped up. She licked her fingers, pushed the wallpaper back down and held it there. "It's dry in here. What do you expect? Nobody lives here." She took her finger off and the wallpaper popped back up. "It's a shame." She cocked her head at him. A gold earring sparkled in the sunlight.

"I guess we're done here." She stood, walked to the front door and looked back at him over her shoulder. "Lock the door on your way out."

***

Burr stopped at the high school on his way out of Petoskey. He thought he might as well see where Brian had coached. He turned off Mitchell into the high school and drove toward the baseball field. Burr saw a man in his mid-sixties standing on home plate, hands in his pockets. Boys were playing catch all around him. There were snowbanks around the backstop and in the shadows of the stands.

The first step is shoveling the field.

Burr walked up to the man.

"I don't think I saw you at the parents meeting."

"I wasn't there," Burr said.

"You want something?"

"I'm Brian Dunn's lawyer," Burr said.

"Dallas Stall." He shook Burr's hand.

"Are you the coach?"

"No, I'm just freezing my ass off out here because I like kids who don't listen and can't hit a curve ball."

"Didn't Brian Dunn coach baseball here?" Burr said.

"Assistant. He'd have been head coach by now and I'd be trolling for browns in the bay if the ice was out."

"Wasn't he kind of old to be an assistant?" Burr said.

Stall put his hand back in his pocket. "I was grooming him." The coach limped to the pitcher's mound, leading with his left leg and pulling his right leg through without bending it. He pulled off his hat and scratched the top of his head. He had short hair, more gray than black. His ears stuck out from his head, and he had a flat nose and thin lips. The coach sent the boys to the outfield to run laps. He stood behind Burr and lit a cigarette.

"Don't let them kids see this."

"Do you think it was an accident?"

"Musta been. Brian couldn't kill no one." Stall cupped the cigarette in his hand, his back to the outfield.

"Why did a dentist coach baseball?"

"It's hard to find somebody who knows baseball around here."

"It's been six years," Burr said.

"I had a guy but he didn't work out. And I couldn't just quit without a new coach. We got good baseball here." Stall inhaled the cigarette. "I don't like the boys to see me smoke. But they probably know."

"What happened?" Burr said.

Stall walked over to the fence on the first base side of the field.

"Brian wasn't that great a dentist. Nobody went to him for anything complicated. Just simple stuff. But he was a hometown boy." Stall kicked at the snow next to the fence. A chunk broke off, and he crushed it with his foot. "Killing his wife, even if it was an accident, sure didn't help his practice."

"Why?"

"How'd you like somebody poking around in your mouth who can't even figure out how to keep from pulling a trigger on a gun that ends up being loaded?"

Good point.

"It don't exactly inspire confidence, what with dentistry being all about fine motor control."

"I guess not."

"And the school board didn't renew his coaching deal. That just about broke his heart," Stall said. "But that ain't what really did it."

Burr looked at Stall.

"Well, if you ain't gonna ask, I'll tell you. Lisa worked for him. Office manager or some such thing. That's no big deal, but then he marries her."

"And?"

"His patients quit coming in. It was like turning off the faucet. Shuts his practice right down. So they moved." Stahl looked out at the boys.

"Do you think they had been having an affair?"

Stall dropped the cigarette in the dirt and crushed it with his foot. He picked up the butt and stuck it in his pocket. "I doubt he had it in him, but he sure had eyes for her." Stall whistled the boys in.

CHAPTER ELEVEN

Burr took Beach Road to the Harbour Inn. The road wound through the woods, then ran along Little Traverse Bay. It was late afternoon. The sun was still high in the sky, and there would be daylight until eight. It was spring downstate, but here there was still snow in the woods and ice in the bay.

It's an odd time of year up here.

He retrieved Zeke from Stewart and wasn't sure which of them was happier to be rid of the other. He spent a martini-free night with Zeke, waking up once to the tapping of rain on Stewart's tarnished copper roof.

The two of them drove back to Petoskey the next morning. The rain had turned to partly cloudy. At US-31, the fast-food restaurants sprung up in earnest.

"Zeke, the Petoskey city fathers have a different idea about tourism than they have in Harbor Springs."

At the crest of the Mitchell Street hill, Burr made a U-turn and pulled up to the curb. He parked the Jeep under a leafless maple tree, cracked the windows for Zeke and stood in front of the Van Arkel Funeral Home, Lawrence Van Arkel, Director. A three-story Victorian that had once been a real home. Burr admired the fresh coat of white paint, forest green shutters and matching gingerbread trim. He walked up to the covered porch and let himself in. An ageless, somber man in a funereal suit met him at the door.

"Jorgenson or Mothershead, sir?"

"Excuse me," Burr said.

"The Jorgenson visitation is in here." The somber man pointed into what once must have been the dining room. Burr peered in and saw a nose sticking out of an open casket.

"Mothershead is under way down there."

That must be the living room.

"Actually, I'm here to see Mr. Van Arkel."

"I'm afraid Dr. Van Arkel is with the Mothersheads."

"Mothershead it is," Burr said. He walked silently on the navy herringbone carpet to the Mothershead funeral. He slipped into the chapel, originally the living room, and slid into a chair in the back.

Burr quite enjoyed the eulogy and thought he would have liked the late Mr. Mothershead. After the service, the mourners departed with the recently departed, all except Burr, still sitting, and Van Arkel, standing over him.

"I came to ask you a few questions," Burr said.

The undertaker took a white, freshly pressed handkerchief from the breast pocket of his equally funereal suit and blew his nose. "I didn't think you came for the service. If you have questions, you may subpoena me."

"I'm trying to save a man's life."

"You know perfectly well that Michigan doesn't allow capital punishment." Van Arkel folded the handkerchief and put it back in his pocket.

"Dr. Van Arkel, I'm defending Brian Dunn on a charge of first-degree murder. He has a wife and child. ..."

"He has two children." The undertaker raised his hand and held out two fingers. "You ridiculed me. That's what you did. You ridiculed me."

So that's what I did.

"It could hurt my business."

It's always about the money.

I'm very sorry," Burr said, who wasn't. "What can I do to make it right?"

"Nothing."

Burr walked over to a bay window and noticed his Jeep. Zeke's nose poked out of the window. "There you are."

"Who?" Van Arkel said.

"My dog."

"What kind of dog is it, and why did you leave it in a car?"

Burr looked back at Van Arkel. "He's a yellow Lab, and I didn't think you'd want a dog in here."

"Your dog is more welcome here than you are." Van Arkel peered out the window. "Do you hunt your dog, Mr. Lafayette?"

"Ducks and geese mostly. Some pheasants. Arthritis has slowed him down on the pheasants."

Van Arkel turned to Burr. "I have two German shorthairs."

"Grouse and woodcock," Burr said.

"I prefer pointing dogs. They have a preciseness about them that flushing dogs do not. But a Labrador Retriever is useful in the water." Van Arkel cleared his throat. "I arrived after Rollie. I had no idea what had occurred or where. Then I saw Rollie at the foot of the basement stairs. I examined the body and took pictures."

"Why didn't the detectives or the crime scene cops take the pictures?"

"This is a small town, Mr. Lafayette. Petoskey isn't big enough for all that. In a murder, the chief would call in the state police. But not for an accident." Van Arkel looked down at his shoes, which didn't need polishing, then at Burr. "There was a great deal of blood. I had forgotten how much, really. I never really see it because I drain it into ..."

"Dr. Van Arkel, I appreciate your ..."

"A touch queasy, are we? Of course. Sometimes I forget," Van Arkel smiled. "I asked Rollie if he had moved the body, and he said no, he hadn't. Except to check for a pulse which, of course, there wasn't. No one could survive a gunshot from a 30:06 at that range."

"First, I took pictures — an entire roll. Then I examined the wound. The entry bullet left a small hole, no bigger than a nickel. The exit wound was much bigger — about two-and-a-half inches across. Normally, a 30:06 tumbles inside the flesh and leaves a gaping hole, but not at this range."

"Where did the bullet enter?"

"As I testified, just below the left armpit, slightly to the rear of the arm. It then exited between the right armpit and the hip, just on the abdomen side of the right side, slightly below the point it entered. Like this." The undertaker drew a line through himself marking the bullet's path.

"Did you see anything that struck you as odd?"

"No. It appeared to be what it was. Accidental death by gunshot."

"Why did you think it was an accident?"

"Who would be so stupid as to shoot one's wife in the basement with one's son upstairs?" Van Arkel said.

"Unless one was very clever."

"Brian's not that clever."

"Maybe he lost his temper."

Van Arkel took a deep breath, then let it out. "I've known Brian since third grade. I never once saw him lose his temper."

"What about the difference in the height of the entry and exit wounds? Doesn't that seem like the gun was fired from the shoulder at an angle?"

"It does. But the angle wasn't acute."

Burr looked back out the window. Zeke and his nose were gone. *It must be nap time.*

Burr turned back to Van Arkel. "Brian said he was cleaning the gun on the workbench. Wouldn't that mean it was flat — horizontal — so the bullet would have traveled parallel to the floor and entered and exited at the same point? But that's not what the laser showed."

"That's right."

"But your autopsy said it was an accident."

"That's also right."

The more I find out, the less I know.

"Did you see where the bullet struck the wall?"

"I did," Van Arkel said.

"Then, how can the laser study be reconciled with your autopsy?"

Van Arkel stiffened. "The facts are that the entry height and exit height of the bullet differed by seven inches. The laser was obviously more precise than my examination, but a variety of other reasons could explain the difference."

"Such as," Burr said.

"What if she wasn't standing up straight? That would explain the angle, wouldn't it?"

"Yes, but not where the bullet hit the wall."

Van Arkel started to chew on his lip. Burr let him chew. Finally, the undertaker stopped chewing and smacked his lips. "If the bullet skimmed ... no, let me be slightly more precise. If the bullet glanced off a rib, that would do it. Not enough to shatter the bone, but just enough to deflect the bullet."

"Gannon testified that the force of the bullet would be too strong, even if it struck a bone," Burr said.

"She said if it struck a bone, not if it glanced off a bone."

"I asked her that question at the preliminary exam."

"No, you didn't," Van Arkel said. "You asked her if it struck a bone."

"She misled me."

"You didn't ask the right question." Van Arkel smiled.

Science has failed me again.

"Dr. Van Arkel, did the bullet glance off a rib?"

"I don't know, but there was no shattered bone."

"But it could have happened," Burr said.

"It could."

"So ... how could we find out what happened?"

"You cannot determine from the autopsy if the path of the bullet was altered when it entered the body."

"Are we euchred?"

"Not we, Mr. Lafayette. You." Van Arkel chewed his lip again. "But there is a way."

"There is?"

"Yes," Van Arkel said. "Exhume the body."

CHAPTER TWELVE

Burr drove around the south side of Crooked Lake to a two-story house that needed a coat of paint. A woman in her late sixties opened the door.

"Rollie ain't here. Come on in and I'll show you where he is."

Burr stepped into the foyer. The house was dark and musty. Five or six cats ducked underneath furniture.

"If you look out the window, you can see his shanty." She pointed to the northeast.

"Isn't it a little late for ice fishing?"

"The old fool don't know when to quit." She shook her head. "Says this is the best fishing. Just before the ice is out. He'll drown one of these days. But that's where he is, all right."

Burr looked out the window. There was a shanty about half a mile out on the ice that also needed a coat of paint. Smoke rose through a chimney pipe and blew off to the northwest. The shanty leaned to the east.

It probably settled when it rained.

The ice was gone at the shore. Burr walked a plank strung from the beach to the ice, then trudged a slushy path in the ice to the shanty. The sun had come out, and the sunlight reflecting off the ice almost blinded him.

Burr knocked on the door. No answer. He looked around and saw a banged-up snowmobile.

How did he get that thing out here?

He knocked again.

"What? What's that? Who's out there?" said a voice from inside.

"It's Burr Lafayette. Your wife said you were out here."

"She did, did she?"

"She did."

"That figures," the voice said.

Burr looked at the snowmobile again. The back end was sinking into the ice.

That thing is as beat up as his house.

A head peeked out the shanty door.

"Mr. Gustafson?"

"Who wants to know?"

"Could I ask you a few questions?"

"You from the DNR?" Gustafson said.

"What?"

"You know, the Department of Natural Resources."

"No."

"How would I know that?"

"I'm Brian Dunn's lawyer. From the preliminary exam."

"I think I seen you before."

How did I ever get sucked into this?

"How did you get that snow machine out here?"

Rollie's shoulders joined his head sticking out of the door. All he had on were jeans, a T-shirt and boots.

"I drove it."

"Isn't the ice getting a little thin?"

"She's starting to rot. One more rain and a little wind and she'll be gone. But now's when the fishing's best."

Gustafson stepped out of the shanty. His belly rolled over the waistband of his jeans. "Get in here. I got to keep an eye on my line."

Burr stepped out of the sun and into the dark shanty. He couldn't see a thing and tripped over a cooler.

"Watch you don't fall in the hole." Gustafson shut the door. "The light spooks the fish, especially the walleye. Just stand there till your eyes adjust."

Burr felt a small bottle pressed into his hand. He took a pull. A sweet and syrupy liquid stuck to the sides of his mouth, oozed down his throat and burned in his stomach. He handed the bottle back.

"If there's anything sweeter than this, I don't know what it is."

"Good, ain't it?"

"It is," Burr said, though it wasn't.

"Betcha can't guess what it is."

Burr did know. Or was afraid he did. "Schnapps. I'll say butter-scotch schnapps."

"By God, that's right. Used to drink peppermint, but it got to taste too much like toothpaste." He sucked on the pint. "What happened to Brian after I left?"

"He was charged with first-degree murder. I was hoping you'd tell me what happened."

"I don't know what happened. I wasn't there when it happened."

If he's an example of Petoskey's former finest, there's probably a lot of unsolved crimes in the city limits.

"Would you tell me what happened after you arrived?"

"I suppose I could." Gustafson took another pull. "'Course, you could read all the paperwork."

"I did that."

"I guess you probably did."

Burr's eyes had adjusted to the twilight of the shanty. He watched the retired cop stumble over to a lawn chair, with green and dirty-white web straps on a beat-up aluminum frame. Gustafson sat, reached into a bucket, caught a minnow and baited a hook. He dropped the minnow in the hole at his feet and started jigging.

"I only have this one chair. You can sit on the cooler. There's cold beer in there. Course we don't need a cooler to keep it cold, now do we."

Burr took out a beer and sat on the cooler.

It's a Labatt. That makes it worth the walk.

"Why don't I join you?" Gustafson said.

Burr stood, fished out a can and passed it over.

"Mr. Gustafson, would you please tell me what happened."

The retired cop leaned back in his chair and took a pull on the Labatt. "I was on duty that night. It was Friday. The Friday before Christmas. Christmas was on a Saturday that year.

"Anyway, I'm cruising downtown by the Perry-Davis. The hotel by the old train station. Lookin' for drunk skiers coming out from the bars. I haven't seen any, but then it's only eight, maybe eight-thirty. All of a sudden the dispatcher comes on, says there's been a shooting. No. That's not what he said — an accident with a gun — over on Waukazoo. I'm only seven or eight blocks away. I was going to turn my flashers on but, hell, I was so close and there wasn't much traffic. I didn't really see the need. I just drove over there quick as I could. Couldn't have taken me more than two minutes. I go up to the door and rung the bell. Nobody answered. But I heard all this hollering inside. I turned the knob and went right in. There's old Brian and he's holding his boy, Chad. He must have been sixteen or seventeen at the time. Brian's got him in a bear hug, got his arms around the boy's chest, got his arms pinned to his chest. You know, like this." Gustafson reached out his arms, in a hug.

"There's blood all over the boy's shirt, so I think he's the one that did whatever it was. Then I start to pick out the words. He's hollering and crying at the same time. 'You killed her. You killed her.' Over and over. Over and over. Brian, he's not saying anything, but his face is real red and I can see he's crying. Well, they're standing right by the basement door. I can see the stairs. So I put two and two together and I run down the stairs. There's blood everywhere on the way down — on the walls, the railing. I figure the boy must of gone down there after he heard the shot. Anyway, there she was all crumpled up next to the wall, lying there in a puddle of blood. A big puddle. She was dead all right. No pulse, but she was still warm. I looked around a little, not too much because that yelling was still going. I didn't want it to get out of hand. I called for help right away. That's just the procedure when something like this happens. Called for an ambulance, too, but Claudia was dead all right."

Rollie took a pull on the schnapps, then chased it with a swallow of beer.

"I seen this rifle on the workbench. I went over and looked at it. It was a deer rifle. Didn't touch it. It was pointed in the general direction of Claudia. I smelled the barrel. I could tell it had just been fired. So then I go over and look at Claudia. I can see where the bullet went in and where it came out."

Gustafson stopped talking and bent down to the hole. He jigged his line twice, then once more. He took another pull on the Labatt.

"I can't think of anything else to do down there, so I start up the stairs. I'm not in too big a hurry because I don't know what I'm going to do when I get up there. I'm hoping the ambulance gets there pretty quick. And I'm going to have to get a statement from Brian, which I won't be able to do until that boy quiets down. I'll have to get a statement from the boy, too, but I don't see how that's gonna happen tonight. All in all, I was wishing I hadn't been so Johnny-on-the-spot when the call came in."

"That's what you remember?"

"Yep, and all before I got to the top step."

This might be a colossal waste of time.

"So I go up there. And old Brian's still got his boy bear hugged. By now the boy's just sobbing. Not saying anything. Just crying. I ask Brian if there's anything I can do. He says no. I start to take my pad out but then I think better of it. Then I just go sit down in old Brian's Lazy Boy. Dark blue. Nice one, too. Then I see it."

"See what?"

"The Christmas tree."

"The Christmas tree?"

"Don't you see?" Gustafson said.

"Yes," Burr said, who didn't.

"Who the hell would kill their wife in the basement with a deer rifle while they was decorating their Christmas tree. Especially with a kid around. Don't make sense."

"What if that's what Brian thought, and that's why he killed her then."

"I thought about that. Truly, I did. But you know what? Brian's not that smart. Oh, he's smart all right. I mean he's a dentist after all. Pretty fair baseball coach, too. But he's not devious smart. Not like a lawyer ... no offense." Gustafson smiled at him.

"None taken."

Gustafson stopped for a moment, then, "You getting all this? I don't see no notes being taken."

"I'm getting it. I just want you to tell it."

"Van Arkel shows up and off we go downstairs. He only needs to look at her once to know she's dead. Asks me what happened. I point to the deer rifle on the workbench.

"Accident?" he says.

"I haven't talked to Brian yet," I said, "but I'd say so." Van Arkel looks at me, looks at the gun, looks at her. Then he yawns. He goes over to Claudia and gives her a good going-over.

"The ambulance guys have now showed up. The neighbor lady comes over. Larson is her name. She holds the boy and asks if she can take him next door. I say yes.

"Brian walks out the front door with them but then walks across the street. Turns around and stands there in the cold, looking back at his house in his shirtsleeves.

"I go back downstairs. They got Claudia in a body bag on a gurney. They start to take her out. On the way, they knock over the Christmas tree. Damnedest thing. I go to the door and wave at Brian to come in. Brian comes in and plops himself down in the Lazy Boy. I sit on the couch. It's his chair after all.

"So now it's just me and Brian. Neither of us saying anything. Finally, I say, 'You feel like talking about this? Not really' he says. 'You want me to come back tomorrow?' Brian shakes his head no. 'You want to come down to the station? He don't say nothing. I get up. No use wearing out my welcome. I figured it could wait so I started for the door."

"You just left?"

"Wait now, let me finish." Gustafson shifted in his chair. "If you're not careful, this chair will make your butt look like a tic-tac-toe game. So anyway, I'm about at the door and Brian says, 'No, let me do it now,' so I sit back down and get out my notebook. Boy, does Brian look bad. Eyes all puffy. Red, too. I just sit there waiting for him. He tells me what happened. I got to get it all down because somebody died, and this is one report that's going to get read."

"What did you think?"

"I thought it was an accident. Any fool could see that. Don't know why anybody would go to all that trouble to murder someone that way. Too much to go wrong."

"What if Brian just got mad and picked up the gun and shot her?"

"I thought about that. But it don't make sense. How does he know she's coming down? He said he didn't call her. It could have been on purpose, but I think it was an accident." The old man shook his head.

"Bad luck. Very bad luck." He took another pull on the schnapps then finished his beer. "How about passing me another beer." Burr stood and opened the cooler.

"Look out!" The fishing pole had dipped into the hole, and line was running off the reel. "Damn. Now that's a fish."

Gustafson let the line play out. When it stopped, he lifted the pole slightly. Burr watched him mouth *1-2-3*, then jerk hard on the pole. Line ran off the reel again. "Gotcha now, you bastard." He tightened the drag two turns and started to reel in. The fish took off again. "It's a pike, see. The way he took that minnow. They grab it and run but can't swallow it until it's head-first in his mouth. He stops and turns that minnow around head-first. Then he swallows it. When he stops, I count to three then I let him have it." The pole bent almost double. Line screamed off the reel. "This here is one big pike."

Five minutes later Gustafson nosed the fish to the hole, and with one quick move, he stuck his free hand in the fish's gill and jerked it out of the water and onto the ice. It was at least two feet long. It flopped on the ice until Gustafson held it down with his boot. "Well, I'll be damned. You know what this is?"

The flopping fish's eyes bulged.

"Walleye," Burr said.

"Sure as shit is. This ain't no pike. I could of sworn it was a pike. Bit just like one. Too bad, though."

Burr looked at Gustafson.

"Best eating fish there is. Eight pounds if he's an ounce." Gustafson looked down at the fish. Then sideways at Burr. "Too bad the season's closed." But the old man didn't put the fish back in the hole. "You sure you ain't from the DNR."

Burr shook his head.

Gustafson opened the door and stepped out, carrying the fish by the gill. Burr followed him. He saw a dozen perch lying on the ice in the shade of the shanty. He hadn't noticed them when he first got there. "All right then, this here will be our little secret." Gustafson kicked at the snow until he found the corner of a board. He kicked the board away uncovering a hole gouged into the ice. He dropped the walleye in the hole. It flopped next to the other five.

CHAPTER THIRTEEN

Burr left Rollie Gustafson to his poaching and made peace with Zeke, who was sulking in the back seat. He decided to take Brian's route on the afternoon the unhappy family cut the Christmas tree. By the time they passed Nub's Nob — still knee deep in snow but no skiers — Zeke was riding shotgun with his nose out the window. They turned on Larks Lake Road, passed three two-tracks, but Burr had no idea which one Brian had taken.

"Zeke, this was a colossal waste of time."

Burr decided to take the scenic way back to Harbor Springs. He turned on M-119 at Good Hart, a narrow two-lane that ran along the edge of a bluff two hundred feet above Lake Michigan. The road twisted through woods and turned back on itself in switchbacks and hairpin turns. The road was so narrow there was no centerline and no real shoulder, just a white line on each edge of the pavement. Not a road to be in a hurry.

The snow in the woods had a blue cast from the late afternoon sun. The beach below was a white ribbon of sand against the blue of the lake, the ice gone here. Trees grew up the side of the bluff, mostly second growth hardwood, right to the edge of the road. When they leafed out, it looked like a tunnel, this part of the road known as the *Tunnel of Trees.*

Burr looked through the trees to the lake.

"Zeke, there may be a more beautiful place than this, but I've never been there."

A white, late model Riviera roared up from behind, then slowed. There was no room to pass. Burr looked in his rearview mirror at the Buick. It was following too close. Burr sped up and the Buick pulled right up, closer than before. Burr touched his brakes, but the car didn't back off. Then it pulled out in the left lane. The road was straighter here, but was still a poor excuse for a two-lane. There was no room to pass and no shoulder.

Burr sped up, but the tailgater stayed to the left. The Riviera downshifted and then was alongside him.

"Damn it all."

The straightaway ended, the two cars still side-by-side, careening around a curve on a road not meant to be driven at anything over thirty-five miles an hour. Burr looked over at the Buick, but he couldn't see the driver through the tinted windows.

"I'll be damned if he's going to pass me."

The road straightened out. The Jeep and the Riviera ran down the road side-by-side. The road was just too narrow, and Burr had to run the Jeep's right tires on what little shoulder there was.

Burr sped up again. Then they were on another curve. The Jeep swayed. The road straightened out and then came a hairpin.

"What in God's name am I doing."

Burr took his foot off the gas, but it was too late.

The Buick kept going straight for a second too long, then roared away.

The Jeep ran off the road and across the shoulder. Burr crushed his foot on the brakes. The Jeep skidded.

Then it was flying, sailing over the bluff, the Jeep's shadow underneath them. Burr reached for Zeke, blissfully unaware that they were flying. He pulled Zeke into his lap, covered him with his chest and ducked. They hit the first of the saplings. The Jeep rolled to the passenger side, hit another tree, breaking its fall. The Jeep righted itself, then crashed into more trees on its way down the bluff. Burr sat up.

The Jeep broke off the tops of the trees as it fell. Branches scraped its sides. A limb smashed Burr's window, and he ducked again. The Jeep bounced off a tree then broke off the top of another. When the Jeep righted itself again, the broken trunk jammed through the floorboards in the backseat and kept going until it struck the roof. They were halfway down the bluff, but ten feet off the ground, impaled by the broken tree and wedged between two others.

Zeke sat up, licked Burr on the face and sat at shotgun again. He pawed at the window.

"Do you have any idea what just happened?"

Burr's hands shook. He grabbed the steering wheel and shut his eyes. Zeke eased over and licked Burr's face.

"Thank you, Zeke."

Burr opened his eyes and looked out. They were in a treehouse with no ladder.

He tried opening the doors, but they were jammed.

"Damn it all."

He crawled into the back, and the Jeep settled. Now they were about three feet off the ground. Burr kicked out the rear window.

"It never worked right anyway."

Burr and Zeke climbed out of the wreck and started up the bluff. About halfway up, Burr saw a bloodroot poking up through the dead leaves. It had eight white petals with a yellow center and a single leaf that wrapped around the blossom like the hood of a cobra.

"Zeke, this is the first wildflower of spring."

The two of them climbed back to M-119 and walked until they found a house with a phone.

***

Burr sat at a window table at Michelangelo's, Zeke at his feet. It had snowed the night before, a heavy, wet, cottage-cheesy, discouraging snow. Eight inches' worth, a late snow, even by Michigan standards. He was on his third glass of a chewy, old-vine Zinfandel when Suzanne showed up in her fur coat.

This has got to be the last outing of the season for that coat.

He stood and pulled out a chair for her.

"You could have been killed."

The waitress brought a glass for Suzanne and poured her the Zinfandel.

"You're awfully calm for someone who flew off a cliff."

"It was a bluff," he said.

"Who was in the other car?"

"I have no idea." Burr took another swallow of the wine. "Raspberries, chocolate, and pepper. A perfect wine for a day like today. I hope we don't get too many more."

"How can you possibly prattle on about wine when you were almost killed by who knows who."

"I had a part to play."

"And you've lost your Jeep."

"I loved that Jeep."

"Don't take it too far."

Burr swirled the wine in his glass.

"And now you don't have a car."

Actually, he did have another car, but this wasn't the time for that.

"Suzanne, as much as I'd like to believe you're devastated by my little mishap, there must be another reason you're here."

"I found us a laser expert."

I knew there'd be something else.

Burr looked at her, admiring her pouty lips and her too big smile.

"Are you listening to me?"

She's not beautiful, but she's stunning.

***

It was the fur coat that had finally gotten things going. Burr had given up on the pretext of the lawsuit and the pretense of client relations. Not only had he offended the firm's sense of propriety, worse, he had courted Suzanne right under Grace's nose, had been courting her for six months. He thought Suzanne enjoyed his company. He hoped she liked him.

She was bright, quick with a word, cynical. Very well read. Clever in a naughty way. He'd virtually lost his mind to her legs, her scent and, of course, her lips.

But she'd parried his every advance until that night in her fur coat. He had the firm's box seats for the Red Wings game at the Joe and a stainless-steel thermos of very dry, very dirty Bombay Sapphire martinis and no expectations. Suzanne had worn her fur coat and not much else.

The Wings were getting the better of the Leafs. The martinis were getting the better of Burr. It turned out that Suzanne loved hockey. She was a student of the game and pretty much ignored Burr. It was chilly at the Joe and she kept her coat on.

She had worn black heels, too formal for hockey, her legs disappearing into her coat. He watched her uncross her legs during the first intermission. Burr saw the top of her stockings and a slice of bare thigh above them. He was instantly aroused and befuddled for the rest of the game. They ended up in the bar at the Pontchartrain and then her apartment. He kissed her as soon as he closed the door, his hands on her shoulders inside her coat. He brushed it off her shoulders, and it fell to the floor. All she had on was her lingerie. Lacy black bra, panties, garter belt and stockings.

That was how it finally started. He'd chased her until she caught him.

***

Burr looped into the circle drive of the University Marriott at 8:20 a.m., precisely twenty minutes late. The hotel stood right next to Burr's building and had upped the value of his building, not to mention his property taxes. Worse, it blocked his view of the campus. All in all, he preferred life pre-Marriott.

Suzanne opened the door of Burr's brand new, secondhand Jeep. "Did you just buy this?"

"Not exactly." Exactly what he'd done was exactly what he didn't want to do. He had a slightly newer, black Jeep Grand Wagoneer. He didn't really like the color, and this one had a rear window wiper that he knew wouldn't work right, but it went perfectly with the rear window that already didn't work right. He loved Grand Wagoneers, but he'd had to trade legal work for it. Silly, mind numbing collection work, but he needed a car.

Zeke tried to kiss Suzanne as she climbed in. She shooed him to the backseat.

Burr thought Zeke had the right idea.

An hour later, Burr parked in the faculty lot at the University of Michigan law school.

"You don't have a permit to park here," Suzanne said.

"I didn't have one thirty years ago, either."

They walked through the law quad, Elizabethan architecture, built in the thirties. Stone buildings with stained glass windows. The oaks were just leafing out. They cut across the Diag to the Physics Building, then up four flights of stairs to Room 434, to brass nameplate Henry R. Pattengill, PhD. Suzanne knocked and the door opened.

"Yes," said the tall, thin, seventyish man with very little hair except what grew out of his nose and ears. Burr and Suzanne sat across from him in two university-issue side chairs. Early indestructible. They sat in silence. Burr already didn't like Pattengill. Finally, Burr said, "I'm told you're an expert in lasers and you'd be willing to testify that the prosecution's laser study was defective."

"I did not say that."

Burr looked at Suzanne. "Isn't that what you told me?"

Professor Pattengill raised his hand like a traffic cop. "Stop. That's not what I said. What I said was, I am an expert in the area of lasers, and I was sure I could find an irregularity in whatever it was."

"And what did you find?" Burr said.

"Nothing," Pattengill said.

Burr turned to Suzanne again. "I thought you said you sent Professor Pattengill the study."

"I did."

"I have the study, but I haven't read it."

"Why not?" Burr said.

This guy annoys me.

"Because I have not received my fee."

"Your fee." Burr decided to try a different tack. "Professor Pattengill, I am most impressed with your vitae," which he hadn't read. "And I'm sure I will be equally impressed with your lab."

"My lab," Pattengill said.

"Yes," Burr said. "May we see it?"

"Mr. Lafollette," Pattengill said.

"Lafayette," Burr said.

Pattengill ignored him. "This is my lab." He held up an eight-by-eleven yellow pad.

"You have no lab."

"I do, indeed, and this is it." He waved the yellow pad in the air. "I'm a theoretical physicist. I have no need for a lab."

"How do you know you can help us if you haven't read the study?"

"I can find something wrong with anything."

I believe that.

"Then you'll help us?"

"I will need my fee."

"Of course," Burr said.

"Twenty-five thousand. Half now and half the day before I testify. Plus expenses."

"That seems a little high."

"I have many projects," Pattengill said.

"How many yellow pads do you think you'll need?" Burr said.

"We'll take it," Suzanne said.

***

Back outside, Suzanne fumed. "Why were you taunting him? He is an expert on lasers."

"Where are you going to get the money?"

"We'll get it."

"Does he get paid before or after I do?"

Burr walked out of the building, Suzanne at his heels.

"Burr, please."

"Even if you get the money, that guy isn't going to be able to help us."

"Why not?"

"He's not exactly Mr. Personality."

"Don't give up."

"I haven't given up."

"What are you going to do then?"

Burr scratched his nose. "I don't know."

"I think we should do what Van Arkel said."

"Which was?" Burr said.

"Exhume Claudia."

Burr shuddered. "We'll need a court order."

Zeke barked at them when they got back to the Jeep. Burr saw a familiar brown envelope under the windshield wiper.

"If we get a court order and we're wrong, it will be a disaster."

"Why?"

"If there's no broken or chipped bone, then we're worse off than we are now," Burr said. "Right now, we can rely on what Van Arkel said could have happened. If we know for sure, and we're wrong, Truax wins."

"Why doesn't Truax exhume the body?" Suzanne said.

"Truax doesn't want to know, either. He's got Gannon."

Burr pulled the envelope off the windshield and opened it. "Twenty-five bucks," he said. "Prices have gone up."

"I thought you said you parked here in law school."

"I got tickets then, too." He crumpled the ticket and stuck it in his pocket.

***

Burr had two bilge pumps going, but they weren't keeping up. He had a hand pump left. He poked the intake hose into the bilge and duct-taped the hose to the mast. Then he ran the exhaust hose out into the cockpit and the self-bailers. He sat on the starboard berth and started pumping.

"If the two electrics won't stop it, I don't really see how one more pump will turn the tide." Zeke looked back at him from the quarter berth next to the nav station on the port side. "Don't just sit there. Do something." The dog started grooming himself.

Kismet was a forty-one-foot cutter-rigged yawl, circa 1937. Stewart said it slept six, laid twelve. She was still in good shape for a fifty-year-old boat, but not like she was when Burr had the money to write checks.

Burr launched her two days ago, and she sat in slings until today. The planking had soaked up, squeezing the caulking and sealing the hull, mostly. But somewhere there was a leak and Little Traverse Bay poured in.

There were footsteps on the dock. Zeke barked.

"Permission to come aboard?" Suzanne peered at him from the companionway. Burr kept pumping. "Need any help?"

"No." Burr kept pumping.

After they'd made love that first time, he had to see her every day, which, of course, was impossible, particularly since he hadn't left Grace. He knew he'd been a fool. Suzanne had never said she loved him. He should have believed what she didn't say.

Suzanne climbed down the companionway. No one looked better in blue jeans. Her running shoes squished on the floorboards.

"My, but it's wet down here."

"You have a remarkable grasp of the obvious." Burr kept pumping.

"Why did you launch *Kismet*?"

"I need a place to live."

"While you're working on Brian's case."

"Yes."

She kissed him lightly on the cheek. "Why don't you stay at the Inn?"

"Stewart won't let me. He's coming into his high season."

"He must have at least one room."

"He says I abuse room service."

"And dogs are not allowed."

"That, too," Burr said, relieved that Suzanne hadn't brought up Aunt Kitty's cottage, enormous, but not big enough for the both of them.

"I'm going to have a phone and fax here. As soon as *Kismet* soaks up, I'm going back to East Lansing. I have three or four cases to finish before the summer recess, then I'm going to live here until the trial is over."

"I'm not sure this is the best way to help Brian."

Burr pried up a floorboard. *Kismet* was still taking on water.

"Did you check all the through-hulls?" Suzanne said.

"Yes."

"Of course you did." She opened the locker under the galley sink and stuck her head in. "These are closed," she said. "Pardon me." She squeezed by him and made her way into the head. "These are closed, too. " She came back to the starboard bunk. "Stand up."

"I'm pumping."

"Pump over there."

Burr knew from experience it was easier to move than argue. He shifted his pumping operation to the port bunk. Suzanne took off the cushion on the starboard bunk, then the wooden lid on the storage locker. She reached inside.

"Here it is," she said.

"Here's what?"

"The open through-hull."

"There's no through-hull there."

"It's the old water intake for the head."

"How did you know?"

"I was here when the holding tank was put in." Suzanne turned the valve clockwise.

"I forgot about that."

"I guess you did."

The electric pumps took hold. Burr stopped pumping.

CHAPTER FOURTEEN

Burr had second thoughts about seeing Kaye. Somehow he felt he was cheating on Suzanne, although he didn't quite see how that could be possible. All he wanted to do was find out more about Truax, and he thought realtors probably knew more about what was actually going on locally than perhaps any other group of people.

He'd called her, and she'd invited him to her condominium at Marina Villa, in Harbor Springs, a long white building fronting Little Traverse Bay. When she opened her villa door, he thought she wanted to give him a hug instead of a handshake, and she certainly hadn't dressed like this was business, wearing black jeans with skinny legs, ballet flats and a fitted coral top that matched her lipstick.

Does she think this is a date?

That morning he had hunted black morels in a secret spot just north of Harbor Springs. He'd brought them along with a bottle of his favorite Pinot. Kaye led him into the kitchen and handed him a knife. He sliced the mushrooms, melted butter in a frying pan and slid them in. He uncorked the wine.

"Let's let this breathe a little."

Burr finished sautéing the mushrooms and took them off the flame. He poured the wine and fed her a mushroom.

"It's ..." she paused. "It's ..."

"Nutty," Burr said. He took a swallow of his wine, still a bit stiff but on the way. "Why do you think Truax is doing this?"

"I beg your pardon."

I may have cut to the chase too soon.

"Do you have a plate for the mushrooms?"

Kaye handed him a serving bowl from the cupboard. She started to get out plates but closed the cupboard. "We can just eat them from the bowl." She led him into the great room, facing south, flooded with light and a stunning view of Little Traverse Bay. A sleek blond dining room table sat under an equally sleek pewter chandelier at the side of the room. She'd set two places at the table.

She does think this is a date, but I was the one who brought the wine.

He looked out at the bay. A soft, cool wind from the southwest, one-foot waves, blue sky and bluer water. It was mid-May, but the harbor was still empty. There'd be a few boats by Memorial Day, but the season didn't really get going until the Fourth of July.

"You have a great view."

"I bought this at a foreclosure sale the last time the car business crashed."

Timing is everything.

Burr sipped his wine. It had opened nicely. "Does your son live with you?"

"When he's not off at college." She pushed the morels toward him. "Eat these while they're warm, and I'll get the salads." She paused, then "Did I tell you about him when we were in that awful house? I must have. And about Maury, too."

Burr nodded.

"What about your family?"

"Divorced. Also a son. Part time."

"I'm sorry. I guess I don't really think about it from the father's point of view very often." She spooned the rest of the morels onto his plate. "Let me get the salads."

This is a date.

Burr poured the rest of the wine. Kaye came back in with two mixed green salads and an herb dressing. After that, leg of lamb with rosemary and garlic, green beans with dill. The lamb fell off the bone, and the garlic filled the dining room. Kaye cleared the table and came back with strawberry shortcake with whipped cream and lemon zest. The lemon zest took the edge off the sweetness of the strawberries and made his lips pucker. After dessert, Kaye poured him a glass of an oaky Chardonnay and led him to an overstuffed white couch in the great room. She sat kitty-corner in a matching easy chair.

I'd better get on with it before I forget the reason I'm here.

"Kaye, that was delicious."

"You're welcome. Thanks so much for coming."

He leaned toward her. "Why do you think Truax is prosecuting Brian? After all this time."

"I don't know. I guess he must think Brian did it."

"I think there's more to it than that."

Kay inched closer to Burr, their knees touching. "He's ambitious and he's smart. And political. Politically correct."

"Is he married?" Burr refilled her glass. "Kids?"

"Three," Kaye said. "Catholic. Anti-abortion. Republican. Law and order. Pro-business. He wants to see Northern Michigan grow. The real estate developers love him." She sat back in her chair. "Does this matter?"

"I like to know who I'm up against."

Kaye nodded but didn't look convinced.

"Any idea what Truax likes to do?"

"Ties flies. Doesn't fish," Kaye said.

"Shoots. Doesn't hunt," Burr said.

"How do you know that?"

"A lucky guess. Would you say he's puritanical?" Burr said.

"Puritanical?"

"Of or relating to Puritans," Burr said.

Kaye scowled at him "I know what it means. It's an old-fashioned word. Puritanical would be good, but proper might be better."

"Proper." Burr thought about that, then, "Do you know what kind of car he drives?"

"Car?"

"A white Riviera?"

"I have no idea."

She must think I'm crazy.

Kaye crossed her legs, then uncrossed them. "Is that why you wanted to see me?"

"No, I wanted to see you. And it's morel season." He smiled at her.

Kaye leaned toward him again. "Would you like to stay?"

There were black flecks in the blue of her eyes. She pushed his hair back, then kissed him. He kissed her back. Then he left.

***

Late the next afternoon, Burr and Zeke stopped at the security point, a small white building at the entrance to Harbor Point.

"Is that a new car for you, Mr. Lafayette," the security guard said.

"Yes, Norbert. Sadly, yes."

"We're on the summer schedule now. You'll have to park in the garage," Norbert said, sixtyish and thin as a pencil. He still had a full head of black hair, neatly parted.

Burr backed up and pulled around to the garages behind the tennis courts. He parked in the stall next to his Aunt Kitty's silver Mercedes and climbed on a bicycle, a red Huffy with a basket on the front and a bell on the handlebars.

Harbor Point, founded in 1896, had been one of Michigan's first gated communities and snooty enough that the cottages didn't have names. They were all numbered. No cars were allowed during the season, just horses and bicycles. As he pedaled, Zeke trotted beside him. Burr cycled past a wooded nature preserve on his right, turn-of-the-century cottages to his left. At the end of the point, the top-drawer cottages fronted both Lake Michigan and Little Traverse Bay.

He dismounted at Cottage Number 59, yet another three-story Victorian, white with forest green trim. A turret on the Lake Michigan side. Three cottages from the end of the point and the lighthouse. He smelled the lake, wet and sandy, and walked up to the porch with white flooring, baby blue beadboard ceiling and white railing.

The cottage was built by his great-grandfather, had been his father's, and now belonged to Aunt Kitty, his father's younger sister, a maiden lady who had become a lawyer long before it was fashionable. She was his only living relative except for Zeke-the-boy.

The family trust specified that the cottage pass by age and blood. Burr was next in line if he outlived his aunt, a feudal way to pass title but one designed to keep the cottage in the family, and the only thing left in the trust, the Lafayettes not what they once were, financially speaking.

Burr knocked on the leaded glass door, then let himself in.

His aunt met him in the foyer. "You're late again."

Aunt Kitty, tall with silver hair pulled back in a ponytail, led him to the kitchen, through a hall with varnished oak hardwood under oriental rugs. She opened the refrigerator and filled two tumblers with ice. "You know where the gin and vermouth are. I have an olive for you, but I will not allow olive juice. It ruins the gin."

Burr rolled his eyes.

"Don't you look at me like that."

Burr opened the liquor cabinet and took out the Bombay and the vermouth. "How long have you had this vermouth?"

"I buy a new one every year."

"As long as it's fresh."

"Don't be smart with me. I'll see you in the parlor." She left.

Burr mixed the drinks. He put four olives in his drink and as much olive juice as he dared, then took both drinks to the parlor.

Aunt Kitty sat in a wingback chair next to the fireplace. It was fieldstone with a bird's-eye maple mantel, and it covered almost half the wall.

Burr handed her the martini, then sat next to her on a matching chair. Zeke curled up at his feet.

She raised her glass, looked out at the big lake and then back at Burr. "To your latest folly."

I guess that breaks the ice.

"What can you tell me about Truax?"

"You have no business trying a murder case. You know nothing about it."

"I'm a litigator."

"Commercial. And a damn good one. Until you started that appellate work. Probably lost your touch by now."

"A trial is a trial." Burr swirled the ice in his glass.

"It's not and you know it. Criminal law is about as much like civil law as dating sex is like married sex." She took a big swallow of her martini. "Why is he doing this?"

"He's got new evidence."

"The state police didn't come up with this on their own. Somebody wanted it reopened," Aunt Kitty said. "Maybe it was Claudia's family. Or the boy. What's his name?"

"Chad." Burr drank.

There's nothing like a good martini.

"You ruin a perfectly good gin with olive juice. You know that, don't you?"

Burr ignored her. "His name is Chad, but I can't find him."

"So you think Calvin Truax is behind this?"

"I can't think of anyone else."

"No one thought he had a chance when he ran for prosecutor," Aunt Kitty said. "Light that fire, will you. I have a chill."

"It's May," Burr said.

"It can get damn cold here in May."

Burr lit the fire. Zeke got up and laid down in front of it. Aunt Kitty edged her chair toward the fire. "Does he have a case?" she said.

"He has some evidence, but he doesn't have a motive," Burr said.

"There's that new young wife. That's your motive."

"It's not in any of the pleadings."

"Not yet."

"All he's got is the laser," Burr said.

"And a dead woman. And a house that hasn't sold in seven years."

"Six," Burr said.

"Whatever. Nobody likes to see a house empty for six years," Aunt Kitty said. "Not anywhere, but really not in a small town like Petoskey. Especially a tourist town."

"So he brings a charge of first-degree murder to get the house sold."

"That smart attitude is what gets you in trouble."

"And?"

"Make me a dividend." She handed Burr her glass. "Go easy on the vermouth."

Burr scooped more ice in her glass, filled it with gin and half a capful of vermouth. Back in the parlor, he handed her the glass. She took a swallow. "Much better, but just a little too much vermouth."

That thing must taste like jet fuel.

"Well then, as to Truax, I think he may want to run for office," Aunt Kitty said.

"He already did."

"No. The House or Senate."

"Congress?" Burr said.

"Is anybody quitting down in Lansing?"

"I don't know," Burr said.

"Term limits," Aunt Kitty said. "I'll bet somebody can't run again. Term limits are a bad idea." She stirred her martini with her finger.

"That doesn't make any sense."

"Then why do you think he's doing it?" Aunt Kitty took her finger out of the glass and licked it.

"For the publicity?" Burr said.

"That's right." She sipped her martini.

"Because it's the best advertising he can get."

"When is the trial?"

"October."

"Bingo," Aunt Kitty said. "A month before the election."

"What if he loses the case?"

"It doesn't matter." Aunt Kitty took a big swallow this time.

She makes drinking a martini an art form.

"Because if he wins, it's justice. If he doesn't, the people have spoken. Either way, he has the publicity."

"He was just doing his job," Burr said.

"He has to file by July 1st."

"Brian is his advertising campaign."

"Despicable." Aunt Kitty threw the ice from her glass into the fire.

***

Burr wasn't surprised when the always affable Deputy Brubaker showed up at Brian's store in Grosse Pointe with yet another arrest warrant.

Truax wanted Brian held without bail because he'd been ordered not to leave Emmet County. This was proof he was a flight risk.

Burr said that Brian had a business to run and that he, Burr, would be personally responsible. Gillis said he wouldn't take that chance and upped the bail to a million dollars, which meant that Brian would be in jail at least until the trial was over. Gillis also announced that the case would be under the jurisdiction of Emmet County Circuit Court Judge Samuel J. Dykehouse, presiding.

After the hearing, Burr walked the parking lot, not a white Riviera to be found. Burr drove to East Lansing after the bail hearing. He spent the next three weeks working on what was left of his paying cases. He tried to collect as many of his bills as he could, collection calls not favored in a silk-stocking practice. In between, he drove back and forth to Grosse Pointe to see Zeke-the-boy.

He moved on board *Kismet* the day after the Michigan appellate courts recessed for the summer.

The day after he moved on board, he sat across from Jacob in a window booth with red vinyl cushions at Juilleret's. Founded in 1898, Juilleret's had the best whitefish in Michigan. They trucked it in fresh every day from Lake Superior, that and the fact the cooks spread butter on it before they broiled it, which was not common knowledge. It was common knowledge that Juilleret's was the noisiest restaurant in the entire state. The ceiling, the original tin, painted white, bounced every sound back to the original creaky hardwood floor. Families with young children produced most of the din, but there was also a jukebox, whose records had not been changed for at least thirty years. Burr rarely ate at Juilleret's because it had no liquor license, but he thought drying out a bit more was a noble idea and picked Juilleret's for that very reason.

"We simply cannot conduct this matter from a diner. Especially with the roar of all these jabbering children," Jacob said. "This place is worse than your boat."

"Not really," Burr said. "It's dry in here." Burr had the leaks below the waterline more or less under control, but it was raining and *Kismet* needed a new cabin top.

The waitress, a college-age girl in red shorts and a white polo that said *Juilleret's*, took their order. Whitefish sandwiches with coleslaw and freshly squeezed lemonade.

"I think we need to find the boy," Burr said.

"Boy?"

"Chad. Brian's son."

"He's hardly a boy now. It's been six years. He must be at least twenty-three."

"Brian hasn't seen much of him since Claudia died," Burr said.

"He's in the Navy. Eve and I haven't been able to find him." Jacob cut the crusts off his sandwich and took a bite.

"I think we need to find him."

"If we can't find him, neither can Truax."

"Don't be so sure."

Their lemonades arrived. Burr fished the cherry out of his lemonade and chewed it slowly.

This is a poor substitute for a gin-soaked olive.

"I don't see why we need Chad."

"He was there," Burr said. "He could help us."

"He could also hurt us."

"I guess we'll find out if Truax knows where Chad is when we get his witness list, but let's keep looking."

Lunch arrived. Burr took a bite of his sandwich. "There is something else I need you to look into."

"Whatever it is, the answer is no." Jacob ate a forkful of coleslaw. "I detest the dives you take me to, but this coleslaw is quite good."

Praise from Caesar.

"I saw Brian yesterday."

"In jail?" Jacob shuddered.

"This is a criminal case."

"How we ever got here is beyond me."

We got here because of Suzanne, but that's for a different day.

"I asked Brian flat out if he was involved with Lisa before Claudia died. He said no. Then I tracked down his former hygienist. She said she didn't really see any monkey business."

"There you have it."

"Lawyers lie, witnesses lie and, most importantly, clients lie." Burr looked at his lemonade but thought better of it. "I need you to do some research."

Jacob beamed. "I'm a master of legal research."

"I want you to check the motels around here and see if Brian or Lisa ever checked in."

"I'm not doing it."

"While you're doing that, I'll talk to the neighbors."

Jacob cut up his sandwich in little pieces and ate them with a fork.

Burr looked outside. The rain ran down the windows in ever so many tiny rivers.

***

Burr met Jacob at Pirate Golf, on US-31 just outside Petoskey. The miniature golf course straddled Tannery Creek, which once had a fine run of steelhead, now ruined by Pirate Golf.

"Sleuthing is a waste of my time, as is this silly miniature golf."

"It's good to do something while we talk." Burr had just made a hole-in-one on the tenth, a tricky hole best played through the tunnel of flowing water.

He'd just finished talking to Dorothy Larson, the neighbor on the driveway side of Brian's house. She was a small woman, close to seventy. She had curly light brown hair. Burr was sure the curls and the color had both come from a bottle.

She said she'd never seen Lisa at Brian's before Claudia died.

Burr twirled his putter like a baton.

"I haven't found anyone or anything that points directly to an affair. But that doesn't mean there wasn't something going on between Brian and Lisa. All it means is that the people I talked to either didn't know about it or didn't want to tell me about it."

"I checked all the motels within twenty miles of Petoskey. Nothing."

Burr parred the eleventh hole. Jacob took a six. "This is the silliest game I've ever had the misfortune to play." Jacob picked up his ball and put it in his pocket. "There were no witnesses when Brian killed Claudia, either. But his fingerprints were all over the gun."

"The gun?"

"Yes, the gun." Burr aimed the putter at Jacob's nose.

"Stop pointing that silly putter at me."

"The gun," Burr said again, still pointing the putter at Jacob's nose.

"Would you please stop that."

"Where's the gun that killed Claudia? Where's that gun?" Burr twirled his putter like a baton again.

CHAPTER FIFTEEN

Burr ended the round, much to Jacob's relief, and drove to the jail. One of the deputies brought Brian to the visitors room. He had on an orange jumpsuit that was tight around the stomach and he had lost all the color in his face.

Burr sat across from him at the table.

"Where's the gun, Brian?"

"What?"

"The rifle that killed Claudia."

Brian looked at him like he was crazy. "I have no idea."

Burr stood and paced around the table where Brian was sitting. He stopped behind Brian. "Where's the gun," he said again. Brian turned around at looked at him.

"Without the gun, there's no murder weapon."

"You're supposed to be getting me out on bail."

Burr started pacing again. "Maybe the gun was defective."

"It wasn't," Brian said. "I need to get out of here. I need to be with Lisa and Becky."

"How do you know it wasn't defective?"

"You're not listening. I need to get out of here."

"Brian, I'm sorry, but you're not getting out. You left Emmet County and you got arrested. Gillis denied bail. You were there."

"I have a business to run."

"Not right now you don't, and you won't until I get you acquitted." Burr stopped in front of Brian. "I need to know about the gun."

Brian sank in his chair. "I was careless."

Burr started pacing again. "Did you unload it before you cleaned it?"

Brian squirmed in his chair. "I thought I did."

"What about the safety?"

"I always kept it on."

"What if there was still a shell in the chamber and the safety was broken? Or the extractors? Or the trigger?" Burr stopped behind Brian.

Brian turned around to look at him. "The gun was fine." Burr started pacing again.

"Would you please sit down."

Burr sat facing Brian. "How do you know there was nothing wrong with it?"

"It was fine when Trevor borrowed it," Brian said.

"Trevor?"

"I lent it to him."

"Who?"

"Trevor," Brian said. "Trevor Farr. It was dirty when he brought it back. That's why I was cleaning it."

"When did you lend it to him?"

"I shot my deer a week into the season. Trevor said his rifle wasn't working right, so I lent him mine."

"You never told me any of this." Burr stood.

"I didn't think it was important."

"You lent it to Trevor Farr," Burr said.

"I just said that."

"Well, that's it."

"That's what?"

"And that was the rifle that killed Claudia?"

"Yes." Brian squirmed again.

"Where is it?"

"I don't know," Brian said. "I already said I don't know. I never saw it after that night."

Burr started pacing again. "Why did you wait until the 17th of December to clean your gun?"

"It was a busy time of year. And the gun was down in the base-ment. I never thought about it until I went down there that day."

Burr stopped pacing. "And?"

"It was dirty, and there was rust on the barrel. Trevor doesn't take very good care of things. I didn't have anything else to do down there, so I thought I might as well clean it."

"Did you check to see if it was empty?"

"Yes." Squirmed a third time. "I thought I did."

"So, it could have been loaded?"

"I suppose so."

"What about the clip?"

"The clip was still in the gun. But I took it out. That's when I racked the gun."

"Start at the beginning."

"Only if you sit down."

Burr sat.

"We were decorating the tree, and Claudia was bitching at me. So I went down to the basement. Anything to get away from her. I saw my deer rifle and started cleaning it."

"So you were cleaning the gun when she came down there?"

Brian nodded.

"Brian, what happened to the rifle. Where is it?"

"I don't know. I never saw it again."

"What kind was it?"

"A Field and Jones. 30:06 bolt."

"What model?"

"Model?" He looked at his hands, then up at Burr. "I think it was a Model 92."

Burr started to say something, thought better of it, then left.

***

Burr and Zeke caught up with Gustafson at dawn the next day at the Waugoshance Point boat launch. The retired cop was already sitting in his boat. It was an old Sea Nymph, a sixteen-footer with a two-cycle, fifteen-horse Evinrude. The motor looked almost as old as the boat, which looked almost as old as Gustafson.

The abandoned lighthouse marked the shoal off Waugoshance Point. It was still in the shadows, but the new lighthouse at White Shoal was lit up by the early morning sun.

Zeke waded into Sturgeon Bay, took a drink and went for a swim.

"Come on. We've got to go before it gets too rough." They were twenty-five miles north of Harbor Springs at the tip of the lower peninsula, and just west of Mackinaw City. Sturgeon Bay was no place for a sixteen-foot boat when the wind picked up.

"I can't go with you."

"Damned if you can't."

"I only have a few questions."

"Ask 'em from the boat. Get in." Gustafson pulled on the starter cord. The engine sputtered. He pulled again. More sputtering. "I flooded the damn thing." Gustafson took a Labatt out of his cooler and drank half of it. He closed the choke, then pulled again. The engine sputtered again, then caught. Burr smelled the sweet smell of the gasoline and the oil in the smoke from the exhaust. Gustafson looked up at Burr. "What questions?"

"About the gun."

"What gun?" Gustafson finished his beer. "If you come, I can fish four poles. If you want to ask me something, you better hop in."

Why can't anything be simple.

"You can bring your dog. I'll have you back before lunch." He handed Burr a Labatt from his cooler. "I like to think of it as liquid grain. Like Cheerios." Gustafson opened another one and took a long drink. "These bass here, the smallmouth, are in to spawn. We'll just troll some Rapalas along the shore and see what happens."

Zeke jumped in the boat. Burr pushed it off and climbed in. He opened the beer and drank.

I never thought about having beer for breakfast.

The sun had broken the horizon now, and the flat gray water had an orange cast.

Gustafson put the outboard in reverse. It stalled. "Damn it." He pulled the starter cord again. It started this time, but the engine smoked. "I maybe put too much oil in the gas." He eased it into reverse again. The engine missed but didn't stall. He shifted to neutral, then put it in gear. "There we go," he said, smiling. "So what gun are we talking about?"

"The gun that killed Claudia," Burr said.

"That gun," Gustafson said. "Deer rifle, a 30:06. What about it?"

"Why didn't you tell me Trevor Farr borrowed it?"

"You didn't ask."

Save me from fools and sinners.

"Wouldn't you think that was something I might want to know?"

"I never thought about it. Hand me that blue Rapala from the big tackle box." Gustafson took the engine out of gear. Burr passed him the lure, and Gustafson rigged the first pole.

"What about Truax?"

"He knew all about Trevor. Hand me that brown one with the orange stripe."

"How do you know that?"

"He asked me about it."

"He didn't ask you at the preliminary exam."

"He asked me before the preliminary exam. When he interviewed me."

Truax knew but didn't want me to know. I'm sure there wasn't anything about it in the autopsy or the inquest.

"What happened to the gun?"

"Damned if I know."

"What if the gun was broken?" Burr said.

"What if it was? It's still an accident. Only more so. Now hand me that black and white Bomber."

Burr passed him the lure. "What did you do with the gun?"

"Never saw it again." Gustafson rigged the third pole. "One more and we're done. That's the thing about having you here. Too bad your dog don't count for two more." Gustafson laughed.

"Where do you think it is?"

"Damned if I know." Gustafson put the poles in the rod holders, then handed Burr a pair of binoculars. "If the fishing's no good, we'll just run on down and check things out at the nude beach. Ever been there?"

"No."

"Me neither, but you can see real good from the lake." He finished his beer and started on another. "If I was you, I'd have another beer. After that, I'd talk to George Maples. He's the only one I can think of who might know." Gustafson put the engine in gear and let the lines out one by one. They started off, dead slow.

***

Burr stood in front of a wire mesh cage. A small, wiry man with thick glasses and a flat top sat at a metal desk inside the cage.

He was in the evidence room in the basement of the Petoskey courthouse in the middle of what he guessed was going to be another pointless conversation.

"I know what's here," Sergeant Maples said. "And that's not here."

"How can you be so sure?" Burr said, standing outside the cage, looking in.

"Because it's my job to be sure."

"When was it here?"

"I don't remember when it was here, but I'm sure it's not here now." The policeman took off his glasses and started cleaning them with his tie.

"How can you be so sure?"

"I told you already. It's my job to know what's here."

"Can I look at your inventory list?"

"No, you can't." Maples put his glasses back on. "And even if you could, that's not as important as what's here." He tapped his temple with his forefinger.

Where do they find these guys?

"Sergeant Maples, can I come in and look around?"

"No, you can't. This is all evidence. And no one can touch it but me."

Burr didn't have much more time. Zeke was in the car and it was getting hot. "Can you at least tell me how your system works?"

"That I can do," Maples said. "Say we get some evidence, like a gun, or we confiscate something, like drugs. It comes to me. I tag it with the case number and put it on the shelf. Then I enter it all on that thing." Maples pointed across the room to a computer the size of a small car. "Pretty good system," Maples cleared his throat, "when it works."

"How old is this system?"

"Three years," the sergeant said.

"And before that?"

"A logbook and index cards."

"Then what happens?"

Sergeant Maples stood up. "When they need the evidence, the

detective, prosecutor or whoever checks it out. When they're done with it, they bring it back."

"Then what?" Burr said.

"Then what, what?"

"When the case is over."

"After two years, say, after all the appeals. Whose-ever it was can come claim it. Unless it's drugs, of course."

"Of course," Burr said. "And if they don't come get it?"

"Then it goes to auction."

"Then what?"

"Then it sells or I throw it away. Or I might keep it if it's any good. You never know. I got this grandfather clock in my den. I still don't know why it didn't go at the auction." Maples winked at him.

"What happened to Brian's gun?"

"That was a long time ago."

"How long, would you say?"

"I don't remember that far back."

"I thought you remembered everything."

"That's not what I said."

"I thought it was."

Maples stood, walked up to Burr and stared at him through the cage. "What I said was, I know everything that's here. I don't know what used to be here. I forget about it when it leaves."

"I see," Burr said, who didn't.

"I only have room for so much up here." Maples tapped his forehead. "That's how I keep it all straight."

"Do you remember the gun?"

Maples opened the door, came out and stood face-to-face with Burr. "What did I just tell you?"

"Was there a logbook with the entry for Brian's gun?"

"Yep."

Now we're getting somewhere.

"Can I see it?"

"Nope."

"Why not?"

"The old ones got ruined in the flood."

"The flood?"

"It wasn't exactly a flood, but it got pretty wet in here when the sprinklers turned on."

CHAPTER SIXTEEN

Burr followed Frieda Deutsch down the ammunition aisle, lit up under the blue glare of fluorescent lights. There were shelves full of ammunition of .32 caliber, .38 caliber, .45 caliber, 22 shorts, 22 longs, pheasant loads, duck loads, goose loads, steel shot, lead shot, lead nose, hollow point, full metal jacket. She even had ammunition for BB guns.

You could start a war with all this.

Burr had asked Eve to find an expert on the Field and Jones Model 92 rifle, and it looked like she had. Burr had driven to Ionia, a small town on the Grand River halfway between Lansing and Grand Rapids. It had once been a boomtown, but when the timber ran out and the freeway passed it by to the south, the little town stayed little. There wasn't much in Ionia except the courthouse, the state prison and Deutsch Arms, the biggest gun store in the state.

She turned the corner at the end of the aisle, and they walked past rows and rows of pistols, shotguns and rifles, gun locks on every one and every one chained to the wall.

At the end of the aisle, she took a key from her necklace of keys and unlocked one of the chains.

"I think I still have one."

She looked through the guns then took one off the chain.

"Here it is."

Burr followed her and the gun to the back of the store. She unlocked a door and went in, Burr right behind her.

She turned and stuck her hand at him again. It was chubby and her fingernails were dirty. "Frieda Deutsch," she said again. She was a large woman, actually a very large woman. She smiled at him through her tan, a tan with rings of white where the fat had blocked the sun. Reading glasses hung around her neck on a silver chain, along with the chain with the keys. She leaned toward him and showed off her ample bosom. "You're awfully cute."

For once in his life, Burr didn't know what to say. He looked down at his shoes, which still needed polishing.

"You don't have to worry. I'm too big for the likes of you."

Burr looked up at her and for another once in his life, didn't know what to say.

"Your assistant said you wanted to talk to me about this gun," Frieda Deutsch said.

Burr nodded, then "I understand that you're an expert on Field and Jones firearms."

"I've worked in this gun shop for thirty-three years. Owned it for the last five, since my father died."

"So you're familiar with the Field and Jones 30:06. The Model 92 bolt action."

"I've been the gunsmith here for the last seventeen years. Smithette, actually." She laughed. "That's a joke."

"Of course it is." Burr looked back down at his shoes.

"Don't be shy."

This is silly.

He looked back up at her. "Does the Model 92 ever malfunction?"

"This way," she said. Burr followed the gunsmith through a narrow hall. She squeezed down the hall, turned sideways but still brushed against the walls.

She's not any thinner sideways than she is front to back.

They walked into a workshop with a firing range off to the side. Burr smelled metal shavings and the sweet smell of gun oil.

Frieda turned on the lights. Row after row of light bulbs, all bare. She laid the rifle on a workbench and sat down on a stool.

She stroked the rifle, then looked at Burr. "I hate fluorescent lights. They make the guns look sick." She picked up the gun and showed it to him. "This is the Model 92. Do you know anything about it?"

"No," Burr said.

"I'm going to keep this simple and not fool around with the clip." Frieda stood and lumbered over to the firing range. "Watch this." She pulled the bolt back and opened the chamber. She loaded a shell in the chamber and closed it. Then she pulled the bolt back ever so slightly. "See how the extractors work? They're like fingers. They grab the rim of the shell casing and pull it out."

Burr looked down at the gun. He saw the jaws of the extractors on the rim of the shell casing. She pulled the bolt all the way back. The shell flipped out of the gun and rang along the floor.

"If the extractors don't work right, they don't grab the shell." Frieda looked at Burr. "The extractors are what pulls the shell out of the barrel. You knew that, didn't you?"

Burr nodded.

Frieda put on her reading glasses and worked on the gun with a tiny screwdriver. She put another shell in the chamber and racked the gun. The shell didn't come out. She racked it again. No shell. "The chamber is supposed to be empty, but it's not."

Burr, encouraged in a dark sort of way, said, "Has this ever happened?"

"Once in a great while."

"Have you ever seen it happen?"

"Once," she said. "Maybe twice. That's why I quit selling them." She shouldered the rifle and aimed at a target there. "I racked this gun twice, so it's supposed to be empty. Move over so I don't ring your ears." She fired at the target, a man's head, which she pierced through the left eye.

***

Burr woke up at 3 a.m., rain tapping on the deck above his head. He heard the drip, drip, drip into the saucepan he'd put underneath the leak.

Suzanne lay next to him in his bunk in the aft cabin. She had appeared after midnight. They had made love, then fallen asleep.

The double bunk was narrower than a queen bed. Suzanne slept as she always slept after they had made love, separate and not touching. She slept with her jaw clenched. She always slept that way, at least with him.

He didn't know if he loved her. He didn't know if she loved him, and he didn't know if she'd loved him the last time. He had loved her the last time, or thought he had, which, of course, had been the problem.

He started counting the drips and fell back to sleep.

***

Burr stood in the sun on the concrete driveway, just outside the garage. The rain had blown through, and it was clear and seventy. A blue pickup perched on a lift. A man stood under it, cutting off a muffler with a torch.

He was so tall that, even with the lift all the way up, he had to stoop at the shoulders. He wore safety goggles but no mask. His shirt didn't quite reach his waist, and the sleeves of his shirt were cut off at the shoulders. His biceps bulged and he didn't have an ounce of fat on him.

He must be Trevor Farr.

When Farr saw Burr, he stood upright and bumped his head on the bumper.

"Damn." Farr dropped the torch. The hose writhed like a snake, spewing flame at the head. He picked it up, turned it off, pushed the goggles on his forehead and looked at Burr. Farr had one long eyebrow that stretched across his forehead. His ears stuck out. He rubbed his head, bald on top, and looked at his fingers. They were smeared with blood from his head. "Damn," he said again. He bent over toward Burr. "Do I need stitches?"

"I don't think so, but it's pretty bloody."

"That's all right." Farr wiped his head with an oily rag. "What do you want?"

"I need to find out about the gun you borrowed from Brian Dunn. The deer rifle."

"The 30:06."

"You borrowed it from Brian," Burr said again.

"That's right," Farr said.

"Can you tell me about it?"

"What's this got to do with me?" Farr rubbed the top of his head. With the safety glasses on his forehead, he looked like he had four eyes.

"I'm trying to help Brian," Burr said. "I'm his lawyer."

Farr looked at the bloody-oily rag, then at Burr. "Well, see, my rifle broke. The firing pin. I had this big buck, maybe twelve points, coming to my bait pile. I shot, but nothing happened. I was really pissed off. I knew Brian had already got his, so I asked if I could borrow his gun."

"And?"

"I borrowed it."

Burr smelled the sweetness of the acetylene underneath the smell of the oil and burned metal. "I think the gas may still be on."

Farr sniffed. "Damn-it-all if I didn't leave that gas on at the tank. Don't smoke or nothin' until I get this gas out of here." He walked to a green tank up against a wall and turned off the gas. Then he flipped a switch and the shop fan started to whine. "We coulda both been blowed up."

If the story about borrowing the gun is anything like this, no jury will ever convict Brian.

"What about Brian's rifle?"

"Like I said, I borrowed it. I went out there, sat for three days. Nothin'. Then, on the fourth day, bingo. He comes right in. I shoot, but damned if I don't miss. I think the scope was off." Farr stuck his tongue in his cheek. "Coulda been the snow that got in my eye when I shot."

That's what they all say.

"When did you take the gun back?"

"Couple days after deer season ended."

"When exactly?"

"I don't know." He shifted his weight from one leg to the other. "What difference does it make? Less than a week after the season. I know that."

"What did Brian say?"

"Nothin'," Farr said. "He wasn't there."

"What did you do?"

"Left it in the garage, next to the door."

"Did you clear the chamber?"

"'Course I did. You think I'm stupid?" Farr said. "You trying to blame this on me? You think it was me?" Farr shifted his weight again.

"No, no, of course not," Burr said. "What was the weather like that day? The last day you went hunting."

"Rain, then snow. This snowflake got in my eye. That's how I missed. But it coulda been the scope."

"Did you clean the gun?"

"'Course I did," Farr said.

"At home?"

"Hell, no. I wiped her down good, soon as I got back to the truck."

"Did the gun work all right?"

"Worked fine," Farr said. "Except the scope might be off."

"Did you clear the chamber?"

"I already said I did," Farr said.

"Where did you get the bullets?" Burr said.

"Brian gave me the bullets and the clip."

"What time was it when you quit hunting that day?"

"I don't know," Farr said. "Dark thirty. That late in the season, those deer don't move until dark."

"Did you drop the gun?"

"No," Farr said.

"Get it wet?"

"Yeah, but I wiped it off. I already told you that."

"Was it muddy?"

"Damn straight it was muddy, with all that rain and snow and the ground not frozen."

"No, the gun. Was the gun muddy?"

"Yeah, but like I said, I wiped it off."

"What about the clip?"

"The clip?"

"Did you take it out?"

"You know, I'm done talking with you. 'Cause I gotta deliver this truck in an hour, and I am not going to make it if I talk one minute more."

"I appreciate that, Mr. Farr, but Brian has a lot at stake." Burr pushed the dirt on the concrete floor into a pile. "The rest of his life."

"He shoulda thought about that before he shot her."

"You must have been pretty good friends," Burr said. "He did lend you his deer rifle."

"I haven't heard from him since he left. So we can't be that good of friends," Farr turned back to the truck.

"I am trying to help Brian," Burr said. "Is there anything you remember? Anything wrong with that rifle?"

"I think the scope was off. He told me he had it sighted in, but I don't think so. That's why I missed."

"Anything else? Did it stick when you racked it?"

"No, not really," Farr said. "Maybe a little."

"Did you drop it?"

"I already said I didn't."

"What did you do with the shell in the chamber?"

"I racked it out," Farr said, shifting his weight again.

"What about the next one?"

"What next one?"

"The next shell," Burr said.

The big man looked at him. "I took the clip off. Because the next shell would rack in when the empty racked out. That's what bolt actions do."

"What then?"

"What do you mean, what then?"

"With the gun and the clip," Burr said.

"I took it back to Brian's."

"What did you do with the clip?" Burr said.

"How should I know? It's been seven, eight years."

"Six, actually. Did you put the clip back in the gun when you returned it?"

"What do I want with the clip? It won't fit my gun."

"What about the shell you racked out?" Burr said.

Farr turned his back on Burr, turned the tank back on and lit the torch. He pulled his safety goggles back down and went back to cutting off the muffler.

***

That evening, Burr sat in *Kismet's* galley sipping a jammy glass of Cabernet, alone again except for Zeke, who was snoring on the quarter berth across from him. The alcohol stove flamed blue underneath the baked beans in the saucepan. He always enjoyed a hearty Cabernet with his baked beans.

Burr didn't believe Farr's story, not all of it. He didn't believe that Farr remembered exactly what happened, and if he did remember, Burr didn't think Farr had told him everything. If he could prove that Farr had returned the gun with a shell in the chamber and that the extractors didn't work right, then he could prove it was an accident. A careless friend. A defective gun. But a very poor witness.

***

Jacob met Burr at *Kismet* in the morning. He stepped aboard and sat down in the cockpit under a bright morning sun.

He looks a little queasy.

"We're going to stop looking for the gun," Burr said.

"I beg your pardon."

"We don't need it."

"Why?"

"If we find the gun, there might not be anything wrong with it. Then we're euchred. This way no one knows for sure."

"What if Truax finds it?" Jacob had gone pale but probably not because of the gun.

"He doesn't want to find it either."

"Why not?" Jacob said.

"Because it might be defective. Then he's euchred."

Jacob leaned over the side and threw up.

CHAPTER SEVENTEEN

Just before dawn on the first of September, Burr and Zeke hid in corn stubble two miles from Cross Village and a stone's throw from Wycamp Lake. He smelled the sweet smell of manure where the cows had grazed. He was pretty sure he wasn't lying in any, but it was hard to tell in the dark.

He had laid cornstalks over Zeke, not enough to cover him, but enough to break up his profile. Burr had covered himself, facing downwind, just outside the decoys. He heard the geese when they got off Wycamp Lake.

They sound like barking dogs.

Five minutes later, he saw seven or eight of them flying toward him. Then he heard a voice.

"Burr. Burr, where are you?"

"Get down and be quiet."

"I've got to talk to you," Jacob said.

"Not now."

"Now." Jacob looked down at him in the chopped corn. Burr smelled the manure again. Jacob waved his arms.

"Damn it all, Jacob. You'll scare off the geese."

"That was my intention."

"How did you find me?"

"Stewart told me where you were."

"Whatever it is, it can wait."

"No, it can't."

Burr sat up. "For God's sake, what is it?"

"I found them out."

"What?"

"I found them out," Jacob said again.

"Who?"

"What is this?" Jacob stood on one foot and looked at the sole of one his Italian loafers.

This isn't the place for those shoes.

"That is cow shit," Burr said.

"Damn it, Burr. You're hunting in the midst of cow droppings?"

"The geese like the chopped corn."

"Damn it, Burr," Jacob said again. He picked up a cornstalk.

"Damn what?"

"Damn you and all your follies. Your leaky boat. This hunting thing. Damn your client. And damn Suzanne." He waved his arms again, cornstalk in one hand.

"Suzanne?"

"She must have known," Jacob said.

"Known what?"

The geese cleared the tree line, set their wings and started gliding in. They were still coming, despite Jacob and his arm-waving. Burr lifted his shotgun and pointed it at the lead bird. They got within thirty-five yards, wings set, then veered to the south. He swung through the lead bird but didn't shoot.

"You may as well have shot," Jacob said.

"I didn't want to kill one that badly." Burr stood and lit a cigarette, his first of the season.

"*Sensible Rates,*" Jacob said. "They stayed at *Sensible Rates.*"

"What?"

"That's what the sign says on the road, underneath the name Indian River Cabins."

Jacob tossed the cornstalk behind him. "They were clever. Clever as they could be. Just outside Indian River," Jacob said. "They trysted there."

Burr spit out the cigarette and ground it in under his heel.

Maybe Truax does know, and I should have known.

"Damn it all. I should have known." Burr kicked at the ground. "How many?"

"How many what?"

"How many motels did you check?" Burr said.

"Seventy-six," Jacob said.

"I thought you gave up."

"I went out to forty miles from Petoskey."

He never gives up. Maybe he should have.

"How did you find out?"

"I was having lunch at Vivio's in Indian River. The manicotti is quite good. I was thinking that, if they were having an affair, they would be smart enough not to stay in Petoskey. And I'd already checked all of the motels in Petoskey and Harbor Springs. So they'd go out of town. But not too far. I'd already tried Pellston, and I thought Charlevoix would be too expensive for a dentist who wasn't doing so well. Indian River is only half an hour from Petoskey, so why not?"

"I tried three other motels, then I saw the sign," Jacob said. "*Sensible Rates*. Six old cabins. Wood siding, white with blue trim."

"Are you sure?"

"Quite."

"How do you know?"

"The motelier," Jacob said. "If you could call him that."

"Motelier?"

"Actually, it was his wife," Jacob said. "She didn't remember Brian specifically, but she remembered an older, middle-aged man and a younger woman. Not that she hadn't ever seen that before. She remembered two cars. *'That always gives them away'* ... that's what she said. That, plus the cash. The motelier kept trying to silence her, his wife. I think he liked the idea. She would have none of it. She said it went on for almost a year, once, twice a week. A few hours at a time. No overnights. Then it stopped."

"Stopped?"

"Just like that." Jacob snapped his fingers, but they didn't snap. He looked at them like a lighter that wouldn't light.

"When did it stop?"

"The summer after Claudia was killed," Jacob said.

"When they married and moved to Grosse Pointe."

"Exactly."

"How do you know for sure?"

"I looked in one of the rooms," Jacob said. "Perfect for an affair on a shoestring budget. Vintage 1950. Perfect. One room with a bathroom. No tub. A white shower stall with rust stains. Iron from the water. Bedspread with fringe. Kitchenette. Hot plate. No microwave."

"Mini bar?"

"That's not funny. The mini bar concept has not come to *Sensible Rates*."

"Do they have records?"

"Mercifully, no. Something about the IRS, I expect."

"This still doesn't prove anything."

"The old girl followed Brian home," Jacob said.

"She what?"

"She followed him home one night."

"She didn't," Burr said.

"She did. She was going to tell Claudia, but her husband wouldn't let her."

"What's her name?"

"Her name?" Jacob said. "Her name is Zolkowski. Bernadette Zolkowski."

"I wonder if Truax knows."

***

Burr paid a visit to Brian as soon as the jail opened.

"It's none of your business," Brian said.

"It is now."

"How did you find out?"

"Does it matter?"

Brian looked down at his hands.

"I asked you, over and over again." Burr stood. "You lied to me. How can I help you if you lie to me?"

"That doesn't mean I killed her." Brian wiped sweat off his forehead. His armpits were wet, and his orange jumpsuit stuck to him.

"You did kill her."

"It was an accident," Brian said. "I swear it was."

"Right." Burr started pacing.

"I love Lisa. I stopped loving Claudia years ago. Our marriage was dead, but that doesn't mean I murdered her."

"No, it just looks like it."

"It doesn't if nobody knows about me and Lisa."

"If I know, Truax knows. Or he can find out. Why didn't you tell me?"

"Lisa said you wouldn't help us if you knew."

Burr paced back and forth in front of Brian.

"Would you please stop that."

"Stop what?"

"Pacing."

Burr ignored Brian.

"Does Suzanne know?"

"No," Brian said.

Burr walked out.

***

Harbor Springs, the next afternoon. The Saturday of Labor Day weekend. Seventy-five and sunny with a ten-knot wind from the north.

A perfect day for a sail.

The summer crowds were mostly gone, victims of the teachers union who, for their own reasons, insisted on starting school in late August instead of post-Labor Day. Burr and Suzanne were going for a sail as soon as they finished their project and as soon as Burr had the answer to one question.

A cormorant had been perching on the wind vane on top of *Kismet's* mast all summer. Nothing Burr had done would keep it off. He had hoisted a plastic owl to the top of the mast. He shot at it with a BB gun until he'd been threatened with arrest for harassing a federally protected bird. Finally, the wind vane sheered. The cormorant left, but now there was no way to know the wind direction.

"Is this a safe thing to do?" Suzanne stood on the deck in the bosun's chair about to be hoisted to the top of the mast.

"Perfectly."

"It's not safe," Suzanne said. "It would be safe if you had someone to tail the halyard."

"I've got it through the jam cleat. Nothing will go wrong. The jib halyard is your safety line." Burr wound the main halyard around the winch, snapped in the winch handle and began grinding. He turned the winch handle two more cranks and Suzanne was off her feet.

Burr clipped a safety line around her waist and tied it to the jib halyard. She wrapped her legs around the mast and crossed her ankles. Burr hoisted her up the mast with the main halyard, pulling her to the first set of spreaders. She let go with her legs and he hauled her up more.

He ground the winch until she was shoulder high with the top of the mast. He cleated off the halyard and sent up the new wind vane and tools in a canvas bag on the spinnaker halyard. Suzanne unbolted the broken vane and bolted the new one on.

Burr lifted the jam cleat and let the halyard play through his hands around the winch, keeping four turns on it. Suzanne slid slowly down the mast. Halfway down, Burr locked the jam cleat and tied off the halyard. Suzanne dangled twenty-five feet above the deck. She looked down at him.

"Get me down."

"Suzanne, I was wondering."

"Don't wonder anything until I'm on the deck."

"Suzanne, I was wondering."

"What?"

"I was wondering how long you've known about Brian and Lisa."

"Known what?"

"Oh, you know." Burr opened the jam cleat. After Suzanne dropped ten feet, he closed it. She jerked to a stop and swung from side to side in the bosun's chair.

"Stop it. Please stop it."

"Tell me about the affair."

"What affair?"

"You're in no position to be cute." He brought her down another five feet.

"Get me down."

"Suzanne, you are perfectly safe up there." The wind had blown her hair into her mouth and she didn't dare let go of the halyard to take it out. He looked up at her as she tried to spit the hair out of her mouth.

"Suzanne, I am greatly disappointed in you."

"In me?"

"Yes."

"Why?"

"Yesterday I learned what I suspected all along."

"What, for God's sake? What?"

"That Brian and Lisa were having an affair before Claudia was killed."

"Please let me down," she said, begging.

"You're her sister, and she never told you?"

"She never told me."

"You're her sister," Burr said again. "You must have known."

"If I'd known, I'd have told you," she said. "You'd have to know that to defend Brian."

"Would I? Or is that why you hired me?"

"What are you talking about?"

"Because I'm not from here. Because I'm not a criminal defense lawyer. Because I'm stupid around you."

"Burr, I love you."

"Right."

"I didn't know. I swear."

"Jacob found out," Burr said. "*Sensible Rates* in Indian River."

"I don't believe it."

"Believe it."

"How can you be sure?"

"Brian admitted it."

"We'll just have to figure out what to do."

"We?"

"Yes, we," Suzanne said. "I swear I didn't know."

"Promise?"

"Yes."

"Cross your heart."

Suzanne crossed her heart. Burr lowered her to the deck. She climbed out of the chair, went down below and came out with her carry-on bag. She glared at him and left.

If looks could kill.

***

Burr decided to go for a sail anyway. He and Zeke motored past the moored boats, then turned back to the harbor into the wind. He set the staysail and mizzen, the rig he used when he was sailing single-handed. Burr brought *Kismet* back around, killed the engine and made for Harbor Point on a broad reach. The wind had freshened to about fifteen knots, and there were whitecaps on the bay. At Harbor Point, he hardened up and headed out into Lake Michigan on a beam reach, *Kismet* making six knots due west. Burr thought she seemed a bit sluggish, but then he hadn't put up the main.

Maybe Suzanne hadn't known about the affair. Lisa might not have told her everything, especially if she thought Suzanne wouldn't ask for Burr's help. But it was a bit farfetched to think that Suzanne didn't know.

Five miles out, Burr tried to come about, but *Kismet* wouldn't respond. He looked down below. The cabin was full of water, over the floorboards and halfway up the bunks.

"That's why there's no steerage, Zeke. We're sinking."

Burr climbed down below, water up to his shins. He turned on the bilge pump, but it couldn't keep up. He reached for the VHF radio.

"Charlevoix Coast Guard. Charlevoix Coast Guard. Charlevoix Coast Guard. This is the sailing vessel *Kismet*, WT 6948." No response. Burr counted to thirty, then "Charlevoix Coast Guard. Charlevoix Coast Guard. Charlevoix Coast Guard. This is the sailing vessel *Kismet* WT 6948." Still no response. He counted to twenty and tried again. "Charlevoix Coast Guard. Charlevoix Coast Guard. Charlevoix Coast Guard. This is the sailing vessel *Kismet* WT 6948.

"Charlevoix Coast Guard. Charlevoix Coast Guard. Charlevoix Coast Guard. This is the sailing vessel *Kismet* WT 6948."

He looked up in the cockpit. With no one at the helm, *Kismet* had gone head to wind, her sails flogging in the wind. Zeke didn't seem to care, blissfully unaware that Burr's beloved boat was sinking.

"Zeke, we're going to have to get off. We can both swim, but I don't know for how long." He slogged back to the radio. "Charlevoix Coast Guard. Charlevoix Coast Guard. Charlevoix ..."

"Sailing vessel *Kismet*. This is the Charlevoix Coast Guard."

"Thank God," Burr said into the microphone. "Charlevoix Coast Guard, this is the sailing vessel *Kismet*. We are taking on water and require immediate assistance."

Static. *Kismet* was settling. Burr stretched the cord on the radio and climbed into the cockpit.

"*Kismet*. What is the condition of your vessel?"

"Charlevoix Coast Guard, we are sinking. Estimate twenty minutes."

"*Kismet*, how many are in your party?"

"Charlevoix Coast Guard. One person. One dog."

"*Kismet*, stand by on Channel 68. We will ..."

The radio went dead. "Damn it all, Zeke." Burr thought the water must have shorted out the electrical system. He looked over the side and saw that *Kismet* had about a foot of freeboard left. Then she would sink. Gone forever. In two hundred feet of water. How could this have happened? Did she blow a seam?

Burr pulled the inflatable life raft from the lazarette. He attached the CO2 cartridge and the raft inflated. "At least we won't drown." Burr reached back down into the cabin and turned off the power. He climbed down into the cabin and sloshed in waist-deep water and found his files. In spite of his protestations, Eve had insisted on storing them in plastic bags. He pried up the floorboards and took out his wine. He found the life jackets and put one on. Then he threw everything — the life jackets, the files, the wine — into the raft and slipped it over the side. He climbed in and called Zeke, who had no interest in the raft. He pulled the dog over the side and into the raft.

Burr cast off and paddled fifty feet off the stern, far enough away to avoid fouling on *Kismet* when she sank. The wind had blown a chop on the lake. The raft tossed in the waves. If the wind blew much harder, the waves would break over the raft and swamp it.

He looked at Kismet for the last time. She was down in the stern, the lake rushing into her cockpit. Water poured into the cabin. She righted herself, water up to the cabin top, but still floating. Then she listed to port and was gone.

"Mother of God. What just happened?"

Burr stared where Kismet had just been. Nothing. There was nothing. Then a life ring. Then a sponge floated to the surface and then his can opener with the wooden handle. He paddled over and rescued the life ring and the can opener.

"The hell with the sponge."

He released the signal dye stored in the raft, then rummaged through the bottles and found a bottle of Veuve Cliquot. It wasn't chilled, but the water in the bilge wasn't much more than sixty degrees. He thought they'd be rescued by the Coast Guard in about an hour, less if a boat close by had heard his transmission. He looked longingly at the champagne.

"Zeke, I hate to waste a perfectly good bottle of champagne."

He had the bottle in his hand when he saw that the raft was sinking.

"Damn it all. Now what am I going to do?" He wrapped life jackets around the wine and the files, then wrestled Zeke into the last one.

"Zeke, you look good in a Mae West."

Burr clipped on Zeke's leash and held the dog close to him. Zeke was scared but not panicky. Burr talked to him softly. He squirmed but didn't growl. The raft filled up with water but didn't sink. They bobbed up and down in the swamped raft and waited.

***

Half an hour later, the Coast Guard rescue boat roared up from the south. The helmsman cut back on the throttle, coasted up to them and put the engine in neutral. Burr grabbed the gunwale of the boat with one hand, Zeke with the other. Zeke panicked and clawed at the hull with his front paws. The seaman grabbed him by the collar and pulled him over the side. The dog fell into the boat, shook himself off, lay down in the cockpit and shivered.

Burr hooked one leg over the side and the seaman hauled him in. He sat against the hull, soaked and shivering like Zeke. Burr was waterlogged, but his files were not. He had managed to rescue the wine. The Coast Guard radioed the Irish Boat Shop in Harbor Springs and took them in. Suzanne met them with towels, handed him one and dried off Zeke with the other.

"My God, Burr, what happened?"

"*Kismet* wasn't handling right. She wouldn't come about, so I checked down below, and she was filling up. I think she may have burst a seam."

"You could have drowned," she said. "Take your shirt off. You'll never warm up this way."

"I'm all right."

"No, you're not. You'll get hypothermia." She started drying off Zeke again. "Zeke, are you all right?"

"He's a Lab, but he was almost gone."

"What about *Kismet*?"

"She's gone."

Suzanne pulled his shirt over his head and wrapped him in a towel.

***

Burr sucked on his finger. He'd poked it on one of Stewart's quilting needles. Not Stewart's exactly, but Stewart had filled the Inn with a quilting bee group, and Burr had found a lost needle. The fall color season hadn't started yet, and Stewart would do anything to fill up the Inn and pay the mortgage. The quilters had commandeered the Inn and its conference room for the quilting bee. When they left, Eve booked it as Burr's trial headquarters.

The conference room was a cinder-block basement paneled over with tongue and groove, varnished knotty pine. The paneling was peeling where it met the floor. The only sunlight came from the window wells. Burr did not like his new headquarters.

He sat at a folding table, like a table in a school lunchroom. A black rotary phone in front of him, its cord snaking off to the wall. Zeke lay at his feet.

I don't like it here.

Shoes clicked down the stairs.

"Isn't this a nice office?" Eve said.

Burr took his finger out of his mouth. "It is, isn't it."

"I thought I found all the needles."

Burr walked over to a window well and looked up and out. "We have a great view of the bushes."

"Since I know how much money we don't have, I found us an office we could afford," Eve said. She handed him the Lafayette and Wertheim checkbook, the big black checkbook with three rings and check stubs.

I hate that thing.

Burr looked back at Eve. He arched his eyebrows and wondered how much it was going to cost him to rent the basement of the Harbour Inn, Stewart's friendship going only so far.

"You're going to update Stewart's estate plan in exchange for renting this wonderful basement," Eve said.

"I don't know much about estate planning."

But I don't think Stewart has much of an estate.

"None of this would have happened if you'd just turned down this case. You'd still have your silly Jeep and your waterlogged sailboat," Eve said.

I miss them both.

Burr sat in his folding chair and sulked. Then he shuffled through the papers on his folding table until he found what he was looking for. "He delivered it right on time."

"Who?"

"Truax. He delivered the witness list just like the court rules say." Burr studied the list. "It's a preview of his case. The laser and ..." Burr ran his finger down the list of names "... and all of these people who are going say that Brian and Lisa were having an affair. If he can do that, he wins." He put the list down. "And we've got a drunken ex-cop, a doctor turned undertaker and a very large gun expert."

"Don't be so optimistic."

Jacob came in, wearing a blue blazer over a starched blue pinstripe shirt and charcoal slacks.

He's switched to his fall wardrobe.

Jacob handed Burr a letter from Emmet County Circuit Court. Burr read it, crumpled it up and threw it where the wastebasket should have been.

Damn it all.

"That's where I'll put the wastebasket," Eve said. "When we get one."

"District judges don't try murder cases," Burr said.

"Gillis isn't a district judge anymore," Jacob said.

"What happened?" More tugging from Eve.

Jacob pulled out a folding chair and wiped it off with his handkerchief. He started to sit but thought better of it. "One of the justices on the Court of Appeals had a stroke. Dykehouse, our trial judge, got appointed to take his place. Gillis is now a circuit judge."

"Tinker to Evers to Chance," Burr said.

"I beg your pardon," Jacob said.

"Baseball," Eve said.

Jacob shook his head. "And Gillis hates you."

***

Burr and Zeke rode the ferry from Walpole to Algonac. They'd just finished hunting the Canadian duck opener with Victor, over the protest of everyone except Zeke. Even Victor thought it was a bad idea. Burr hadn't missed opening day in twenty years and he was damned if he'd miss this one.

The ferry churned across the St. Clair River. Burr looked at the witness list Truax had served him with. The cop, the undertaker and the laser lady. No surprises there. The baseball coach, friends, neighbors, employees. He'd talked to them all and hadn't found anything damning. Burr didn't think there was anyone on Truax's witness list who was going to speak to any possible motive Brian might have had for murdering Claudia. The Indian River motel owners weren't on the list, but there was the motive, Brian's affair with Lisa.

"Zeke, if I know, I have to assume Truax knows."

In the back seat for once, the aging Lab, tired from retrieving ducks, snored softly.

"No one listens to me."

As for Burr, he had Maples and the missing gun and Frieda Deutsch and the defective gun, if it was defective.

"Zeke, it's not much, but it's all I've got."

CHAPTER EIGHTEEN

"I refuse to accept another of your challenges," Judge Gillis said.

"Yes, Your Honor, but ..."

"Don't interrupt me, Mr. Lafayette. You may use your peremptory challenges. Let's see here ..." Gillis looked through his reading glasses, eyes crossed slightly. "I see. Yes, here it is. You have one left. Do you wish to use it?"

"No, Your Honor."

"Mrs. Horton, you are hereby impaneled."

"Your Honor," Burr said, standing.

"Yes, Mr. Lafayette."

"May I approach the bench?"

"No," Gillis said. "Whatever you have to say, say it from there."

"Your Honor," Burr said. "I think it may be prejudicial."

"Prejudicial to whom?"

"To my client."

"Why would that be?" Gillis said.

Burr ran his hands through his hair, front to back, then picked up the Michigan court rules. "Your Honor, the court rules regarding jury selection require that a juror be disqualified if he or she is prejudiced regarding the matter at hand."

"I am well aware of that provision."

"Your Honor, I submit that Mrs. Horton should be disqualified for that reason."

"For what reason?"

"That she is prejudiced and has a preconceived opinion regarding this case."

Gillis took off his glasses and held them up to the light from the windows. The October light was pale in the afternoon but not as weak as it had been at the preliminary exam in February. Gillis breathed on both lenses and rubbed them with the sleeve of his robe.

Why didn't he hand them to Miss Long Fingers?

Gillis put his glasses back on. "Mr. Lafayette. It is beyond me how this poor woman – poor I say because she will undoubtedly have to listen to you dither during this trial – is by any fathomable reason prejudiced."

"I believe she has already made up her mind, Your Honor."

"And why would that be?"

"Because ..."

"Never mind." Gillis pointed at him, then curled his forefinger. "Come here, Mr. Lafayette, and I'll tell you."

Burr slipped quietly to the bench.

I don't think I'm going to like this.

"This is why you want her disqualified," Gillis said, not especially sotto voce, "because she is overweight, not particularly attractive, quite likely unhappily married, and resents the hell out of your client who she probably thinks killed his wife so he could marry a younger woman." Gillis was out of breath. "That's your theory of jury selection, isn't it," Gillis said, not asking.

"Your Honor, I object. I ask that the prospective jurors all be disqualified."

"Nonsense"

"You've prejudiced all of them."

Gillis turned red. "They didn't hear me."

"Your Honor, I'm sure they did."

"Mr. Lafayette, I'm a simple man. Nonetheless, I have sat on the bench for thirty years. While this is my first murder trial, I've conducted more jury trials than I can remember." Gillis put his glasses back on, then took them off. "If it was up to you, the jury would be composed of men over fifty, each married to a woman under thirty. Isn't that about right, Mr. Lafayette?"

"No, Your Honor," Burr said, lying.

"The juror you don't want is female, at least fifty, divorced, husband remarried to a younger woman. Like Mrs. Horton."

"Mrs. Horton is married, Your Honor."

"She's your second worst juror. Female over fifty, unhappily married. Is that right?"

"No, Your Honor," Burr said.

"Mr. Lafayette, the facts are that most people here are married. Probably not happily married. More than half of the prospective jurors are women because their husbands have predeceased them." Gillis shook his head. "While I'm at it, I'm sure you would prefer there were no Catholics on the jury, but Emmet County is over sixty percent Catholic. It's so nice to see you again. I didn't think I'd ever again have the pleasure." Gillis waved his glasses at Burr. "You may proceed."

"Your Honor, respectfully, I ask that you disqualify Mrs. Horton for cause and that you disqualify the jurors who heard your outburst."

***

Gillis adjourned for the day at 4:30 p.m. He'd impaneled a twelve-person jury and two alternates. Eight women and four men. The two alternates were men. Of the eight women, five were over fifty, three of whom were divorced. The other three were married with children at home. Five were Catholic.

Of the four men, one did have a younger second wife, but only by four years. The other three were married. Burr thought that, unfortunately, they were happily married.

***

Burr tapped his brand new No.2 yellow pencil, Brian next to him, Jacob next to Brian. Lisa, Suzanne and Eve in the first pew behind them. The gallery full to overflowing. The fall colors were past peak, the tourists were long gone, and a murder trial didn't happen in Petoskey very often. Gillis, Miss Long Fingers and Swede were in their places. Truax was droning on about the civic duty of a juror, but none of them appeared to be listening.

Then Truax started with the Dick and Jane version of first-degree murder. "We will prove that Mr. Dunn committed first-degree murder, which is premeditated murder. All that means is that Mr. Dunn killed his wife on purpose and that he had a plan for doing it. That's all it means. It's very simple."

Truax put his hands in his pockets and rocked back and forth on his heels.

He looks like an Ichabod Crane version of a metronome.

"This case is simple because it only has three pieces. Three easy pieces. When I prove each piece — which I will — there will be no choice but to convict the defendant of murdering his wife. No choice whatsoever."

Truax stopped rocking.

"Three pieces. Piece one." He raised his hand and stuck one finger up. "Brian Dunn killed his wife. We know it's true. How? He said so. Over and over. *I killed my wife.* The first piece has already been proven."

"Piece two." A second finger shot up. "Brian Dunn killed his wife on purpose. How do we know that? We have an expert — an expert from the state police — who has proven that, from the way the bullet entered Claudia Dunn's body, it could only have done so if the gun had been picked up and aimed at poor Claudia."

"Like this." Truax turned and aimed a pretend rifle at Brian.

Burr jumped to his feet. "I object, Your Honor."

Gillis glared at Truax over his reading glasses. "Stop it, Calvin. We've only just started."

Truax nodded. His Adam's apple bobbed, but he didn't say anything.

That slowed him down a little.

But not for long.

"Third," now a hand with three fingers. "Mr. Dunn had a plan. That's what premeditated is. Mr. Dunn had a plan to kill his wife. He called her down to the basement. That was his plan. He called her down to the basement and he killed her. He murdered her. And do you know why he murdered her?"

Here it comes.

Truax put his hand down. He rocked back and forth, then stopped dead still. "I'll tell you why. Because he was having an affair, a sordid affair, with a woman almost twenty years his junior. With a woman who could have been his daughter. That's right, his daughter. He could be her father. Brian Dunn made a plan to kill his wife so he could take up with a younger woman."

Burr snapped his pencil in two.

Truax looked at Burr and the broken pencil and smiled at him. He turned to the jury and looked at each of them, one by one. "That's the third piece. A sordid, wretched affair." He rocked again, then stopped. "Three pieces. That's all. That is what we will prove. After we do that, we'll ask that you find the defendant, Brian Dunn, guilty of first-degree murder."

Truax turned away from the jury. "And here," he said, pointing at Lisa, sitting primly in the front row, just behind Brian, "is the wanton woman, the reason for this heinous crime. This is the younger woman, the woman who threw herself at him."

Damn it all.

Lisa met Truax's look. Burr had told her that, if she were drawn in, to look at Truax, then Brian, then at the jury, then to her lap. Not a defiant look, but a concerned look.

At least she did what I told her to do.

She'd also dressed as Burr had told her. A black dress, slightly matronly, and as far from a little black dress as possible. He had Brian in a blue suit that didn't fit him too well. His tie was too wide, and Burr had it tied slightly crooked. Brian had put on weight in jail, which suited Burr just fine. The round face and too small clothes gave him a harmless look, like the bumbling fool Burr thought he was.

Now I'm the fool.

Truax sat down. His lips stretched wide in a self-satisfied smile.

Like the cat who swallowed the canary. And I'm the canary.

Gillis looked down at Burr. "Mr. Lafayette, you may proceed."

Burr stood. He had on his favorite suit, the one he always wore for opening and closing arguments. His charcoal, tropical wool suit, maybe a bit threadbare. Baby blue, pinpoint oxford button-down. Red tie with black diamonds. He was at home, in spite of what had just happened.

"Ladies and gentlemen," he said, looking down at his shoes. He didn't want to look them in the eye, not yet. He walked toward the jury. Now he looked them in the eye, one by one, left to right, like he was reading a book.

"Ladies and gentlemen," he said again. "My name is Burr Lafayette. This is my partner and co-counsel Jacob Wertheim. We represent Brian Dunn and, as a practical matter, we also represent his wife, Lisa, who has been pointed out to you, and his children, Chad and Becky, who are not here today. You may know Brian or know of him. His family lived here for a long time, and he did, too, until recently. Until the accident."

Burr slid his hands into his pockets and talked to his shoes again, the tasseled cordovan loafers that still needed polishing.

"You see, I really don't know why we're here. Why you've been taken from your lives, what you do each day. And why Mr. Dunn has been ripped from his life. He's been in jail since December, unable to work, unable to provide for his family, unable to be with his wife, his son or his daughter. His daughter is five years old. She doesn't understand why her daddy isn't home at night. She's mad at him for not being there.

"It's terrible to be ripped out of your home at gunpoint, thrown in jail and kept there for almost a year." Burr turned to Brian, who gave him a sorrowful look, as instructed. "And for Brian, it has been terrible." Burr turned back to the jury.

"Murder, of course, is terrible. If you murdered someone, you'd deserve to be in jail, you'd deserve it for what you did. I believe that. I'm sure you all do, too."

Burr looked at the jury. They all nodded.

"But if you were accused of murder and thrown in jail because of an accident, that would be terrible." Burr looked down at his shoes again. Then up at the jury. "Wouldn't it?" They nodded again.

"And that's what happened here. An accident. A horrible, tragic accident. Would you like to know what happened?"

Of course they would. He had them now. He had them, and he knew it. They did, too, and they were glad of it.

"This is what happened. Brian lent his deer rifle to a friend. His friend went hunting with it. Then he brought it back and left it in Brian's garage because no one was home. When Brian got home, he took it down to the basement. It was dirty and needed a good cleaning, but Brian didn't have time to do it just then.

"Two weeks later, Brian, his wife, and their son go out to cut their Christmas tree, like they did every year. They come home. Brian puts the tree in the stand. They string the lights. They take a break while Claudia makes spiced hot cider. Brian goes down to the basement. He sees his deer rifle and thinks that this is a good time to clean it.

"And you know what?"

No, they said with their eyes.

"He's a little upset with his friend, who he thought would have taken better care of his rifle. It's dirty. Really dirty. And his friend left the clip in the gun. Can you imagine that? Then Claudia comes down the stairs and tells him it's time to put the angel on top of the tree. And that's Brian's job. Brian looks up at his wife, gun on the workbench where he's cleaning it. He's a little distracted. Then, *bang*," Burr said, clapping his hands. They all jumped. The jury, Brian, Lisa, Suzanne, Jacob, the gallery, Gillis. Even Truax.

"The gun went off. His wife falls. There's blood. Brian runs to her. Chad starts down the stairs. Brian stops him and won't let him come down, takes him upstairs. Then you know what Brian does? He calls the police. Chad is taken to the neighbor next door. The police come and they ask Brian what happened.

"He says 'the gun went off.' As you might imagine, he's in shock and doesn't really know what happened, but he thinks that the cleaning rag might have gotten tangled around the trigger. He thought the rifle was empty. He was careful. He took the clip out. He racked the gun, threw the bolt, but somehow there was still a shell in it. Perhaps the gun had been returned broken. But it was an accident. A terrible accident.

"And you know what? That's what the police thought, too. They called it an accident. A terrible accident. But an accident. The coroner thought so, too.

"There was an inquest," Burr said. "An inquest is an investigation to see if charges should be filed. But do you know what happened?"

The jury didn't know.

"The people at the inquest thought it was an accident. There were no charges filed. They thought it was an accident."

"And then you know what happened?"

They didn't, but they wanted to.

"Brian was devastated. He mourned for a long time, but finally he started living again. He remarried, had another child. He got on with life. That makes sense, doesn't it? Of course it does." Burr looked at the jury one by one. "But then do you know what happened?"

They didn't, but they wanted to.

"Six years later, after everyone's forgotten what happened, after the evidence has disappeared. Did you know the police have lost the gun? It's been six years, not six months. Six years after this terrible tragedy, an ambitious prosecutor arrests Brian for murder. Right out of the blue. Six years after it happened. After the police said it was an accident. After the coroner said it was an accident. An ambitious prosecutor, this man, arrested Brian Dunn for murder." Burr pointed at Truax, who turned redder than Gillis had.

Right on cue.

"And do you know what? Until that time, Brian had never been arrested for anything. Never in his whole life. A long time ago, he got two points for going 65 on US-31, ten over, between here and Boyne Falls."

Two of the jurors snickered.

"The points expired fifteen years ago. But Mr. Truax arrests Brian for murder because a laser, a laser like in *Star Wars*, says it couldn't be an accident.

"And you know what else?"

They didn't, but they wanted to.

"Mr. Truax doesn't even have the gun. He doesn't know where it is. What if the gun was defective? What if it didn't work right? Then what?"

"And you know what else? This man," he said, pointing to Truax again, "This man has refused to let Brian out on bail. So he's spent almost a year in jail. He can't provide for his family in jail, can he? No, of course he can't." They agreed. "And do you know why? Because this man believes Brian is a threat to society and might run away. A flight risk. Brian, a flight risk. I don't think so, do you?" They didn't.

The jury was ready to let Brian go, right then and there.

"To find him guilty, do you know what you must do?" He had them.

They leaned toward him. "To find Brian guilty, you must believe that Brian murdered his wife beyond a reasonable doubt. Beyond a reasonable doubt. Not a hunch. Not a guess. Not an *I suppose so*. You've really got to believe it. Ladies and gentlemen, I just don't see it.

"Why bring a case like this? Why do it? Why, after all this time, when the evidence is old — what there is of it — when Brian has led an exemplary life. Husband, father, breadwinner, coach. A dentist. Why do it? I'll tell you why we're here."

Burr walked up to the jury box. He walked right up to them, his eyes in their eyes.

"I'll tell you why. I'll tell you why you're here. It's not about justice. It's not even about Brian. It's about him." Burr pointed at Truax. "It's about him." Then he whispered so only the jury could hear, not Truax, not Gillis, not anyone but the jury. "It's because he wants to be a state senator, that's why. He wants publicity. It has nothing to do with Brian."

Truax shot up. "What? What did he say? I object. What did he say? I couldn't hear."

"Mr. Lafayette, you must speak so that we all can hear you," Gillis said.

"Yes, Your Honor," Burr said.

"Strike that from the record," Gillis said.

Miss Long Fingers turned to Judge Gillis. "Your Honor, I didn't hear what he said."

"Mr. Lafayette, please repeat what you said to the jury so that we all may hear it."

"With all due respect, Your Honor, if I repeat it, so you can hear it so you can strike it from the record, wouldn't it be better not to repeat it?"

Gillis thought this over. It looked to Burr that the judge's eyes crossed when he concentrated. He looked over his glasses, "Mr. Lafayette, I must know what you said." Burr looked at Gillis but didn't say a word. "What was it that you said, Mr. Lafayette?"

Burr turned from the jury to Truax and then to Gillis. "I said that the real reason for this trial was to get Truax publicity for his election to the state senate."

Truax launched himself to his feet. "I object, Your Honor. I object." He turned redder than before.

"Strike that from the record," Gillis said, turning redder than Truax. *These two are having a 'who can turn redder' contest.*

"I have nothing further, Your Honor," Burr said. He walked back to his table and sat.

Gillis looked at Truax. "You may proceed."

Truax didn't call either the retired cop or the undertaker. He proved his first easy piece by introducing Gustafson's police report and Van Arkel's autopsy into evidence and reading from them. Burr had no choice but to accept the reports.

Truax then called Ellen Gannon. The bailiff swore her in. She sat, pulled down and straightened her skirt and crossed her legs.

"Dr. Gannon, in your own words, in lay terms, please tell us about the laser technology and what you found."

Burr thought it also smart of Truax to start with his best witness. Truax had done a good job with her credentials and the technology.

"It's very simple, really." She uncrossed her legs and put her knees together. "A laser shoots a straight line. We can determine the path of the bullet because we know where the bullet struck the wall, where it exited the victim's body and where it entered. Because we know the victim's height, we can connect those three points. The result is a line that points to where the bullet came from. Because the murder weapon..."

"Objection, Your Honor," Burr said. "It is a rifle. It is up to the jury to determine if a murder was committed."

"Sustained," Gillis said. "Please continue, Dr. Gannon."

"The gun has a long barrel. We place the rifle barrel on the line, and it tells us from where the bullet was fired."

"And what did it tell you?" Truax said.

"It told us that the gun could not have gone off from the workbench. The angles don't work."

"Where would the gun have to be?"

"May I show you?"

"Please."

Gannon stood. She picked up her arms as if she were shouldering a rifle. She swung them, pointed at Brian. He ducked.

"Objection, Your Honor," Burr said.

"What for?"

"The witness is intimidating my client."

"There is altogether too much pointing going on. Sustained." Gillis scowled. "You may proceed, Mr. Truax."

"What you're saying is that when the entry, the exit, and wall points are connected, it's not possible for the gun to have been on the workbench," Truax said.

"That's correct," Gannon said.

"The way they line up, though, fits with a gun that had been shouldered and fired," Truax said.

"Exactly," Gannon said.

"Dr. Gannon, I think I understand, but could you demonstrate it graphically?" Truax said.

"I have two charts that illustrate my point. May I?"

Of course you may.

Truax walked to his table and picked up the charts. "Your Honor, the people would like to introduce these diagrams as People's Exhibits One and Two."

"Let me see them." Truax handed the two charts to the judge, who made a show of studying them. Gillis passed the charts back to Truax. Burr walked up to Truax and looked at the charts.

Two poster boards, each showing a woman, a wall, and a man aiming a rifle. The wall, the entry wound and the exit wound were all marked. A line was drawn through each one. On the first poster, the line ran up to the man aiming a rifle at the woman. A straight line connected them all. On the second poster, the gun was on a workbench. The line ran up from the entry wound just as in the first drawing. When it reached the height of the workbench, though, it angled parallel to the gun on the table, a crooked line. Clearly not possible, at least according to the laws of physics.

They were everything Burr hoped they wouldn't be. Much better than the toy rifle at the preliminary exam.

There's nothing I can do to keep them out.

"No objection, Your Honor," Burr said.

Truax showed the charts to the jury then walked back to the

witness. "Dr. Gannon, how could the workbench drawing occur in the real world?"

"It couldn't."

"Why not?"

"Because the trajectory of a bullet is straight, especially at close range. Its path won't change."

"I see," Truax said. "Suppose the gun had fired, gone off, say, accidentally from the workbench. How would that look?"

"That would be the third chart," she said.

Truax walked to his table and retrieved another poster, which he introduced as People's Exhibit Three. This showed a line drawn from the gun on the workbench to an entry wound just below the armpit, an exit wound at the same height, and a mark on the wall at the same height.

"Dr. Gannon, please tell us about People's Exhibit Three."

"If the gun had gone off from the workbench, the path of the bullet would be very close to parallel with the workbench and the bullet would have ended up in the wall at the same height it left the gun."

"And the wounds?"

"They would be in line with the two end points. Here and here," she said pointing.

"But?"

"But the bullet hit the wall substantially below the height of the workbench, and it entered the body above the level of the table. Both of these points are inconsistent with the gun going off from the workbench."

"Inconsistent?"

"Impossible."

"Impossible?" Truax said. "What are you saying?"

"I am saying that there is no way that Mrs. Dunn was killed by a bullet from the workbench."

"It's impossible."

"Yes," she said. "It is impossible."

"How was she killed?"

"Objection," Burr said. "Calls for a statement of fact which the witness cannot know."

"I withdraw the question." Truax gave him a peeved look. "Let me restate the question. In your opinion, how was she killed?"

"She was killed by someone who aimed a rifle," Gannon said.

"Objection," Burr said. "It has not been established, even by these voodoo physics, that the gun was aimed."

"Sustained," Gillis said.

"Ms. Gannon, please give us your opinion as to what occurred," Truax said.

"In my opinion, the gun could only have been fired from the shoulder."

"Which diagram is that?"

"This one." Gannon pointed to People's Exhibit One, the man firing the gun from his shoulder.

"Let the record show this is People's Exhibit One," Truax said. "Please show us once more what that would look like."

"I beg your pardon."

"Demonstrate like you did before. But don't point it at Mr. Dunn this time." Truax backed up. "This time aim at me."

Gannon picked up an imaginary rifle, shouldered it, and aimed it at Truax.

"Now, pull the trigger," Truax said.

The laser expert pulled an imaginary trigger. "Bang," she said, and Truax clapped his hands. Just like Burr. They all jumped, just like before.

"No further questions, Your Honor," Truax said.

"Your witness, Mr. Lafayette," Gillis said.

Burr started his cross-examination of the comely Ellen Gannon with her credentials.

"Objection, Your Honor," Truax said. "The qualifications of the witness have already been established, and, I might add, they are impeccable."

"I agree, Your Honor," Burr said, "but as to expert witnesses, the court rules clearly allow cross-examination regarding qualifications."

Gillis looked like he was thinking over the objection. Burr had no idea why he had to think it over. It was one of the clearest rules about experts. Finally, "You may proceed, Mr. Lafayette."

"Thank you, Your Honor." Burr walked to the witness stand.

"Ms. Gannon, you have testified that you have degrees in physics. Is that correct?"

"It's Doctor."

"Of course it is."

"You have degrees in physics. Is that correct," Burr said again.

"A master's and a doctorate."

"Any other degrees?"

"My bachelor's degree was in astronomy."

"I see," Burr said, leaning on the railing even closer. "Comets and meteors."

"Objection, Your Honor," Truax said. "Counsel is taunting the witness."

"Watch your manners, Mr. Lafayette."

"Yes, Your Honor. Ms. Gannon, do you have any other degrees?"

"It's Doctor," she said again.

"I'm so sorry," Burr said, who wasn't. "Do you have any other degrees?"

"No," she said.

"Any other course of study or specialties? For instance ..." Burr looked at the jury, then back at Gannon. "... did you ever study anatomy? Human anatomy?"

"No, I did not."

"You haven't studied human anatomy, but you have applied the principles of physics to the human body."

"That's right."

"Dr. Gannon," Burr said, backing away, "a laser is nothing more than a beam of light. Is that right?"

"Yes."

"And the whole point of your laser analysis is based on the premise that light travels in a straight line. Is that right?"

"Yes," Gannon said.

"Objection, Your Honor," Truax said. "This is going nowhere."

"Your Honor, if Mr. Truax would afford me the simple courtesy of listening politely, we would be there by now."

"Proceed, Mr. Lafayette," Gillis said.

"Ms. Gannon. What happens if, for example, I take this ..." Burr fished around in a jacket pocket and came out with a small pocket mirror "... simple mirror and place it in the path of the laser? What happens to the beam of light then? What happens to its path?"

"Its path changes such that the angle of reflection equals the angle of incidence."

"Spoken like a physicist," Burr said. "Now, in plain language, is it true that, when the laser — the light — hits the mirror, its path is changed? It no longer travels in a straight line."

"Yes, that's true."

"Suppose a bullet strikes a bone, would that change its path?"

"No," Gannon said. "Not in this case."

"No? How do you know?"

"Because the shot was fired at close range. The bullet would be traveling too fast. It has too much force to alter its path."

"Have you studied anatomy, Ms. Gannon?"

"Yes."

Burr leaned on the railing. "I thought you said you hadn't studied anatomy."

"I studied it for this case."

"But not formally." Burr looked back at the jury.

"No, not formally."

"Would you consider yourself an expert on anatomy?"

"Objection. That is a legal question," Truax said

"Sustained," Gillis said.

Burr shook his head. "You have no training in anatomy, yet you studied it enough to know that if the bullet hit a bone, its path wouldn't change."

"Yes, that's right," Gannon said.

Burr had just enough light from the windows so the light from his mirror flashed into Gannon's eyes. She blinked, then moved her hand to block the mirror.

"Objection, Your Honor," Truax said. "Counsel is taunting the witness again."

"I'm so sorry, Ms. Gannon. The light must have gotten in your eyes." Burr pocketed the mirror. "Ms. Gannon, your findings on the entry and exit wounds were from what source?"

"From the coroner's report. And it's *Doctor*."

"The coroner's report," Burr said.

"Yes."

"And did they indicate the location of the wounds?"

"They did."

"And where were they?"

"The bullet entered here." She pointed to a spot on her left side just below her armpit. "And exited here." She pointed to a spot just above her right hip. "Approximately."

"You said *approximately*."

"Yes," Gannon said. "The report is very specific. Where I am showing you on my body is only approximate."

"I see," Burr said. "And what was the size of the entry wound."

"The diameter of the bullet. Very small," Gannon said.

"The size of my little finger," Burr raised the pinkie of his left hand, made sure the jury could see it.

"Approximately."

"Approximately," Burr said. "You are fond of that word. And what was the size of the exit wound?"

"It was circular. About six centimeters in diameter.

"So the hole was almost a two-and-a-half-inch circle. Is that right?"

"Approximately," she said again.

"Come on, Ms. Gannon. That's a big hole." Burr made a circle with his thumb and forefinger, two inches-plus in diameter and looked through it. First at Gannon, then the jury. "I'd say that's a big hole. A big hole to guess at where the actual path of the bullet was. A guess, that's what I'd call it. A big guess to determine a man's fate."

"That is not the critical hole," Gannon said.

"I didn't ask you a question, Ms. Gannon. Now, I'd like you to look at this chart." Burr strode to his table. Jacob handed him a poster board. Burr introduced it into evidence. "Ms. Gannon, I would ask you to tell me what you see here."

"Objection, Your Honor," Truax said. "That is speculation. An expert witness need not give credence to speculative evidence by reading it."

"Sustained," Gillis said.

They're both right. For once.

Burr held the poster so that Gannon and the jury could see it. There was a rifle on a workbench and a line drawn to a woman standing. The line entered the body, glanced off a bone then changed direction slightly, angling downward.

"Suppose a laser is placed on the workbench where this rifle is, as in this exhibit, and the beam of light is directed on the path of the rifle, and when it gets here," he touched the bone, "there is a mirror, what would happen?"

"The path of the light would change."

"Down this line?"

"Yes."

"And, similarly, if the bullet hit a bone, might it not deflect down this path?"

"No."

"Why not?"

"Because the bullet has too much force."

"Ms. Gannon, did you examine the body?"

"No, of course not," Gannon said. "It was six years ago."

"My point exactly," Burr said. "It has been a long time, hasn't it?"

"Objection," Truax said.

"I withdraw the question." Burr took the poster back to Jacob, then walked back to Gannon. "The point is, Ms. Gannon, you don't know, do you? This is a fine theory except you didn't examine the body. It's certainly possible that the bullet could have glanced off a bone and changed its path. Isn't that possible?"

"No," she said. "It's not."

"This is nothing more than a theory. It's not proof."

"Objection, Your Honor," Truax said.

"Sustained," Gillis said.

She's getting angry. That's perfect.

"Ms. Gannon, one more question." Burr leaned in again. "How many times before have you used this laser analysis in a murder trial?"

"This time," she said.

"Ms. Gannon, please don't be cute. How many times before this time have you used this?"

"None."

"This is the only time?"

"This is the first time," she said.

"The only time."

"Yes."

"No further questions, Your Honor."

"We reconvene at 1:30." Gillis banged his gavel and waltzed out, his robes flowing.

***

Burr reprised lunch at the Park Garden Café. When he squeezed the lemon on his whitefish, it squirted on his tie. Eve dipped her napkin in her water glass and wiped it off.

"It won't stain. I Scotchgarded it yesterday, so it's bulletproof."

That's a poor choice of words.

***

After lunch, Truax began with his third finger, the motive finger and last of the three easy pieces. Burr thought he'd hurt Truax with the second piece, which required Brian to have killed Claudia on purpose, but that wouldn't matter if Truax could show that Brian killed Claudia because of the affair. Truax was well on his way with Dallas Stall, the baseball coach.

"And where did Mr. Dunn place his hand?"

"On her bottom," Stall said.

"On her bottom?"

"Yes."

"Mr. Stall, please go back and tell us again."

"Objection, Your Honor," Burr said. "We've already heard this."

"Overruled," Gillis said.

They must be in cahoots.

"At the awards ceremony for baseball, I saw him open the door for her at the school entrance, then she walks through."

"Who is she again?"

"Her," Stall said, pointing at Lisa.

"For the record, *her* is the current Mrs. Dunn," Truax said. "And?"

"She starts to go in and he puts his hand on her bottom."

"Couldn't he have just been helping her through the door?"

"Not that way," Stall said.

The courtroom snickered.

"Why not?"

"If it was me, I wouldn't touch anybody there unless I knew they'd like it. Otherwise, you could get sued."

Why didn't Stall tell me?

"I have no further questions, Your Honor."

"You may proceed, Mr. Lafayette," Gillis said.

Thank God Truax hadn't thought to ask what Lisa had been doing at the awards ceremony in the first place.

Burr stood. "Mr. Stall, did you ever see Mr. Dunn kiss Miss Fairchild before Mrs. Dunn died?

"No."

"Did you ever see them hold hands?"

"No."

"Did you ever see any other public displays of affection?"

"No," Stall said again.

"Did Mr. Dunn ever speak romantically about Miss Fairchild to you?"

"No."

"Yet you believe they were having an affair."

"I saw what I saw."

Burr approached Stall. "Please answer the question, Mr. Stall."

"I don't know. Maybe not an affair, but he had a crush on her. I know that."

"A crush, Mr. Stall, is not an affair." Burr looked at the jury. One of the jurors nodded.

Truax then called Elizabeth Lisecky, a tiny, fiftyish woman with a round face like a pumpkin and matching orange hair. She was the hygienist Burr had found, and she, like Stall, hadn't told him everything. Her answers weren't quite as graphic as Stall's, but they were still damaging.

Now it was Burr's turn.

"You were a hygienist in Brian Dunn's dental office?"

"Yes," she said.

"Please tell us what you told Mr. Dunn," Burr said.

"I told him to keep his distance from her."

"From whom?"

"Miss Fairchild," Ms. Lisecky said.

"Why did you say that?"

"Because he was married. Isn't that pretty obvious?"

"But why, specifically, did you tell him that?"

"I saw them holding hands."

"Where?"

"In the office," she said. "And I saw it in his eyes. Like a puppy."

"Just answer the question, Ms. Lisecky," Burr said. "Did you ever see Mr. Dunn kiss Miss Fairchild?"

"No," she said.

"Touch her breast?"

"No." She blushed.

"Put his hand on her bottom?" Burr said.

"No," she said, still blushing.

"But he held her hand?"

"Yes, in the office."

"When was that?"

"I don't remember," she said.

"You remember he held her hand, but you don't remember when?" Burr stared at her. "Could it have been at the office Christmas party?"

"I don't remember."

"You remember that you saw them holding hands, but you don't remember when or where," Burr said again.

"That's right," she said.

"I see," Burr said. "Well, Ms. Lisecky, isn't it possible that you are slightly overzealous in your pursuit of decorum?"

"I know moon eyes when I see them."

"Where and when did you see them holding hands?"

"I don't remember," she said for a third time.

"Please answer the question," Burr said.

Truax popped up. "Objection, Your Honor. 'I don't remember' is an answer."

"Sustained."

"I have no further questions."

Gillis adjourned them for the day.

CHAPTER NINETEEN

The next morning, Truax called more witnesses to testify about the affair. All of them testified that they thought Brian and Lisa were having an affair, but none of them had actually seen anything more than hand holding or a kiss here and there. But it was still damaging.

Thank God he hasn't found the woman from Sensible Rates.

Truax called Connie Cusack, the last witness on his list. A middle-aged woman with bifocals took the witness stand. She wore a mail carrier's uniform. The bailiff swore her in.

"Ms. Cusack, did you ever see Mr. Dunn and Miss Fairchild together before Claudia Dunn was killed?" Truax said.

"Yes."

"And where would that be?"

"In Lisa Fairchild's garage."

"Ms. Fairchild's garage? And where is that garage?"

She took off her glasses. "It's next to her house."

Where else would it be?

"And what did you see?"

"I was delivering her mail when I saw Miss Fairchild pull up in her car. She didn't see me." The witness smiled at Truax. "I was behind a tree, bent over petting her cat."

Truax smiled a *get on with it* smile.

"The garage door opens up and she drives in. Then the door closes. I don't think too much about it, but then nothing happens."

"What do you mean 'nothing happens'"?

"The garage isn't attached to the house, so you have to come out to get to the house. But she doesn't come out of the garage. I get curious and go over to the garage window. The engine is running. I wonder, *is everything all right?* So I go up to the window. I can't quite see in. I cup my hands like this." She shaded the sides of her face with her hands. Then she leaned toward Truax. "I'll tell you what I saw. I saw Mr. Dunn in the car with her."

The mail carrier pointed at Lisa. Lisa's jaw dropped, then she put her head in her hands.

Burr bit his cheek. *That's the first time she's lost her composure during the trial. Not a good time to do it.*

"What do you think happened," Truax said.

"Mr. Dunn must have ducked down when they drove up."

"What were they doing?"

"He was kissing her."

Damn it all.

"Anything else?"

"I don't like to say this, but since you asked, he had his hand up her skirt."

"He did?" Truax said, incredulous.

As if he didn't know.

Burr jumped to his feet. "Objection, Your Honor. This is not necessary."

"Your Honor, this is certainly necessary. It shows motive."

"Overruled," Gillis said.

"How far up her skirt was his hand?"

"All the way up. All the way up so you could see her underpants. They were black."

"Ms. Cusack, when did you see this?"

"Well, it was before my route got changed. So it must have been 1976."

Truax looked at the jury. "Ladies and gentlemen, Claudia Dunn was murdered in 1977 so it's clear that this happened before she was murdered." Truax looked over at Brian, then back at the jury. "If it wasn't clear before, it's painfully clear now that Mr. Dunn was having an affair with Ms. Fairchild before the late Mrs. Dunn was murdered." Truax looked at Brian, then back at the jury. "And that's why he murdered her." Truax looked at Burr. "Your witness."

Burr looked at Brian, who didn't look back at him.

Now what do I do?

He stood and walked up to Ms. Cusack.

"Ms. Cusack, did you tell either Ms. Fairchild or Mr. Dunn that you spied on them?"

"Objection, Your Honor. Irrelevant," Truax said.

"It most certainly is relevant, Your Honor. My client had a right to know he was being spied on."

I'm never going to win this one.

"Sustained."

"Did Mr. Truax tell you to keep this to yourself?"

"Objection," Truax said.

I'm not going to win this one either.

"Sustained."

Burr looked at Gillis. "I have no further questions." Burr walked back to his table and sat. He picked up his pencil. It was all he could do not to break it. "Goddamn it, Brian. What else haven't you told me?"

Suzanne leaned over the rail. "Be quiet, the jury will hear you."

Burr broke his pencil.

Gillis looked at Truax. "I believe that was your last witness." The judge looked at Burr. "Mr. Lafayette, you may begin your defense."

Truax stood.

"Mr. Truax, that was your last witness. You may as well sit down."

"Your Honor," Truax said.

Gillis shuffled through the papers on his desk. He picked one up and waved it at the prosecutor. "There are no more witnesses on your list."

"I have one more witness, Your Honor."

Burr looked at Truax's witness list. He'd crossed out all of the names. Burr stood. "Your Honor, the prosecution has called all of its witnesses."

"Your Honor," Truax said, "I have just now been able to locate Chad Dunn, the defendant's son."

Damn it all.

"Your Honor, I object. This witness was not on the prosecution's list."

"Mr. Dunn is in the Navy, Your Honor," Truax said. "We were unable to locate him until now."

"Nonsense," Burr said. "The court rules require the prosecution to notify the defense in writing of all witnesses it intends to call at least twenty-one days before trial."

"Mr. Dunn was at sea, Your Honor. We were unable to reach him."

"That is patently untrue, Your Honor." Burr pointed at Truax. "The prosecutor is lying."

"Mr. Lafayette," Gillis said.

"Your Honor, is Mr. Truax aware of the U.S. mail, telephones, or telegrams?"

"Mr. Dunn was at sea, Your Honor."

"The radio was invented seventy-five years ago," Burr said.

"Be quiet, Mr. Lafayette," Gillis said.

"If you allow this witness, I will move for a mistrial," Burr said.

Gillis looked over his reading glasses. He rubbed the end of his nose. "Mr. Truax, you may call your witness."

"I move for a mistrial."

"So noted," Gillis said. "Proceed, Mr. Truax."

"Your Honor, the defense requests a thirty-minute recess."

"Mr. Lafayette, the court will recess for the day after it hears this witness."

Truax is coming after us with Brian's son.

Truax called Chad Dunn. He sat tall and straight, hat in his hands, just like a zealous young sailor. And he looked like a zealous young sailor. Broad shoulders, square jaw, clean shaven, hair cropped short. And, of course, in uniform.

Brian looked like he was delighted to see Chad.

Damn that Truax.

Truax asked a few introductory questions, then cut to the chase.

"Mr. Dunn, how do you think your father felt about your mother?"

"He hated her."

"Hated?" Truax said. "Isn't that a bit strong?"

"No, sir. It's not."

"How do you know he hated her?" Truax said.

"I lived there." Chad wrung his hat like a wet washcloth. "I saw it."

"Did they argue?"

"Yes, sir," he said in a military fashion that meant more than what he actually said.

"Fight?"

"Yes, sir."

"They argued and they fought," Truax said.

"Yes, sir."

"Tell me, Chad, why do you think he hated her?"

"Objection," Burr said.

"Overruled," Gillis said.

"I don't know, sir. I really don't know."

"Was she a good mother?"

"Yes, sir."

"A good wife?"

"Yes, sir."

"Objection," Burr said.

"In your opinion, was she a good wife?"

"Yes, sir."

The beloved mother and dutiful wife.

Burr tapped his pencil. Burr thought that by the time Truax was done with Chad Dunn, Claudia would be up for sainthood, which was the very reason Burr had left Claudia out of his defense. The living couldn't compete with the dead. He'd wondered why Truax had left her out. He hadn't. He'd just waited until the end.

Truax lies and cheats, but he's plenty smart.

"Mr. Dunn, where were you on the night your mother was killed?"

"I was in the living room."

"What were you doing?"

"We were decorating our Christmas tree."

"Would you please tell us what happened."

"They were arguing about something. I don't remember what they were arguing about, but Mom said something to Dad. I don't know remember what she said, but I heard him swear at her."

"What did he say?"

"I'd rather not say, sir."

"Please," Truax said.

He knows the answer.

"He said, 'Go fuck yourself.'"

The courtroom twittered. Feet shuffled.

Gillis rapped his gavel.

"Then what?"

"He went down to the basement. Then he told her to come down there."

"He what?"

"He told her to come down there."

"And then?"

"Then she went downstairs. I heard him yell at her. And then he shot her."

"Objection, Your Honor. Calls for a conclusion," Burr said.

"Sustained," Gillis said.

"Mr. Dunn, you say your father called to your mother from the basement, your mother then went down to the basement. You heard your father yelling at her and then you heard a gunshot. Is that what happened?"

"Yes, sir."

"No further questions." Truax looked grimly at the jury, marched to his table and sat. Burr stayed in his chair.

"Mr. Lafayette, I believe it's your turn," Gillis said.

"Your Honor, may I have a ten-minute recess?"

"No, you may not."

"Your Honor, we've had no opportunity to prepare for this surprise witness."

"Proceed, Mr. Lafayette, or you forfeit your opportunity."

"Your Honor," Burr said.

"Now," Gillis said.

Burr knew he was in dangerous territory. He didn't think Truax would be able to produce Brian's son, and he'd believed that Truax had provided him with a complete witness list.

Shame on me.

He'd wondered why Truax had based his entire defense on a laser. Why hadn't Truax tried to show that Brian and Claudia had a bad marriage? Now he knew why. Truax had planned to lull him to sleep. Why did he ever think Truax would base everything on a laser? Because that's what Truax wanted him to think.

I underestimated him.

"Mr. Dunn," Burr said, as kindly as he could.

"Yes, sir?"

"How old are you?"

"Twenty-two, sir."

"And how long have you been in the Navy?" Burr said, still kindly.

"Four years, sir."

"And how old were you when your mother died?"

"Seventeen."

"Seventeen," Burr said. "And your birthday, I believe, is in January?"

"Yes, sir."

"You'll be twenty-three in January."

"Yes, sir."

"Wouldn't that make you sixteen when your Mother was killed?"

"I was almost seventeen," Chad said.

"Yes, almost, but not quite. But that was almost seven years ago. That's quite a long time, isn't it?"

"Yes, sir."

If he says 'sir' one more time, there's going to be another murder trial.

"Do you remember everything that long ago?" Burr said, still as kind as kind could be.

"Not everything," the boy said, "but I remember that night, sir."

"Do you? Do you recall what your parents argued about that night?"

"My mom didn't like the way my dad strung the garland on the tree."

"You just told Mr. Truax that you didn't know what they were arguing about."

"I remember now."

"I see," Burr said. "What did your father do after your mother said she didn't like the way the garland was strung on the tree."

"He took it off."

"Did she say anything then?"

"I don't remember."

"You don't remember."

"No, sir."

"You don't remember," Burr said again. "You remember what your father said, you remember what your mother said. You remember that your father took the garland off, but you don't remember what your mother said after that. Is that right?"

"Objection," Truax said. "Asked and answered. The witness already said he didn't remember."

"Sustained."

"Mr. Dunn, did your father go down to the basement after he took off the garland?"

"Yes, sir."

"Do you remember if your mother said anything to him when he went downstairs?"

"I think she said something."

"What would that be?"

"I don't really remember." Catching himself "... I remember she said something to him about the angel."

"Was your mother particular about the Christmas tree, about how it was decorated?"

"Yes, sir."

"She wanted it done in a particular way, in a particular order."

"Yes, sir."

"When your father went downstairs, were you finished decorating the tree?"

"No, sir."

"What was left?"

"The angel was crooked."

"Did the angel go on last?"

"Yes, sir."

"And where did the angel go?"

"On top of the tree."

"Who put the angel on?"

"My father."

"Did he put it on?"

The boy nodded.

"Please answer the question out loud."

"Yes."

"Wouldn't it make sense that your mother would call him up to straighten out the angel?"

"I don't know."

"Isn't it possible that she called him, told him to come upstairs and fix the angel? I mean, if she was as particular as you say, might she have called him?"

"Objection," Truax said. "Counsel is leading the witness."

"I simply asked a question, Your Honor," Burr said.

"Overruled, but watch yourself, Mr. Lafayette." Gillis turned to Chad. "You may answer the question."

"She might have," Chad said.

"Isn't it possible that she called your father, and when he didn't come upstairs, she went down to get him?"

"No, sir," Chad said.

"Mr. Dunn, I remind you that you are sworn to tell the truth. Isn't it possible that your mother went down to get him?"

"I don't know." Chad wrung his cap again. "She might have."

"Is it possible that you don't really remember exactly what happened?"

"Objection," Truax said.

"What now, Mr. Truax?" Gillis said.

"Counsel is badgering the witness," Truax said.

"Your Honor, I am trying to determine what actually took place that night."

"This is irrelevant, Your Honor," Truax said.

"It is extremely relevant. If Mrs. Dunn went downstairs to get her husband so he could straighten the angel, that categorically refutes the prosecutor's claim that my client called her down to the basement to shoot her, which, by the way, seems preposterous with their son upstairs in the living room."

"Mr. Lafayette, save your theory for your summation," Gillis said.

"Yes, Your Honor."

I made my point.

"Mr. Dunn, would you say you have a close relationship with your father?"

"Close?"

"Are the two of you close?"

"Objection," Truax said. "Too vague."

"Sustained," Gillis said.

"Mr. Dunn, when, before today, was the last time you saw your father?"

"I don't remember," Chad said.

"You don't remember," Burr said.

"No, sir."

Burr leaned on the railing of the witness stand with his left arm. "You don't remember when you last saw your father, but you remember that he called your mother downstairs that night almost seven years ago?"

"Objection," Truax said. "Rhetorical question."

"Sustained," Gillis said.

"Mr. Dunn," Burr said, "According to your father, this is the first time he's seen you since you joined the Navy, over four years ago. Is that right?"

"Yes, sir."

"But you do get leaves?"

"Yes, sir."

"How many leaves have you had in the past four years?"

"I don't know," Chad said.

"Twelve?"

"I don't know," Chad said. "Probably."

"Twelve times and you haven't seen your father once," Burr said, facing the jury.

"No, sir."

Burr turned back to Chad. "Would it be fair to say that you hate your father?"

"No, sir."

"Mr. Dunn, where did you live after your mother was killed?"

"With my best friend's family."

"Here in Petoskey?"

"Yes, sir" Chad said.

"And why was that?"

"I didn't want to live in that house."

Burr looked at Chad. "And what about when your father lost his job and moved to Detroit? Did you go, too?"

"I wanted to stay by my friends," Chad said.

"And what do you think of Lisa Dunn?" Burr asked.

"I don't know," Chad said.

"Do you like her?"

"She's all right."

"Mr. Dunn, you have been recently at sea?"

"Yes, sir."

"How long?"

"Four months."

"That would be since May."

"Since June."

"Since June." Burr walked toward Brian and the defense table. "And do you receive mail while you're at sea?"

"Yes, sir."

"How often?" Burr said.

"It depends, but usually every two weeks."

"Telephone calls?"

"Yes, sir."

"How often?"

"It depends."

"Monthly?" Burr said. "At least once a month?"

"Yes, sir.'

"Mr. Dunn, your ship landed in the last few days then?" Burr said.

"No, sir."

"Really." Burr feigned surprise. "When did you return?"

"Maybe two weeks ago," Chad said.

"And did Mr. Truax contact you then?"

"Yes, sir."

"And did he contact you before that?"

"Yes, sir."

"How many times?"

"I don't remember."

"Was it more than once?"

"Yes."

"More than twice?"

"Yes, sir."

"More than three times?"

"I don't remember."

"More than four times," Burr said.

"Objection, Your Honor," Truax said. "The witness says he doesn't remember, and this has no bearing on this case whatsoever."

"Sustained. Stop this line of questioning Mr. Lafayette."

"Yes, Your Honor." Burr walked back to the defense table and put his hand on Brian's shoulder. "Chad Dunn has been in contact with the prosecutor at least twice in the last two months, yet he has not seen his father in at least four years." Burr walked over to Truax. "And the prosecutor, the would-be state senator, said that Chad Dunn has just now been located. That until now he has been totally unavailable and unreachable. Which appears to be a bald-faced lie." He turned to Gillis. "I have no further questions."

***

Burr barely beat the broom out the door. After Gillis adjourned for the day, Burr, Zeke and a bag of decoys headed for a marshy spot hidden away on Crooked Lake.

He pulled off the road and parked on the side of a two-track. He took off his jacket and tie and then his shoes. He put on his waders, his duck coat and hat. He threw the bag of decoys over his shoulder, grabbed his shotgun and started off for the lake with Zeke. At the water, he threw out the decoys and hid in the cattails. The decoys floated quietly, not a breath of air. He lit a cigarette and watched the smoke drift off. Not a duck in sight, but he didn't care.

"Zeke, I'm missing something."

He picked up the decoys at sunset, walked back to the Jeep and drove to the Side Door Saloon in Petoskey to meet with Jacob and Eve and then Lisa and Suzanne for dinner.

The Side Door, next to Pirate Golf and eponymously named, had no front door but did have good sandwiches if you kept it simple. Burr ordered a Labatt. Jacob ordered his *de rigeuer* club soda with a lime. Eve nursed a Bloody Mary.

The Side Door was dark inside. Burr had picked a table in a corner, which made it even darker. There was a glass on the table with a flickering candle.

That's about all the ambience we're going to get.

"We must resign," Jacob said. "Your client, your client's wife, and quite possibly your paramour are all lying to you."

"Do you mean that Suzanne is quite possibly my paramour or that Suzanne is quite possibly lying?"

"You know very well what I mean."

"I'm not going to resign."

"Why not?"

"Because I don't believe Brian murdered Claudia."

"It certainly looks like he did," Eve said.

"There's something else."

"What?" Eve stirred her bloody mary with her pickle.

"I'm not going to lose to Truax." Burr took a big pull on his beer. Jacob stared at him.

"I suppose it's my ego."

"Bingo," Eve said.

"There's something else."

"Whatever it is, I don't want to know," Jacob said.

"Do you think Becky might be a bit big for her age?"

"Who?"

"Brian's daughter." Eve stopped stirring and bit off the end of her pickle.

"What does that have to do with anything?" Jacob sipped on his club soda.

"I'd like to know how old she is."

"Why don't you just ask Brian or Lisa?"

"I mean exactly how old. Like, when is her birthday?"

"I am a writer of appellate briefs."

"Yes, you are."

"I have no idea where to begin."

"I think we need a birth certificate. You could start at the city-county building."

"In Detroit?"

"We worked in Detroit for twenty years," Eve said.

Jacob kept whining but was cut short when Lisa and Suzanne came in. Burr ordered another Labatt.

"I hardly think it's appropriate to try to catch ducks at a time like this," Lisa said.

"I wasn't trying to catch them," Burr said.

"What were you doing then?"

"I was trying to kill them."

Eve kicked Burr under the table.

Lisa didn't miss a beat. "Truax lied to us about Chad, and I'd like know what you're going to do about it."

"We preserved our rights for an appeal," Jacob said.

"An appeal? Do you mean we're going to lose? After what Truax did to us."

Burr started on his fresh Labatt. "What exactly would you say he did to us?"

"He snuck in Chad," Lisa said. "Truax cheated and lied. That's what he did."

"Are you suggesting that I do the same?"

"I am suggesting that you win and I don't care how you do it."

"Before you advise me to cheat and lie, you might consider why we're here right now."

"And why is that?"

"Because you lied to me."

Suzanne put her hand on Burr's arm. He shook it off.

"Did it ever occur to you that I might have done things differently if I'd known the two of you were screwing each other's eyes out while Brian was married?"

Lisa reached over and poured the Labatt in his lap.

***

Burr turned on his other side so the moonlight wouldn't be in his eyes. He tried to push Zeke, who was snoring, over to the other side of the bed. The dog didn't budge.

"Damn it all."

It was two in the morning and he couldn't get to sleep. His room was furnished, like all the rest, in early cottage with a wrought iron headboard, a dresser with spindly legs and a chair that didn't match either bed or dresser. The room smelled like an attic. That was the best part. He liked the moonlight, but the curtains didn't work and the moon was so bright he could read a book by its light.

He knew that wasn't the real reason he couldn't sleep. It was Suzanne. It was her hand on his arm at the Side Door. He'd brushed her hand off, but it made him think of her. He wanted to believe her, but he knew she must somehow be involved in Brian and Lisa's carrying on. What difference did it really make? At least for now. He was in up to his neck with this trial and he was damned if he was going to lose to Truax.

"Maybe I still love her."

Zeke looked at him, jumped down and curled up on the rug at the foot of the bed.

CHAPTER TWENTY

Burr paced in front of Lawrence Van Arkel, the physician turned mortician, part-time coroner and the first witness for the defense.

It's finally my turn.

He thought Van Arkel could do the most damage to Truax and his laser theory. He thought Truax probably thought so, too, which was why the prosecutor hadn't called Van Arkel as a witness.

Burr led Van Arkel through his credentials, all of Burr's criticisms forgotten now that Van Arkel was on his side. The undertaker testified that he'd performed the autopsy, a standard procedure when the cause of death is by gun.

Then Burr took him to the heart of the matter, so to speak. "Dr. Van Arkel, do you believe that the cause of death was accidental? In spite of the fact that the exit wound was lower than the entry point of the bullet?"

"Yes," Van Arkel said.

I'm on safe ground here.

"Let me go back a step. Would you please explain what you saw and what you concluded?"

"The bullet entered here," Van Arkel said, touching his jacket just under his armpit. He touched his right forefinger under his left armpit. "And then it came out here." He touched a spot about four inches above his waist.

"If the gun went off parallel to the floor, is it possible for the bullet to exit lower than where it entered?"

"Yes."

"Why is that?"

Please answer just the way we practiced.

"If the bullet glanced off a bone, either when it entered or as it exited, its path could change."

Perfect.

"So ... a bullet entering on a path parallel to the floor could be deflected downward? Is that right?"

"Yes," Van Arkel said again.

"And the result would be a wound of the type suffered by the deceased."

"Yes."

"Thank you, Dr. Van Arkel. And how big would the size of the entry hole be?"

"It would be about this size. The size of the bullet." Van Arkel held up his forefinger.

"And the size of the exit wound?" Van Arkel made a larger circle with his thumb and forefinger.

"And is this consistent with a bullet that has struck something?"

"It is."

"Why is that?"

"When a bullet enters flesh, animal or human, if often spins off the path it entered. Sometimes it even tumbles, particularly when it strikes a bone."

"Could you determine exactly the path of the bullet when it left the body of the deceased?"

"No," Van Arkel said.

"Why is that?"

"Because the exit wound was so much larger than the diameter of the bullet."

"Then the laser would be useless to determine the path of the bullet by using the exit wound," Burr said, not asking.

"That is correct," Van Arkel said.

Truax stood. "Objection, Your Honor. The witness is not qualified to speak about the science of lasers."

"Sustained," Gillis said. "Strike the question and answer from the record."

Truax sat.

No matter. The damage was done.

Burr turned to the jury. "Ladies and gentlemen, I submit that the testimony of Dr. Van Arkel casts grave doubt on the scientific theory of the prosecution. This is simply another example of voodoo science. And in this case, voodoo science wrongly applied."

Truax jumped to his feet. "I object, Your Honor. You already instructed that be stricken from the record."

"Strike Mr. Lafayette's last comments from the record." Gillis turned to the jury, "You are to disregard Mr. Lafayette's comments regarding voodoo science." To Burr, "Mr. Lafayette, if you disregard one more of my orders, I will hold you in contempt, and your partner will be the one to finish this trial."

The jury heard Gillis say "voodoo science."

"Yes, Your Honor. I have no further questions."

Burr walked back to the defense table and sat.

That went well.

Van Arkel stood up and stretched.

"Dr. Van Arkel, are you quite through?" Gillis said.

"Yes," he said, still stretching.

"Then please sit down."

That doesn't help your credibility.

Van Arkel sat. Truax stood. "Dr. Van Arkel, when you performed the autopsy on the accused's wife," he pointed at Brian, "did you follow the standard autopsy procedure for gunshot wounds?"

"I did."

"What exactly is that procedure?"

"I take a steel rod, insert the rod into the entry wound and push it through the body and then out the exit wound."

"And did you do this?"

"I did."

"Were you able to push the rod all the way through?"

Van Arkel squirmed. "Yes."

"Easily?" Truax chewed on his cheek. "Did it slip through easily, Dr. Van Arkel?"

"I don't remember." The coroner squirmed again.

Stop squirming.

"Surely you would remember something like that," Truax scowled at him. "After all, how often do you get a case like this?"

"I really don't remember," said Van Arkel.

"Dr. Van Arkel, please," Truax said.

"Objection, Your Honor," Burr said. "He said he didn't remember. 'I don't remember' is an answer."

"Sustained," Gillis said.

"Dr. Van Arkel, you did push the rod through?"

"Yes," Van Arkel said.

"Did the rod strike anything on the way through? Say ... a bone?"

"Objection," Burr said. "Calls for speculation."

Truax opened his mouth but nothing came out. Finally, "It most certainly does not call for speculation, Your Honor."

"Answer the question," Gillis said.

Burr knew Truax was right, but he wanted to give Van Arkel time to settle down.

"I don't recall that the rod struck a bone," Van Arkel said.

Truax smiled. "Is your answer, you don't remember what happened, or you don't recall if the rod struck the bone."

"The latter," Van Arkel said.

"The latter," Truax said, disgusted. "Dr. Van Arkel, do you mean that you don't recall the rod hitting a bone?"

"Yes," Van Arkel said.

"Thank you," Truax said. "Dr. Van Arkel, it is customary to take photographs of the body with a rod like the one you used in place. Is that correct?"

"Yes."

"Did you do that?"

"Yes."

Truax marched to his table and snatched a manila folder. "Your Honor, the prosecution would like to introduce these photographs as People's Exhibit Four."

Where did he get those?

Burr jumped to his feet, "Objection, Your Honor. The prosecution has presented its case. If he wanted that evidence introduced, he should have done it then."

"Your Honor, the court rules permit the introduction of physical evidence if it is used to rebut the proofs offered by the defense."

"They're not being introduced for that purpose," Burr said,

although he knew they were. "They're being introduced to horrify and repulse the members of the jury."

"Nonsense," Truax said. "If you want to talk about angles of entry and exit, I'll show you angles of entry and exit."

"Stop it, both of you." Gillis said, like a parent to quarrelling children. "Let me see them." Truax passed the folder to Gillis, who shut his eyes, exhaled, then paged through them.

"I'll allow them," he said.

"Thank you, Your Honor," Truax said.

I knew they were coming in. They were in the autopsy, but it was worth a try.

Truax handed the folder to Van Arkel. "Are these the photographs?"

"Yes."

"Did you take these photographs?"

"I did."

"What do they show?"

"They show the rod going into and coming out of the body of the deceased," Van Arkel said.

"They show rather more than that, don't they?"

"No," Van Arkel said. "No, I don't think so." Van Arkel started squirming again. Truax walked over to the foreman and handed her the first photograph. She looked at it, turned away, then stared at it again.

"When you're done, please pass it to your left," Truax said.

Like the stuffing at Thanksgiving dinner.

Truax handed her the next photograph, and so it went until they had all been passed around. Each of the jurors looked horrified, repulsed and fascinated, all at the same time. Truax collected them at the back row, like an usher collecting the offering tray in church. He took the pictures back to Van Arkel.

"Dr. Van Arkel, what, in fact, do these pictures show?"

Burr knew exactly what they showed. Claudia on a stainless-steel gurney, naked from the waist up, with a stainless steel rod the diameter of a coat hanger sticking into her left armpit and out from her right side at a forty-five-degree angle. She looked like she had been speared.

Van Arkel didn't say a word.

"Let me tell you what they show." Truax turned to the jury. "These pictures, taken by Dr. Van Arkel himself, show that the accused shot his wife with a rifle mounted on his shoulder. That's what they show."

"Objection, Your Honor," Burr said. "Calls for a conclusion."

"Sustained," Gillis said. "Watch yourself, Mr. Truax."

Dr. Van Arkel started to stand, his hands on the railing.

"I'm not quite through," Truax said.

"Oh," Van Arkel said, almost standing.

"Dr. Van Arkel, please sit down," Gillis said.

The coroner sat.

"Dr. Van Arkel, do you have a relationship with Mr. Dunn?" Truax said.

"No, not really. He moved away, you know."

"I am aware of that," Truax said. "Prior to that, did you?"

"No. No, I guess not."

"You weren't friends?"

"No, we weren't friends."

"But you knew him."

"It's a small town," Van Arkel said.

"So you did know him."

"Yes."

"You have two sons. Is that right."

I was afraid this might happen.

"Objection," Burr said. "Irrelevant."

"I will connect the dots, Your Honor," Truax said.

"Do connect the dots," Gillis said."

"Yes, Your Honor," Truax said. "Your boys both played baseball. Is that right?"

"Yes."

"Was Mr. Dunn their coach?"

"Yes."

"Were they good baseball players?"

"I thought so." Van Arkel smiled.

Don't smile.

"Were they starters?"

"Yes," Van Arkel said, still smiling.

"And you went to the games," Truax said.

"I did," Van Arkel said.

Burr jumped up. "Your Honor, I haven't heard anything that remotely connects the dots. This line of questioning is totally irrelevant. I move that it be stricken from the record."

Gillis looked down at Van Arkel, then at Burr. "Mr. Lafayette, your objection is overruled, but Mr. Truax, get to the point."

"Yes, Your Honor." Truax looked at the smiling witness. "Mr. Dunn coached your sons and they were good baseball players who started and you went to their games."

"Yes."

"But you had no relationship with Mr. Dunn," Van Arkel said.

"He coached my sons."

"I would say that that is a relationship."

Here it comes.

Truax turned to the jury. "The defendant coached two of Dr. Van Arkel's sons." He pointed at Brian, then turned to Van Arkel. "And that is a relationship that might influence your findings."

Van Arkel stopped smiling.

"Objection," Burr said. "This is irrelevant. I move that all of this baseball folderol be stricken from the record."

"Mr. Truax, I agree with Mr. Lafayette. This testimony will be stricken from the record."

But the damage has already been done.

"Thank you, Your Honor," Burr said.

Van Arkel started to stand again.

"Just a few more questions, Dr. Van Arkel."

Van Arkel sat.

"Are you a physician?"

"Yes."

Truax is going to do to me what I did to him at the preliminary exam.

"Are you also the county coroner?"

"It's a part-time job," Van Arkel said.

How many times do I have to tell them to just answer yes or no?

"You are a physician and a part-time coroner."

"Yes."

"Do you practice medicine for a living?"

"No."

"Really?" Truax said. "What do you do for a living?"

As if he doesn't know.

"I'm a mortician."

"A mortician." Truax rolled his eyes. "An undertaker. You're a licensed physician, but you are an undertaker. That's odd."

"It's a family business."

"Of course it is." Truax turned to the jury and smiled. They smiled back at him. And back to Van Arkel. "When you performed the autopsy, the process is to remove certain of the internal organs and examine them. Is that correct?"

"Yes."

"Did you do that?"

"I did."

"And what did you find?"

"There were abnormalities in each lung and in the heart."

"And what were these abnormalities?"

"The bullet passed through both lungs and the heart."

"I see. And the cause of death was?"

"The cause of death was a bullet wound to the lungs and heart," Van Arkel said.

"The heart." Truax dropped his head and didn't say a word. He looked at Van Arkel and then at the jury. "Mrs. Dunn died of a broken heart."

***

Burr called Rollie Gustafson, who didn't look like a policeman. He didn't even look like a former policeman.

He had on a brown suit and what Burr thought must have been the same white shirt he'd worn at the preliminary exam. The white shirt with the collar that was still too small for his neck. His turquoise tie was just that, turquoise, with no pattern. It was tied, but not in any kind of a knot Burr had seen before.

Burr knew it was risky to call Gustafson, but he wanted to have the retired cop say he thought it was an accident.

After qualifying Gustafson, Burr got right to the point. "Please tell us in your own words what happened when you arrived at Mr. Dunn's house."

"Brian was crying. He was real upset. I thought that, if you was going to kill your wife, there's way better places to do it than at home with your kid upstairs. It looked like an accident to me."

"You believed it was an accident."

"I sure did."

Just the way we practiced.

"I have no further questions."

Then it was Truax's turn. "Mr. Gustafson, did you retire from the City of Petoskey police force?"

"Objection, Your Honor," Burr said. "Irrelevant."

"This goes to the question of competency, Your Honor," Truax said.

"I'll allow it," Gillis said.

"Mr. Gustafson, did you retire from the City of Petoskey police force?"

"Yes."

"You did?"

"Yes," Gustafson said again.

"Did you retire or were you fired?"

"I retired," Gustafson said. "I'd been in law enforcement for thirty-three years."

"I see," Truax said. "Did you retire or were you forced to resign? And if you didn't resign you would be fired?"

Just what I was afraid of.

Burr stood. "I object, Your Honor. The witness already answered the question."

"I am merely trying to give the witness the opportunity to tell the truth," Truax said.

"Proceed, Mr. Truax," Gillis said. "But do not badger the witness."

"Yes, Your Honor." Truax turned on his heel, like an about-face, and walked to his table. He picked up a file and walked back to Gustafson. "Mr. Gustafson, I have your personnel file here. Would you care to comment on it?"

"No."

Burr stood again. "Your Honor, this has not been admitted into evidence."

Truax turned to Burr and whispered at him. "I hoped you'd do that." Then to Gillis, "Your Honor, the people would like to introduce Mr. Gustafson's personnel file into evidence." Truax turned back to Burr and smiled.

"I object, Your Honor. This is irrelevant."

"Your Honor, Mr. Gustafson's qualifications are of the utmost relevance."

Gillis thumped his forehead. He took his glasses off, passed them down to Miss Long Fingers, who cleaned them and passed them back to Gillis. "I'll allow it reluctantly."

Truax introduced Gustafson's personnel file, then, "Mr. Gustafson, it says here that you were suspended without pay for six months, then you retired. Would you care to comment on that?"

"No," Gustafson said.

"Mr. Gustafson, according to your file, you were suspended on three different occasions, the last time, as I said, for six months. You retired just before your hearing." Truax looked at the jury, then back at Gustafson. "Why did you retire?"

"I had enough time in for my pension," Gustafson said.

Well done, Rollie.

"It also says in your file that you were suspended for drinking. No, let me be precise. You were suspended because you were drunk on the job. Is that right?"

"I was not drunk," Gustafson said.

"That's not what your file says." Truax stepped in for the kill. "Mr. Gustafson, were you drunk the night you went to Mr. Dunn's house? So drunk that you couldn't do, didn't do, a proper and complete investigation?"

"No," Gustafson said.

Burr leapt to his feet. "This is outrageous, Your Honor."

"Sustained," Gillis said. "That's enough, Mr. Truax."

"Your Honor, I am trying to show that the investigation may have been corrupted by Mr. Gustafson's inebriation," Truax said.

"You haven't shown it," Gillis said. "Strike the last comment by Mr. Truax." Gillis looked over his glasses at the jury. "Ladies and gentlemen, you may consider the competency of Mr. Gustafson. You may not consider that Mr. Truax has showed that he was intoxicated on the night of the killing."

"Mr. Gustafson, did you have a personal relationship with Mr. Dunn?"

"Personal relationship?"

"Did you know him prior to the killing?"

"Yes."

"Were you friends?"

"No," Gustafson said.

"But you went to the same church. Immaculate Heart. Is that right?"

"Brian didn't go too often."

"Answer the question, please," Truax said. "And was Mr. Dunn your son's baseball coach?"

"Brian coached everybody's son."

"Answer the question please," Truax said.

"Yes."

Truax walked to the jury box. "Ladies and gentlemen, I submit to you that Mr. Gustafson, the officer-in-charge, the first one at the scene, had a drinking problem. He was a friend of Mr. Dunn's and bent over backward to make this out to be an accident."

Gillis tore his glasses from his face. "Calvin, for once I agree with counsel for the defense. This is outrageous. If you have more of these antics, I will throw you out. Is that clear?"

"Yes, Your Honor." Truax smiled at the judge. "I have no further questions."

"Don't be smug with me, Calvin." Gillis shook his gavel at him, then adjourned for the day.

***

Burr sat at a window table in the Resorter. The restaurant was empty except for the bartender and Zeke, at his feet. Burr nursed his third martini. The first two had gone down a little too quickly.

"Zeke, I fought to a draw today. That's the best I can say."

The aging Lab wagged his tail.

"All I have to offer you is an olive, which you don't like."

Burr sipped his martini and looked out the window, the wind howling.

The bartender walked over to Burr's table with a telephone and plugged it into a wall jack. "Call for you, Mr. Lafayette."

"I'm not taking any calls."

"He said it's urgent." The bartender set down the phone and left. It rang a minute later. It rang and rang. Burr looked at it. It kept on ringing.

"Persistent devil." Burr took a gulp of his martini. He answered the phone but didn't say anything.

"Burr, Burr, is that you?"

"Jacob?"

"Who else would it be?"

"Where are you?"

"I'm at the Pontchartrain."

"What are you doing there?"

"I've been at the city-county building all day, and now it's too late to come back." The line went dead, then, "How old did you say Becky was?"

"I didn't. I think she's six and was born in December."

"I checked November through January."

"And?"

"And nothing."

"Keep looking." Burr hung up.

CHAPTER TWENTY-ONE

The next morning, Burr made sure he was the first one in the court-house parking lot. He parked in the back of the lot and watched them all arrive. The bailiff, the jurors, the witnesses, his merry band and Truax, who parked a tan Oldsmobile as close to the door as he could.

So that's what he drives.

***

After Swede called them to order, Burr called Sergeant George Maples. The policeman still had his flattop and looked as solid as ever.

Just the way I'd expect a property manager to look.

If Burr had fought to a draw yesterday, he'd have to win today to have a chance of acquitting Brian.

"Sergeant Maples, was it your responsibility to keep track of the evidence for the Petoskey Police Department?"

"Yes," Maples said.

"And that would include Mr. Dunn's deer rifle?" Burr stayed as far away as he could from '*the gun that killed Claudia*' and especially '*the murder weapon.*'

"Yes," Maples said.

"Did you take custody of the deer rifle?"

"Yes."

Burr smiled at the property manager. "Where is Mr. Dunn's rifle?"

"I don't know."

"You don't know?" Burr said, sounding incredulous.

Sergeant Maples started to redden underneath the pincushion of his flattop.

"What happened to Mr. Dunn's rifle."

"I don't know." Now he was beet red.

Burr looked at the jury, then back to the policeman. "Sergeant Maples, let me make sure I have this right. You were in charge of the evidence in the death of Mrs. Dunn, and you don't know what happened to the alleged murder weapon or where it is." Burr looked over at the jury, then back at Maples. "Is that right?"

Maples nodded.

"Please answer the question aloud. For the record," Burr said.

Truax popped up. "I object, Your Honor. Asked and answered."

"Your Honor, a nod is not an answer for the purpose of making a record."

Gillis shook his head. He looked down at Sergeant Maples and his flattop. "Please answer the question."

"I don't know where the rifle is or what happened to it."

"Thank you, Sergeant. Earlier you said that you took custody of the rifle after the accident."

"Yes. I did."

"Please tell us the procedure."

"Back then, before we had a computer, I would record the item in a logbook, what it was, date, case number. Then I'd put it in the cage, find a place for it and then record that in the book."

"What is the cage?"

"Down in the basement of the police station, there's a room with wire mesh in front of it, and a chain link door. That's the evidence cage."

"And it locks?"

"Yes, sir," Maples said.

"Who has the key?"

"Me," Maples said. "Me and the chief. That's it."

"I see," Burr said. "And that's where you put Mr. Dunn's rifle?"

"Yes."

"You said that all of the information about the rifle would be recorded in a logbook." Burr put his hands in his pockets. "Where is the logbook?"

"I don't know."

"You don't know?" Burr said, incredulous.

"That's what I said."

"How could you not know?"

"That file, along with a bunch of others, was destroyed in a flood."

"A flood?"

"Not exactly a flood, but somebody was having a smoke, and the sprinklers turned on. Ruined a bunch of files. But you already know ..."

Burr raised his hand and cut Maples off.

This is my show.

"You don't know where Mr. Dunn's rifle is. You don't know what happened to it, and you have no records about it. Is that right?"

"Yes." Maples' ears turned red.

Burr turned to the jury. "Ladies and gentlemen. The prosecution has brought Mr. Dunn before you on a murder charge, an open murder charge, which means you could conceivably cause him to be imprisoned for the rest of his life." Burr stopped, turned to Brian, then to Truax, then back to the jury. "But Mr. Truax has no weapon. He doesn't know where it is. The police can't find it. They can't even find the file. And yet, Mr. Truax wants you to find Mr. Dunn guilty. And he can't find the gun. This is important." Burr walked to the jury. He put his hands in his pockets. "Why is this important? Because the gun may well have been defective. That's why." Burr turned to Gillis. "I have no further questions, Your Honor." Burr walked back to his table and sat.

Truax stood. "Your Honor, the prosecution asks that the testimony of Sergeant Maples be stricken from the record."

"What on earth for?" Gillis said.

"Sergeant Maples' testimony is irrelevant and designed to confuse the jury. Somehow the police lost the gun. But the gun is not the issue. Everyone admits that the defendant killed his wife with his deer rifle. Where the gun is doesn't matter. Who has it, if anyone does, doesn't matter. The gun doesn't matter. What matters is Brian Dunn killed his wife with that gun."

Oh, but the gun does matter.

Gillis thought so, too. "Counselor, I will not strike the testimony of Sergeant Maples. You may question him if you wish."

"The people have no questions," Truax said.

Gillis dismissed Maples, and Burr called Frieda Deutsch, the key to his defense, especially since he'd shown that the gun that killed Claudia was missing.

If they don't have the gun, no one can prove it wasn't defective. All I need is a reasonable doubt.

Frieda made her way to the witness stand. Swede swore her in. Her glasses still hung on the silver chain.

At least she isn't wearing her keys around her neck.

"Mrs. Deutsch," Burr said.

"It's Miss," she said. "I'm a widow."

"I see," Burr said, who didn't. "Miss Deutsch, what is your occupation?"

"I'm a gunsmith," she said.

"A gunsmith," Burr said. "What does a gunsmith do?"

"You know what a gunsmith does. A gunsmith repairs guns."

"Do you do anything else?" Burr said.

"I also own Classic Arms. It's a gun shop," she said.

"Miss Deutsch, as you know, I've been to your gun shop. I'm not sure a gun shop is a fair description. To me it seems at least like a store, maybe a superstore."

"Objection," Truax said. "Counsel is not the witness."

"Sustained," Gillis said.

"Miss Deutsch, how many guns do you sell in your store a year?"

"About four hundred," she said.

"Four hundred," Burr said. "That's a lot of guns."

"I sell a lot of guns."

"And how long have you been in the business?"

"I've worked there thirty-three years. My father started it fifty years ago, and I took it over when he died. That would be five years ago."

"I'm sorry," Burr said.

"It was tragic."

I have to get her focused.

"Miss Deutsch, how many guns do you repair in a year?"

She scrunched her nose. "About a hundred and fifty, I'd say."

"A hundred and fifty," he said. "Year in and year out?"

"Yes," she said.

Here we go.

"Miss Deutsch are you familiar with the Field & Jones, Model 92. The bolt action 30:06?"

"I am."

"And why would that be?"

"I sold them in the shop for a while."

"You sold them?"

"Yes."

"How many?"

"Eleven."

"Eleven," Burr said. "Miss Deutsch, you said you sell four hundred guns a year. If my math is right, that's almost twenty thousand guns in fifty years. Classic Arms is one of the biggest gun stores in Michigan, and I believe deer rifles are one of your specialties. But you only sold eleven Model 92s? Why is that?"

"Two reasons," Frieda Deutsch said. "They were only out for three years, but I quit selling them before Field & Jones stopped making them."

"Why was that?"

"Bad design."

"Really," Burr said, feigning surprise. "Could you elaborate?"

"They weren't safe. In fact, they were dangerous. So Field & Jones took them off the market."

"What about them was dangerous?"

"Sometimes they wouldn't eject a live shell."

"What does that mean?"

"The Model 92 is a bolt action rifle. You rack in a shell. After you shoot, you rack the bolt. The extractors are like fingers. They grip the shell by the rim and pull it out. While that's going on, another shell gets pulled up from the clip. When you push the bolt back it pushes the shell into the chamber. It works fine. If you shoot. But if you leave a live one in the chamber and don't fire and then pull the bolt back to eject the live shell, once in a while the shell won't eject."

"And," Burr said.

"Well, you think you emptied the gun, but you didn't."

"And," Burr said again.

"The gun you thought was empty, isn't."

Burr turned to Gillis. "Your Honor, to make this perfectly clear, may we demonstrate?"

Truax ejected himself from his chair. "Objection, Your Honor. This is sheer speculation."

"Your Honor," Burr said, "if the prosecution could produce the rifle that killed Mrs. Dunn, this would not be necessary."

"I'll allow it," Gillis said. "Mr. Lafayette. Do not endanger anyone in this courtroom."

"We won't, Your Honor." Burr turned to the jury. "Ladies and gentlemen, we will demonstrate that the rifle in question, which as you now know is missing, may have been loaded. The rifle may have discharged accidentally despite Mr. Dunn's efforts to handle it safely."

Burr nodded at Swede, who took a rifle case from the storage closet. Swede handed Burr the case. Burr started to unzip it.

"Bring that up here," Gillis said. "Take it out of the case where I can see it."

Standing below Gillis, Burr finished unzipping the case and took the rifle out. The jury recoiled. "The defense would like to introduce this rifle as Defense Exhibit Two."

"Mr. Lafayette, are you sure that gun is empty?" Gillis said.

"I am, Your Honor."

"Rack it for me."

Burr pulled back the bolt. Then closed it.

"Open it again," Gillis said. "Let me look through the barrel." Burr slid the bolt back then handed Gillis the rifle. Gillis peered through the chamber. "All right," Gillis said. "I can see daylight. Where's the clip?"

Burr reached into his pocket and pulled out the clip, a thin metal case about the size of a pack of cigarettes, open at the top and the bottom. He handed it to Gillis, who turned it over and over in his hands. "Where are the bullets?"

Burr fished five three-inch bullets from his pocket. He held them in his palm so the jury could see them.

"Are they live?"

"Yes, Your Honor."

"How do you expect me to allow a loaded gun in my courtroom?"

"The safety is on, Your Honor."

"Apparently that is what Mr. Dunn thought," Gillis said.

"I am afraid I must object, Your Honor," Burr said.

"I apologize, counsel," Gillis said. "Strike that from the record."

Burr felt the tension in the courtroom. They were all nervous. He was sure the jury could feel the rifle's killing power.

That helps, and it'll be even better if this works the way it's supposed to.

"Mr. Lafayette, what do you propose to do?"

"I am going to ask Miss Deutsch to demonstrate how this gun might malfunction."

"She's not going to fire it."

"No, Your Honor."

"All right, then, go ahead." Gillis looked over his glasses at Frieda, "Don't point that thing at anyone." Gillis took off his glasses. "Stand over there." He pointed to the far wall. "Do it over there. Face the back wall, and keep the barrel pointed at the floor."

She held the railing of the witness stand and pulled herself to her feet. Gillis handed her the gun.

"Be careful," Gillis said.

"Your Honor," Truax said, "I object. This demonstration has no bearing on what actually occurred."

"Your objection has been noted. Okay, let's see this."

Gillis is curious.

He handed the clip to Burr.

Burr prayed that Frieda would do the demonstration the way they'd practiced. And practiced and practiced. Until she refused to practice anymore. It was true that the Model 92 did occasionally malfunction, but not very often.

She had to do it just right for the extractors to fail, which could be guaranteed with a slight adjustment. He didn't want to know if she had done anything to the gun.

Showtime.

"Ladies and gentlemen," Burr said, "Miss Deutsch will show you how the gun is loaded and how it malfunctions."

"This clip holds the bullets," she said. "There's a spring in here to force the bullet up in the chamber when the bolt is pulled back. Here's how you load it."

She pushed a bullet in the clip, took another from Burr's open hand, and pushed it in. She did this until all five bullets were in the clip.

Burr handed her the gun. "The clip goes here, underneath the rifle in the breech. Right here. Where it's open." She fit the clip in. "Now, to put a shell in the chamber, you rack back this bolt."

"Miss Deutsch, is the safety on?" Gillis said.

"Yes."

"Proceed."

"When you rack the bolt, it pulls a bullet up into the breech ... like this." She showed the bullet, then rammed the bolt shut. "Now it's ready to fire. Let's say that man was a doe." She shouldered the gun and pointed it at a portrait of a long-dead Petoskey luminary on the wall.

"Be careful," Gillis said.

She ignored him. "Let's say it was a doe. You don't want to kill a doe, so you don't shoot." She dropped the gun to her waist. "And now, let's say you're done for the day. So you unload the rifle. Here is where you have to watch yourself. If you take off the clip, like this." She snapped it off and put it in the waistband of her stretch pants.

I wish she hadn't done that.

"And then you rack the gun like this." She pulled back the bolt; the extractors grabbed the shell. It flipped out. She picked it up. Then she unloaded the clip. Four shells here. Five altogether. The gun's empty."

"Watch what happens if you change the order you do things." She put the shells back in the clip. "Five in the clip." She snapped the clip back into the rifle. "Clip in the gun. Now I rack one in the chamber."

She mounted the gun to her shoulder. "Another doe. I put the gun down again. Watch closely," she said to the jury. "This time I rack the gun first, with the clip still in." She racked the gun. The bullet ejected. "Out comes the bullet. Here it is," she said showing it to the jury. "Now I close the bolt." She slid it shut. "You know what just happened?"

The jury didn't.

"Another shell just went into the chamber when the first shell ejected. That's how a bolt action works. So when I take the clip out there's three bullets in the clip." Frieda Deutsch took the clip off the rifle and handed the rifle to Burr. She then emptied the clip. Three bullets came out.

"Now I have these three bullets, plus the one I ejected," holding the four bullets in the palm of her hand.

"Where's the fifth shell?" she said to the jury. "I'll show you." She traded Burr four bullets for the rifle. "The fifth shell is still in the chamber.

"But that shouldn't be a problem," she said. "Why? Because every hunter knows enough to rack the gun again just to be sure. Out comes the shell. Like this."

Frieda racked the gun. No shell.

"I'll rack it again."

"Stop right there," Burr said. "Ladies and gentlemen, there's still a shell in the chamber. It didn't come out."

"I was getting to that."

I guess it's her show.

"Now I rack it again." She racked the gun. "Still nothing. No shell." She racked the gun a third time and then a fourth. Then a fifth. This time the shell came out. "Here it is. Five tries to get out a live shell." She handed the gun back to Burr.

"Thank you, Miss Deutsch," Burr said.

She started toward the gallery.

"Miss Deutsch," Burr said. "I have a few more questions."

She walked back to the witness stand, slowly and deliberately, like a freighter changing course. She lowered herself to her seat.

"Thank you for the demonstration, Miss Deutsch. What exactly does it mean?"

"It means that if you take the clip off first, the gun works fine. But if you eject the shell that's in the chamber first, the next shell goes into the chamber, and it might not eject because sometimes the extractors don't grab it."

"How many times did it take you?"

"Five," she said.

"And what does that mean?"

"It means that you might think the gun is empty when it's not."

"Have you ever seen this happen?"

"Only on this model," Frieda said.

"How many times?"

"Twice," Frieda said.

"And how did you find out about this?"

"Two different guys brought in guns just like this. They knew how many shells were in the gun, and they knew something was wrong."

"What happens?"

"Over time, with use, the extractors can loosen up."

"Is this dangerous?"

"I should say so."

"And what would you recommend?"

"I wouldn't use this gun."

"Did you notify the manufacturer?"

"I did," she said.

"What did they say?"

"They said it wasn't a problem. But they quit making them."

Burr looked at the jury, then back at Frieda. "So it's possible that someone could borrow a gun and return it thinking it was unloaded when it's not."

"I object, Your Honor," Truax said. "This is speculation."

"Overruled," Gillis said. "You may answer the question, Miss Deutsch."

"Yes," she said. "Someone could return a loaded gun."

"And then if the person who got it back racked the gun, the shell still might not come out," Burr said. "The gun might still be loaded. Is that right?"

"Yes."

"So the gun could go off by accident even if you tried to make sure it was empty."

"That's right."

"Did the manufacturer ever issue any warnings about this gun?"

"No," Frieda Deutsch said.

"Would you say this gun is defective?"

"Yes."

"Even if you exercised gun safety," Burr said.

"Yes."

"Miss Deutsch, if the gun were dirty, is it more likely to malfunction?"

"Yes."

"Why is that?"

"If the action is dirty, the extractors are more likely to stick."

"One more question," Burr said. "Is it conceivable that Mr. Dunn could have reasonably thought that the gun was unloaded, could have taken precautions to make sure it was unloaded, and still the gun could be loaded? Could it have gone off and killed his wife?"

"Objection," Truax said. "Calls for a state of mind, which the witness could not know."

"Sustained," Gillis said.

Burr knew her answer wouldn't be allowed. He wanted to ask the question anyway so the jury would understand what all this meant. "Thank you, Miss Deutsch. I have no further questions."

Truax uncoiled, speaking as he stood. Burr could see his tongue darting in and out of his mouth. "Mrs. Deutsch."

"It's Miss," she said again. "I'm a widow."

"Actually, it is *Mrs*. Widows are referred to as *Mrs*."

"I'm a *Miss, not a Mrs*."

"Have it your way," Truax said. "Miss Deutsch, you testified that the gun could malfunction and appear to be empty when in fact it was loaded. Is that right?"

"Yes."

"But the gun doesn't fire on its own, does it?"

"What do you mean?"

"Miss Deutsch, for the gun to fire, the safety must be off," Truax said. "Is that right?"

"Yes."

"And the trigger must be pulled."

"Yes."

"So, even if the gun malfunctioned, someone still must have turned off the safety and pulled the trigger."

"Objection," Burr said. "It hasn't been established that the trigger was pulled."

"How else would it go off?" Truax said.

"Overruled," Gillis said.

"Miss Deutsch, as to your demonstration, did you adjust the gun in order to make it malfunction?"

"I beg your pardon," she said.

"Did you adjust the demonstration gun to make it malfunction?"

"No," she said, but she was sweating through her blouse under her arms.

"Miss Deutsch, did you rig this demonstration?" Truax said.

"What do you mean by that?" the gunsmith said.

Say you didn't. Even if you did.

"Did you intentionally tinker with this rifle in order to make it malfunction?"

"No." She wiggled in her chair.

You could have been more convincing.

"Don't you think it a bit odd that you were somehow able to locate one of the very few Model 92's that doesn't work right?"

"Objection, Your Honor," Burr asked. "Asked and answered."

"Mr. Lafayette, that was not asked and answered. You are overruled." Gillis turned to Frieda. "Please answer the question."

"It's a bad design. That's why they quit making them."

Truax turned to the jury. "Of the thousands of Model 92's manufactured, you so conveniently found one that didn't work right."

"Objection, Your Honor," Burr said.

"That's enough, Calvin," Gillis said.

"No further questions," Truax said.

"You may step down," Gillis said.

She smiled at Burr as she walked by.

"Your next witness," Gillis said.

Burr couldn't risk putting Brian on the stand, and Truax couldn't call Brian if Burr didn't. There was no telling what Truax might drag out of Brian. His marriage, the affair, the gun. Truax couldn't call Lisa, because a wife couldn't be required to testify against her husband. Truax had missed his chance to call Farr, and Burr didn't want to call him as a witness, because Farr was dead certain he'd unloaded the gun.

Truax is on the ropes.

Burr stood. "We have no further witnesses. We're quite through, Your Honor."

"Very well." Gillis made a show of pulling up the sleeve of his robe to look at his watch. "I see it's two-thirty. We shall adjourn for the day. Closing arguments tomorrow, gentlemen." Gillis waltzed out of the courtroom.

Burr rushed out of the courtroom, the first one to leave. He took a one-pound bag of sugar from the Jeep, hurried over to the tan Oldsmobile and poured it into the gas tank.

***

Jacob called Burr at his basement headquarters.

"You were right," Jacob said. "And wrong."

"What?"

"Becky. She was born in August," Jacob said.

"Really," Burr said. "She is young."

"Not exactly," Jacob said.

"What?"

"The prior August. August 1978. I had to go backward. She's not five, she's six."

CHAPTER TWENTY-TWO

The next morning, Burr saw a white Riviera where Truax had parked the tan Oldsmobile the day before. He smiled a wicked smile and dashed up the steps. He settled into his chair just as Swede announced the entrance of Gillis.

Gillis looked at Truax. "We will proceed with the closing arguments, Mr. Truax."

Truax popped up like a jack-in-the-box. "Your Honor, the prosecution would like to offer a rebuttal witness."

"A what," Gillis said. "The prosecution concluded the day before yesterday."

"Your Honor, the prosecution has a rebuttal witness. It's critical to our case."

"Who is it?" Gillis said.

It was Burr's turn to pop up. "Objection, Your Honor. The prosecutor has completed his case."

"Your Honor, the prosecution has one more witness," Truax said.

Gillis looked at his watch. "I thought you were finished."

"This witness has just come forward, Your Honor," Truax said.

"And who might that be?" Gillis said.

"Roman Yatchek, Your Honor, the family priest."

"Objection, Your Honor," Burr said again. "The prosecutor has had ten months to prepare his case."

Gillis thumped his forehead. "Counsel?"

"Your Honor, I apologize, but the witness has just now come forward," Truax said again.

"Nonsense. This is part of his plan, just as the son was. The defense is entitled to notice. It's clearly stated in the court rules."

"Objection noted" Gillis took off his glasses, looked through them and put them back on. "Mr. Truax, you may proceed."

Burr sat. He broke two pencils.

"The people call Tomaz Yatchek."

The bailiff swore in the priest, who wore a black jacket and a clerical collar.

This is terrible.

He had short white hair. His face was flushed, and he had a big, red, bulbous nose.

I'll bet he drinks.

Truax sauntered up to the priest.

"Father Yatchek, how long have you been a priest?"

He had to say "Father." I'd have said the same thing.

"Forty-two years," Yatchek said.

"Forty-two years," Truax nodded. "That's a long time. And how long have you been at Immaculate Heart?"

"Nineteen years."

"That's also a long time," Truax said again.

Spare me.

"Father, how long did you minister to the Dunns?"

"Eighteen years," the priest said.

"Eighteen years," Truax said. "How can you be so sure?"

"I remember that Claudia came to me when she was pregnant."

"Really," Truax said. "Why would you remember that?"

"She said Brian wanted her to have an abortion."

Burr flew out of his chair. "I object, Your Honor. This is privileged communication between a priest and a parishioner."

"Your Honor, the privilege does not survive death." Truax sneered at Burr.

"You're quite right, Mr. Truax," Gillis said. "The privilege does not survive death."

That's the first time he got anything right.

Burr just couldn't leave well enough alone. "You have no idea what the law is."

Gillis roared at him. "Once more, Mr. Lafayette, and I will eject you. No, I will not eject you. I will throw you out by the collar of your thousand-dollar suit."

It was a thousand dollars when I had a thousand dollars to spend on suits.

"Please preserve the objection of the defense for appeal."

"Along with the other fifty-two."

Truax started in again. "Father Yatchek, you said that Mrs. Dunn sought counsel regarding pregnancy. Can you elaborate?"

Truax knows exactly what Yatchek is going to say because he coached him. Although he has just now come forward.

"She told me that Brian didn't think their marriage was going well and didn't believe that having a child was a good idea."

"And what did you advise?"

"We talked about the issue at length. She came to her own conclusion. Abortion was not the right choice."

"And what occurred?"

"Claudia and Brian married, and they were blessed with a son."

Are the secrets ever going to end?

"Thank you, Father," Truax said. "Did you counsel with Mrs. Dunn at any other time?"

"I did."

"Please tell us about it."

"Their marriage was trying," the priest said. "Mrs. Dunn worked very hard at it. I know she loved her husband, but he wanted a divorce."

"Father, what did she tell you?"

"She told me that Mr. Dunn wanted a divorce," Yatchek said. "Many times. She told me that many times."

"When was the last time?"

"Just before she was killed."

"And what advice did you give her?"

"I advised her to pray, to work on the marriage."

"Did she tell you what she decided to do?"

"She said that she believed that God wanted her to have no part in ending her marriage. I tried to see them both, but he refused. I never thought it would come to this."

"Do you believe that Mrs. Dunn was afraid of her husband?"

"I do."

"Why do you say that?"

The priest rubbed his nose. "She said he had a very bad temper," Yatchek said.

"Really?" Truax feigned surprise. "Did this come up very often? Her being afraid?"

"A few times."

"How many?"

"I don't really remember. Two or three times, I suppose."

"When was the last time?"

"In November, before she was killed," Father Yatchek said.

"And what occurred then?"

"She said he lost his temper and screamed at her."

"Father, are you saying that Mrs. Dunn told you that she was afraid of her husband?"

"Yes."

"I have no further questions." Truax gave Burr a *now-you're-really-cooked* look on his way back to his table.

Burr walked to the jury.

I've got to be quick.

"Ladies and gentlemen, you should know that a last-minute witness, like this one and also like Chad Dunn, is very irregular. In fact, I've never seen it done. In fact, the court lets the prosecution do anything ..."

"Stop it right there," Gillis said. "You may question the witness. You may not criticize the court. Is that clear?"

"Yes, Your Honor," Burr said.

Burr had no idea where to begin, but he didn't think the priest had hurt him much. He thought Truax was desperate. He had never even heard of Yatchek before, much less seen him.

"Your Honor," Burr said, "the defense requests an adjournment so that it may properly prepare its cross examination."

"Denied," Gillis said. "It's now or never."

Burr clenched his teeth.

If I ask a few questions, I may be able to improve things.

"Father Yatchek, you were the Dunn family priest for how long?"

"Eighteen years," the priest said.

"Did you ever meet with Mr. Dunn?"

"No."

"Did you meet with their son, Chad?"

"No."

"I see," Burr said. "How could you be the family priest if you only ministered to Mrs. Dunn?"

"She talked to me about the family." The priest started to turn red.

"I see," Burr said. "Wouldn't it be more accurate to say you were her priest, not the family priest?"

"I ministered to the family."

"Father Yatchek, was Mr. Dunn a Catholic?"

The priest turned redder yet. "No."

"Did he attend Mass regularly?"

"No," the priest said.

"Did he attend at all?"

"I don't know," Father Yatchek said.

"You don't know," Burr said. "Is it possible that you bore him some ill will because he didn't attend Mass. Because he wasn't Catholic?"

"No."

"Of course not," Burr said. "Father Yatchek, you testified that Mrs. Dunn was afraid of Mr. Dunn because of his temper. Is that right?"

"Yes."

Burr looked at the jury then back at the red-faced priest. "Well then, Father, what did you do about it?"

"What do you mean, do?"

"About Mrs. Dunn being afraid of her husband."

"What?" the priest said.

"Did you tell the police?"

"No," the priest said.

"Did you call social services?"

"No," the priest said again.

"What exactly did you do in the face of Mrs. Dunn's fear?"

"I listened," the priest said.

"You listened," Burr said. "Mrs. Dunn was afraid of her husband and you listened. That doesn't seem very proactive, does it?"

If he gets any redder, he's going to explode.

"Objection," Truax said. "He is badgering the witness."

"Sustained," Gillis said. "Mr. Lafayette, what point are you trying to make?"

"Your Honor, I am trying to show that Father Yatchek did not like Mr. Dunn. Because he wasn't Catholic. Because he didn't go to Mass and because he wanted his wife to have an abortion, and finally because he wanted a divorce."

"So far you haven't shown much," Truax said.

"Stop it. Both of you," Gillis said.

This case wasn't about what he had been told. It was about what he hadn't been told. Without knowing how the priest would answer, Burr was loath to ask any more questions, but he was angry.

"Father Yatchek, you testified that Mrs. Dunn was afraid of her husband. Is that right?"

"That's right."

"Did you ever see any physical marks on her that would indicate that she had ever been struck by her husband?"

The priest cleared his throat but didn't say anything.

"Answer the question, please."

"No."

"No physical signs of being struck?"

"No."

"Did she ever say that her husband beat her?"

"No."

"Did she say her husband slapped her?"

"No."

"Did she ever say he threatened to kill her?"

"No."

Now we're getting somewhere.

"So, what you're saying is that Mrs. Dunn was afraid of her husband, but she had never been so much as slapped." Burr put his hands in his pockets. "Isn't that a bit farfetched?"

Father Yatchek was fire engine red. "She said she was afraid because she wouldn't give him a divorce, because he was having an affair with her." The priest pointed at Lisa. "And he wanted a divorce so he could marry her. That's what Claudia was afraid of."

"Your Honor, I move to strike the witness' last answer as non-responsive," Burr said.

"Objection, Your Honor," Truax said. "Counsel asked an open-ended question. He gets what he gets."

"I will let the answer stand," Gillis said.

"Your Honor, this entire proceeding has been a sham from start to finish. It is a mockery of the court rules. A fraud on fairness. I move for a mistrial," Burr said.

"Denied," Gillis said. "Any further questions?"

"Just one," Burr said. "Which matchbook cover did you get your law degree from?"

"Get out, Mr. Lafayette. Get out of my courtroom this instant. We will recess for the day. Closing arguments will be tomorrow at 10 a.m. sharp." Gillis blasted out of the courtroom like he had been shot from a cannon.

***

Burr left without a word. He got into his Jeep and drove to Don's Bar, the darkest, dingiest, closest bar, and a bar where he was sure he wouldn't run into anyone he knew. He hadn't been in Don's for at least ten years. There still weren't any windows, and it still smelled like flat beer and ashtrays. He sat at the bar and was alone in the place, except for the bartender.

How does this place stay in business?

He was furious with himself. He'd botched it with Yatchek. Forget the fact that Gillis never should have allowed the priest to testify. Truax had hurt with Yatchek, but Burr had made it worse. Much worse. He'd pushed his luck and lost.

I knew better.

The bartender came over, the same bartender as the last time he was here. He had a round face and one continuous eyebrow, thick like a cat's tail. It was black as night and divided his head into two pieces. It looked like he was chewing the same half-chewed cigar. He never lights them, just chews them.

"I'll have a boilermaker."

The bartender delivered him a shot of Jack Daniels and a Budweiser. *I might as well make this a depth charge.*

He picked up the shot glass and was about to drop it into the beer when Kaye sat down beside him. She had on black wool slacks, an ivory sweater with a wine-colored blazer, dangly gold earrings, and a gold necklace. Her jacket and her lips matched nicely.

He'd seen her in court but hadn't spoken to her since their date with the morels. "How did you find me."

"I followed you."

That's just ducky.

The bartender came back. He cocked his head at Kaye.

"I'd like a glass of Chardonnay. From a box, if you've got it."

"Very funny," the bartender said. He walked away and came back with the wine in a plastic glass.

"Only the best here," Burr said.

"Why are you here?"

"I wanted to be alone."

Kaye drank a little of her wine and made a face. "You're very handsome. You're a great kisser. But you're a jerk."

"I beg your pardon."

"We had such a nice time and then I never heard from you. Typical guy."

She came here to tell me I'm a jerk?

"It's that girl sitting next to Lisa. I can tell by the way you look at her." She took a bigger swallow. "You could be her father, you know."

I probably do have some unfinished business with Suzanne.

"That's not why I'm here." She reached into her purse, took out and handed to Burr a gold locket about the size of a quarter. It was tarnished and had the letter *L* on it.

"Where did you get this," Burr asked.

"I found it," Kaye said.

"Really?"

Kaye looked straight at him. "Don't be a smart ass or I won't tell you."

"I'm sorry. Where did you find it?" He set it down on the bar.

"I thought maybe we could have something together."

Now what do I say?

Burr picked up the locket, made a show of studying it, then put it back on the bar. "We could. We could have something together."

"The three of us?"

I deserved that.

"I found it at Brian's house," Kaye said.

"You did?"

"About three years ago. I wasn't the first realtor. I picked up the listing after the first agent dropped it. Who could blame her? Anyway, I went through the house, like I always do with a new listing. With a vacant house, I take a shoebox and pick up what's been left behind. You'd be surprised what you find." She sipped her wine. "Maybe you wouldn't. Earrings, rings, change. I usually keep the change. Keys, combs. I put the address on the shoebox and when I see the owners, I give it to them. They always appreciate it. One time I found a guy's wedding ring. He asked me not to tell his wife I found it. Like she didn't know it was missing."

"Anyway, I went through the house. There was more stuff for the shoebox than usual. He just moved out and left everything. So I found a lot of stuff."

Burr put the shot glass to his lips, thought better of it and set it back down.

"There was stuff all over in the basement. Tools, mostly. I found a lot of loose stuff, too. Drill bits, safety glasses, screws, bolts. But I only put the good stuff in the box.

"I'm scrounging around the floor, on my hands and knees. I see something under the workbench. It was just a quarter, but I put it in my purse. While I'm down there, I see something else. Just the edge of it. It's in the floor drain where you can hardly see it. I pried off the grate, and this is what I found."

Burr picked up the locket again.

"I didn't think anything about it until the business about the affair came up. I got Brian's shoebox and dug this out." She took the locket from Burr and opened it up. There was a picture of Brian inside.

"How long have you had this?"

"Since I got the listing. Three years. Maybe a little longer. I forgot about it."

"Have you got the key?"

She rummaged around inside her purse. She took out a key ring with at least three dozen keys. "These keys are worth about five thousand dollars each to me." Every key had a piece of tape with a name on it. She ran through the keys, one by one. "Is this it?" She held the key at arm's length and squinted at it. "I need longer arms. Here it is."

He threw down the whiskey and put the locket in his pocket.

***

Burr followed Kaye down the basement steps. He sucked in the damp air and tasted the mildew. The corners of the basement were dark where the lights didn't reach.

All I thought about was the missing gun.

"Show me where you found it."

"Here." She pointed at a floor drain under the workbench.

The grate was about a foot in diameter, cast iron with half-inch slits running across it.

Burr got down on his knees and ran his forefinger across it. Dirt and grease came off on his finger. He tried to pull it up but couldn't get a grip.

"Where did you find it?"

"In there," she said, pointing with the lacquered nail of her forefinger. "Inside the drain."

"Did you find the chain?"

"The chain?"

"Wouldn't a locket hang on a chain?"

"This is all I found."

"Show me what you did."

She found a screwdriver, pried up the edge of the grate and slid it aside. "Damn it."

"What happened?"

"I broke a nail." She looked at her fingers. "I've got nine left."

Burr peered into the drain. It smelled like a sewer.

Why would anyone look in here?

"This is where I found it. On this ledge."

There was a ledge about two inches down. It was an inch wide and ran all the way around the drain. He touched it with his forefinger. The grease stuck underneath his fingernail.

"It's just a locket. What does it prove?" Kaye said.

Burr reached in his pocket for the locket.

Where is it? Where is the damn thing?

He emptied his pockets. Keys, change, his comb, a pen. It wasn't there. Then he found it. He took it out and held it in the palm of his hand.

"What if ..."

"Burr, what are you doing here?"

Burr looked up at Suzanne peering at them from the top of the stairs. Burr closed his hand around the locket.

"You're supposed to meet us for dinner," she said.

Burr watched her eyes dart around the basement. They flashed at him, then fixed on the drain.

"What's going on?"

"I wanted to have another look around," Burr said. "In case I missed something."

Suzanne took two more steps down the stairs. "What are you doing with the drain?"

"I wanted to see if there was anything in there."

"And?"

Burr squeezed his fist. "We didn't find anything." He wasn't sure she believed him, and he wasn't sure why he didn't tell her.

***

After dinner, Burr drove back to Brian's house and parked in the driveway. He told Suzanne he'd left something there, but he didn't think she believed him.

Fog had blown in off the lake, and Brian's house was a hazy silhouette. Next door, Mrs. Larson's lights glowed through the fog. Another look in the basement couldn't hurt. He walked to the side door of the garage. The knob turned in his hand, and he stepped inside.

If only Farr hadn't left the gun in here. Or if he hadn't borrowed it in the first place. Or if Brian had been more careful. Or maybe that wasn't it at all.

Burr slid his hand into his pants pocket and found the locket. He dropped it when he took it out of his pocket.

"Please don't let there be a drain."

He fell to his knees and slid his hands along the floor, scraping his fingers on the uneven concrete. He couldn't find it. He panicked.

He ran his fingers across the floor again. "There must be a light switch somewhere." He looked up and saw a silhouette in the window of the door. He launched himself at the door, but the shadow had disappeared. He flung open the door and ran outside. No one.

Mrs. Larson's house was just across from him, about twenty feet away. The home had a front porch that ran the length of the house. The porch had a solid wooden wall railing, waist high. Burr edged along the side of Brian's garage to the backyard. At his feet, what was left of a vegetable garden tangled him up in frosted tomato vines.

Who would have a garden at a house that's been empty for six years?

He turned back to the street and saw a car glide by in the fog. The headlights looked like they were pulling the car. He walked back to the Jeep, scuffing his shoes on the sidewalk, not noisy but not quiet either. He opened the door on the driver's side and rolled down the window. Then he slammed the door shut. He leaned through the window, poked the key in the ignition and turned it. The engine fired.

If this doesn't work, I'm euchred. He started counting to himself. *1, 2, 3, 4 ...*

A head popped up over the wall of the porch. It looked straight at him, then dived back down.

"Hello, Mrs. Larson."

Silence.

"I know you're over there."

More silence.

Maybe she thinks I didn't see her. Maybe she thinks I'm stupid.

He walked over to the porch and peered over the wall. There was Dorothy Larson, hiding in a corner.

"There you are, Mrs. Larson," Burr said in his most charming *I found you* voice, like in a game of hide-and-seek. She didn't move. "I'm right here you know. Why were you spying on me?"

More silence.

"Mrs. Larson. I saw your head pressed against the window of Brian's garage door."

"It wasn't me," she said.

"I think it was."

"No, not me."

"If it wasn't you, who was it?"

"How would I know?" Mrs. Larson said.

"Who else could it be?"

"Lots of people come by here."

"Like who?"

"You did this afternoon. With that real estate woman."

"Who else?"

"I don't know her name. That tall woman with the green eyes."

Suzanne?

Mrs. Larson stood. "You seen my cat?"

"Your cat?"

"That's why I'm out here."

I don't believe you.

"How did your tomatoes turn out?"

"What?"

"Your tomatoes. In the garden."

"How do you know they're mine?"

"Whose else's would they be?"

"It's got the best sun on the block."

"Did Brian say you could?"

"He sure did."

Burr looked at his shoes and kicked at the grass.

"Mrs. Larson, what about Lisa? Did she ever come over?"

"No."

"She never came over?"

"Nope."

"Mrs. Larson."

"Just the one time."

"The one time? When I talked to you before the trial, you said you'd never seen her here."

"I didn't want to get Brian in trouble."

"It's a little late for that."

"Maybe so." It was Mrs. Larson's turn to stare at her feet.

"You were friends, weren't you?" Burr said. "With Brian."

She nodded.

"How about Claudia?"

The old woman didn't say *boo*.

"Mrs. Larson."

"I always liked Brian. He was good to me. Shoveled my walk. Mowed my lawn. But that Claudia, she was about the meanest I ever seen. She didn't like Brian helping me out. Even though I got no man around here no more."

"You told me you never saw Lisa here."

"It was just the one time. I probably shoulda told you, but I told that other lawyer I never seen her here."

"Truax?"

She nodded again.

That's why Truax never called her as a witness.

"Mrs. Larson, when did you see Lisa?"

"Just the once."

"When was it?"

"You seen my cat?" she said again.

Burr shook his head.

"That's why I'm out here, looking for the cat. Orange one. Pumpkin's her name."

"I'll keep my eyes open."

"You do that."

"When did you see Lisa here?"

She started for the door. Burr ran up the steps.

"When was it?"

"That night."

"What night?"

"You know. The night that ..."

"The night that Claudia was killed?"

It can't be true.

She nodded. "I really got to go in now. It's cold out here."

"You saw Lisa here that night and you didn't say anything to anyone?"

"I didn't want Brian to get in trouble."

"It could have made a big difference in the trial."

It probably would have made it worse.

"Mrs. Larson. Tell me what happened."

"The three of them. Brian, Claudia and Chad left. While they was gone, I seen Lisa walk up from the backyard and go in through the garage. Then Brian and them came back with the tree. There's going to be hell to pay, I think. That's the last I seen of her."

Burr made her repeat the story.

I can't believe it.

She started for the door again. Burr let her pass.

"Let me know if you see Pumpkin."

Burr nodded.

"Bye now."

Burr walked to the Jeep and turned off the engine.

I'm glad it didn't overheat.

He went back into the garage, opened the garage side door for the second time that night and flipped the light switch. The locket was at the edge of the floor drain. He picked it up and rubbed the gold where the *L* was. He opened it. Brian's picture smiled at him.

What really happened that night?

He unlocked the door to the house with the key he'd borrowed from Kaye. He stood on the landing at the top of the stairs and opened the door to the garage. He stepped into the garage and picked up an imaginary deer rifle.

I'm going to have another look in the basement.

He went down to the basement and walked over to the workbench. He held an imaginary rifle in his hands, then racked the imaginary gun. He set it down on the workbench and started to clean it with an imaginary rag.

"The gun probably would point to the stairs."

He mounted the imaginary gun to his shoulder and aimed it where Claudia had been standing. He pulled the imaginary trigger.

"Bang." He set the imaginary gun down on the workbench. "It could have happened that way. But if that's what happened, it is murder. Unless ..."

Burr got on his hands and knees at the foot of the stairs. He ran his hands over the fieldstones' cold, smooth surfaces, smooth except for the spot where the bullet had struck the granite after passing through Claudia.

He smelled smoke.

Where's that coming from?

He could taste it. He ran up the stairs. It was leaking under the door and burned his eyes. He tried the door, but it was locked. The doorknob burned the palm of his hand. He tried the door with his shoulder, but it wouldn't give. He could feel the heat from the other side of the door.

Fire. The house was on fire.

How did that happen? When did it start?

He crashed into the door again, but it wouldn't budge. The smoke began to pour underneath the door. He couldn't breathe, so he ran back down the stairs. The fire above him hissed like a snake. The house groaned. Smoke poured under the door and drifted down through the floor.

Brian's house is going to fall down on me. If the smoke doesn't kill me first.

Burr found a hammer and screwdriver, wrapped a rag over his nose and mouth and started up the stairs. The smoke and the heat drove him back down.

The fire department should be here any minute. Mrs. Larson or one of the other neighbors must have called by now. They'll see my Jeep in the driveway and come get me. If they can get in.

The basement was filling up with smoke. Burr couldn't breathe.

He fell to his knees and covered his mouth and nose with his coat.

I'm going to die here unless I can find a way out.

The floor joists creaked. The floor sagged, then broke open. He saw the fire above him. The floor joists gave and part of the floor fell into the basement. He backed up, tripped and fell backward.

The air was sweet here. Where was it coming from? Where was he? He stood up. He was in the doorway of the coal room, the old coal room. He rushed to the sweet air. It was coming from the boarded-up coal chute. He stood underneath it and filled his lungs. The fire was sucking in fresh air from the chute and stoking the flames.

At least I can breathe.

Burr pushed on the boards, but they were above his head and he couldn't get any leverage.

He crawled back to the workbench on his hands and knees. He pushed it up against the wall below the chute. He climbed on top of it, lay on his back and kicked at the boards. Nothing. The floor above him was so hot it was going to burst into flames.

He kicked again. Nothing. Behind him, the dried paint in the roller pan caught fire. Flames shot into the coal room. Burr kicked more at the boards, but they still wouldn't give. He kicked again and again. One of the boards cracked. He kicked again and it gave way. He could see outside, but the fire was in the coal room now, right behind him. He kicked again, and another board broke. He clawed it out of his way and dragged himself out of the burning house.

***

The fire department arrived just after Burr moved his Jeep onto the street.

Suzanne showed up just after the fire trucks. Then Jacob, Eve, Kaye, Lisa, Truax, and Frieda. Stewart, too. Mrs. Larson, of course. They were all there. The whole dysfunctional lot of them watched Brian's house burn.

The fire department hosed down the neighbors' houses and the big sugar maple in the front yard. They hosed Brian's house, too, but it was too far gone. It would burn to the ground, and they all knew it. They all watched it go. All except Brian. It was his house, but he was in jail.

"I'm told you were the last one seen here," Truax said.

"Really?"

"I'm going to charge you with arson."

"Leave me alone," Burr said. "I've got some marshmallows to roast."

"After I get the warrant, shall I have you arrested at the Harbour Inn? The officers will be discreet and won't disturb your roommate. Ms. Fairchild, isn't it? Although I see your whole harem is here."

"Touché," Burr turned back to the fire. It blew a hot wind on his face. Kaye stood next to him in a long black wool coat.

"The coat suits you," Burr said.

"Thank you," Kaye said. "It goes well with my nightgown."

"There goes your listing."

"My listing. I hadn't even thought about it." Kaye put her hands in her pockets. "Do you have the locket?"

He put his hand in his pocket and made sure it was still there.

***

Burr sat in the lumpy upholstered chair in Jacob's room. It was two a.m., and Jacob was annoyed with Burr, again. Jacob sat up in bed in navy-blue pajamas with white piping.

"Someone's trying to kill you. You know that, don't you?"

"It's crossed my mind."

"First, your Jeep. Then your boat. Now the fire." He lit a joint. "But that's not why you're here.

Burr reached in his pocket, took out the locket and held it up.

"What's that?"

Burr told Jacob the story, from Kaye to Mrs. Larson to the fire.

"There are many ways that locket could have gotten in the drain. It doesn't mean a thing." Jacob sucked on his joint.

"What if it does?"

Jacob got out of bed and took the locket out of Burr's hand. "Even if this does matter, you've got at least two problems. First, there's the evidentiary chain."

I don't want to hear this.

"Who's to say that Kaye is the one who found it. Who's to say that she's had it all this time. And, most importantly, who's to say that she found it in the basement." Jacob sucked on his joint again. "Truax will eat you up on that."

"Second, you did a great job with the gun. Now you're going to start over with this silly locket. You have no idea how or when it got there, and it just makes Brian look worse. You'll undo all of the good you've done if you try to introduce this."

"What if the gun wasn't defective?" Burr said.

"This would just confuse the jury."

"I want the truth," Burr said.

"The truth stopped mattering a long time ago." Jacob dropped the locket back in Burr's hand.

***

Standing outside Suzanne's door, Burr remembered the *other thing* and how things had come apart.

How long has it been?

Three years. It had been a Tuesday three years ago. His night with Zeke-the-boy. They'd gone to Chuck E. Cheese in Eastland, not Burr's favorite, but at least they served beer. He may have had one more than he should have. He was going to say his good-byes at the front door, but Grace looked good in her tight jeans. He'd invited himself in to use the bathroom, then asked if he could put Zeke to bed. After that, he lingered over a glass of wine. One thing had led to another.

They'd been separated for over a year, and they both knew better.

When Burr walked out to his Jeep the next morning, Suzanne was parked in the driveway.

That was the other thing.

Burr, still standing in the hall in front of Suzanne's door, was about to knock. He shook his head and walked away.

CHAPTER TWENTY-THREE

Burr sat on the beach on Crooked Lake in the cover of a fallen spruce, his waders on over his suit, Zeke next to him. The decoys drifted in front of him.

A creek ran through a DNR hatchery, underneath US-31, then another two hundred yards to Crooked Lake. He'd set up where the mouth of the creek emptied into the lake. Not a particularly good spot, but it was only twenty minutes from the courthouse.

He'd been up all night for the first time in ... he couldn't remember when. He had a splitting headache but didn't know if it was from the fire, the lack of sleep or the locket. He had a thermos of coffee and a cream-filled long john with chocolate frosting. He took the long john from the bag, careful not to rub off any of the frosting. His hand began to shake. He grabbed his shaking hand by the wrist. Both hands shook. He lost his grip on the long john and it fell in the sand, frosting side down.

"Damn it all."

Zeke ate the long john.

"At least it didn't go to waste."

Burr lit a cigarette and looked out on Crooked Lake. It was even foggier now than it had been last night.

He thought he had it figured out, but it was too late to do anything about it. He couldn't start over, but he couldn't let it go. He felt around for the locket in the breast pocket of his suit coat, underneath his chest waders.

There was no wind, and the fog laid over him like a blanket. It would take a wind to blow it off or the sun to burn it off. It would be at least nine before that happened. He'd have to make up his mind by then. He heard wing beats and a soft call. He called back, softly. It was a hen mallard. She called again. He called again. Then he heard a flutter and a splash. He was sure she landed in his decoys, but he couldn't see her.

***

"The Honorable Judge Benjamin Gillis," Swede said. "All rise."

Feet shuffled. Chairs scuffed the floor. The bald judge appeared as if by magic.

"Be seated," the bailiff said.

More clothing and furniture noises.

"Gentlemen," Gillis said. "Your closing arguments, please."

"Mr. Truax," Gillis said.

"Yes, Your Honor," Truax said, standing. He walked to the jury. "Ladies and gentlemen, a life has been taken. We know that. We also know that the defendant killed his wife. He admits it." Truax pointed his long, bony finger at Brian.

I hate that finger.

Truax turned back to the jury. "This is about murder." He paused, then "Brian R. Dunn lured his wife to the basement of their home and deliberately shot his wife." He paused again. "With his son upstairs."

Truax droned on. And on.

He's taking too long.

The jury was tired. They were tired of it all, and they'd probably already made up their minds.

Burr tapped his pencil.

Truax droned on.

"Ladies and gentlemen, this is a very simple case. Brian Dunn killed his wife. The people of the State of Michigan submit to you that he did it on purpose. It was not an accident. The accused planned the murder. The laser evidence proves that he picked up the gun and fired it. He did it on purpose."

"Why did he do it? Because he was having an affair with that woman." Truax pointed his long, bony finger at Lisa.

Truax walked back to the jury. "Why? Because his wife wouldn't give him a divorce. As Father Yatchek told us yesterday. That's the why of it."

"And finally, Brian Dunn had a plan," Truax said. "First, he went downstairs and got the gun ready. Then he called his wife. His own son said so. Then he shot her. With his son upstairs. Can you imagine anything more terrible than a father killing his son's mother? With his son just a few feet away? Why would he do that?" Truax looked at the jurors one by one. "Brian Dunn wanted to make sure it looked like an accident. Can you imagine anything more horrible?"

The jury couldn't.

"Ladies and gentlemen, this is first-degree murder. An intentional killing with a plan. Can there be any doubt that the defendant killed his wife? No. Can there be any doubt he intended to do it? No. Can there be any doubt that he had a plan? No."

"Ladies and gentlemen, the people of the State of Michigan ask that you convict the defendant, Brian R. Dunn, of first-degree murder." Truax walked toward the defense table and pointed at Brian.

If he gets any closer, I'm going to break that finger.

"Thank you, Mr. Truax," Gillis said. "Mr. Lafayette?"

"May we have a moment, Your Honor?"

"You may have a moment that lasts no longer than one minute."

Burr took the locket from his pocket. He hid it in his fist. He stood up and leaned over the railing toward Lisa and Suzanne. He opened his fist. Burr felt their eyes on his hand. He looked at Suzanne, looking at his hand, no expression on her face. After a lie that had gone on for almost seven years, he didn't expect to learn much from her, and he didn't.

"What's that?" Lisa said. "What's that got to do with anything?"

"What are you doing?" Suzanne hissed at him.

"Mr. Lafayette, you are about to lose your opportunity to make your closing argument."

Suzanne grabbed at Burr's hand. He snatched it away. He caught her wrist with his free hand.

"What are you doing?" Suzanne said again, pleading this time.

"You will sit there and be quiet," Burr said under his breath.

"I will not."

Burr flung her hand away.

"Will this circus never end?" Gillis thumped his forehead.

Burr put the locket back in his pocket. He walked toward the jury. He pulled his cuffs down and straightened his tie.

"Ladies and gentlemen, it's an injustice that we're even here today. My client has spent almost a year in jail. He was not allowed bail. He was taken away from his family, from his wife and daughter." Burr looked over at Lisa.

Burr fished the locket out of his pocket again. He walked to the empty witness stand and set it on the railing where Gillis couldn't see it. Burr stood where Truax couldn't see it either but where Suzanne and Lisa had no choice but to see it. Burr turned to the jury.

I can feel Suzanne's eyes burning a hole in my back.

"Ladies and gentlemen, this is what happened, and this is why you must find Mr. Dunn not guilty. Mr. Dunn lent his deer rifle to Mr. Farr. Mr. Farr returned it. No one was home, so he left it in the garage. Where it stayed until the night that Mr. Dunn, his wife and son returned with their Christmas tree. They had cut their tree in the woods. A family tradition. Then the three of them decorated the tree, as a family, just like they always did.

"Mr. Dunn took the deer rifle to his workbench in the basement so he could clean it. And being a careful owner of firearms, he checked to make sure the gun was unloaded.

"Mrs. Dunn came downstairs while Brian was cleaning the gun. While he was cleaning it, the gun accidentally discharged, killing Mrs. Dunn. That is what occurred. It was a horrible tragedy, but a tragedy is not a murder. It was an accident.

"Why was it an accident? First, because the police determined it was an accident. The investigating officer, a man with over thirty years' experience, said so. The county coroner said so. An inquest was held and the judge at the inquest said it was an accident. This all occurred almost seven years ago, and it was ruled an accident then. What has changed in almost seven years?"

Burr looked at the jurors, one at a time. "Nothing. Nothing has changed.

"But the prosecutor would have us believe that Mr. Dunn killed his wife intentionally in his son's presence. Why would he have us believe that?" Burr walked toward Truax, "his political aspirations notwithstanding ..."

"Objection," Truax said.

"I withdraw the statement."

Damage done.

Burr looked back at the jurors. "The prosecutor claims he has new evidence. From a laser, of all things. He says that proves the gun was picked up and fired. Nonsense. The evidence just isn't there.

"What else does the prosecutor say? He says Mr. Dunn had an affair. He says Claudia wouldn't give him a divorce so Mr. Dunn killed her. Why does Mr. Truax say this?"

Burr looked at Truax, then back at the jury. "He says it because a few neighbors think Mr. Dunn might, I repeat, *might*, have had an affair. No one saw it. No one is sure."

I'm sure Brian had an affair, but that's for another day.

Burr walked toward the jury.

"None of this adds up. Why?" Burr put his hands in his pockets. "Suppose, just suppose, Mr. Dunn did want to marry Lisa. All he would have to do is file for a divorce. In Michigan, anyone who wants a divorce can get one. Mr. Dunn could have just filed for divorce. Why kill Claudia? Especially with your son upstairs."

Burr took his hands out of his pockets and put them on the railing of the jury box. "I don't understand why, after all this time, anyone would bring a charge like this."

Burr took a step back.

"Do you know why, after all this time, a murder charge should not be brought? Because evidence has a way of disappearing over time. In this case, the prosecution doesn't even have the gun. Can you imagine that? A murder case with no weapon? Mr. Truax cannot produce the gun that killed Mrs. Dunn. The only gun we have is the one introduced by the defense, and the expert witness says the gun that killed Mrs. Dunn may have been defective.

"It's one thing to pick up a gun, aim it at someone and fire. It's another thing if it goes off accidentally. But it's still another thing if the gun goes off because, even if you're careful, the gun doesn't work right. And that, ladies and gentlemen, is what we have here.

"And after all this time, people have trouble remembering what happened. Think about the inconsistencies in the testimony of the witnesses. Time has a way of fogging the memory.

"One more thing. Brian Dunn was never in trouble with the law before this tragic accident or after. Not once. Never.

"And let me ask you this. Is it so unusual for a man, a widower, to remarry and start a new family?

"This man," Burr said, now pointing toward Brian, "lost his dental practice. He lost his life here in Petoskey. He had to move away. He's spent the past twelve months in jail and may now lose his business. If you convict him, he'll spend the rest of his life in jail.

"Ladies and gentlemen, Brian Dunn is not a murderer. If anything, Brian Dunn is a victim. A tragic accident occurred a long time ago. It was terrible, but it was not murder. I ask you, ladies and gentlemen, do not convict Brian Dunn of murder. He is not guilty."

Burr walked back to the witness stand and slipped the locket back in his pocket. He walked back to his table and sat.

"Ladies and gentlemen," Gillis said. "In spite of what these two able advocates have argued, you have more choices than guilty of first-degree murder or not guilty because of accidental death. It is my job to instruct you in the various decisions you may make. It is your job to determine guilt or innocence of three crimes of which I will now instruct you. It is not your job to determine a sentence if you find guilt. That is my job.

"Your job is to determine guilt or innocence. Is that clear?"

They nodded at him.

Gillis picked up a book with jury instructions.

"The defendant is charged with the crime of first-degree premeditated murder. To prove this charge, the prosecutor must prove each of the following elements beyond a reasonable doubt:

"First, that the defendant caused the death of Claudia Dunn. That is ... that Claudia Dunn died as a result of a gunshot.

"Second, that the defendant intended to kill Claudia Dunn.

"Third, that the intent to kill was premeditated. That is ... thought out beforehand. That the killing was deliberate, which means the defendant considered the pros and cons of the killing, thought about it, and chose to kill."

Burr leaned toward Brian. "This is what Truax tried to prove."

"You may also consider the lesser charge of second-degree murder," Gillis said. "To prove this charge ..."

Burr turned to Brian. "For second-degree murder, you kill someone on purpose but without a plan. An intentional killing with no premeditation. You lost your temper and killed Claudia. No plan in advance."

"I didn't do that."

"I know you didn't."

"You may also consider the charge of involuntary manslaughter with a firearm," Gillis said. "This crime is an accidental death caused by the careless use of a firearm. To determine guilt you must find four elements. One, the defendant caused the death of Claudia Dunn. Two, the death resulted from the discharge of a firearm. Three, at the time the firearm went off, the defendant was pointing it at the deceased. Four, the defendant intended to point the firearm at the deceased."

"He is saying that you meant to point the gun at Claudia, but the gun went off accidentally."

"I didn't do that either," Brian said.

Burr didn't say anything.

"Are there any questions?" Gillis said. They shook their heads. "The bailiff will escort you to the jury room. Please ask him if there is anything you need. Remember, your verdict must be unanimous."

"Now what?" Brian said.

"Now we wait."

***

"You son of a bitch," Suzanne said. "Just who do you think you are? Who gave you the right to play with Brian's life because of your own ego." Suzanne spit the words at him like venom.

I've never seen her this mad.

Swede had given them a windowless room in the courthouse. Jacob, Eve, Lisa, and, of course, Suzanne. He'd known since last night that it would come to this. They sat at a long table, with Burr at one end and Suzanne at the other. There were cigarette burns on the table. Burr ran his fingers over them.

Smooth to the touch but black underneath.

"How dare you?" Suzanne said.

I hope I played it right.

He'd taken a chance with the locket. He had done it to shock Suzanne and Lisa and flush them out. If the jury, Truax or, worse yet, Gillis, had seen it, there would have been hell to pay. Burr wasn't entirely sure what was going on, and he really had no right, but he'd done it anyway.

He reached into his jacket pocket and took out the locket again. He held it between his right thumb and forefinger, then set it down on a burn mark, 'L' side up. Suzanne and Lisa stared at it but made no move to pick it up.

"Suzanne," he said. "How dare I? How dare you. And to you, the second Mrs. Dunn, the same thing. Only more so.

"I was taken in and played for a fool. There was no reason to hire me, of all people, to try this case. I knew that. I allowed myself to believe there were good reasons for it. I thought I could do it. And I think I did a pretty good job. The gun was genius on my part, and I think we pulled it off."

Burr looked at Suzanne "I thought maybe we could start over. Until I finally figured out you were lying to me about Brian and Lisa. You had nothing to do with my Jeep. But there's *Kismet*. When you went below to get your bag, did you open a through-hull just to spite me? Or did you mean to drown me because I was getting too close to the truth." Burr looked at Lisa then back at Suzanne. "Which one of you set the fire? Did you think I'd been as useful as I was going to be, and it was time to be done with me. Once and for all."

Burr picked up the locket and tapped it on the table.

"But ladies, the genius is truly yours. All you had to do was convince me there'd been a terrible injustice. Turn me loose and tease me with a second chance at love.

"You sent me on a fool's errand. Give me just enough rope. Don't tell me everything. Just enough. Lie a little when you need to. Enough to keep me going. But never, ever, tell me the whole truth.

"Suzanne, my dear, you spread your legs just enough and at just the right times to keep me believing. Yours is the grandest performance."

Suzanne stood. "I won't listen to another word."

"Sit down," Burr said.

She didn't.

"Sit." Burr stared at her. She stared back and kept standing, then she sat, slowly, like a dog who knew what it had been told to do but didn't want to do it.

"This is what really happened," Burr said. "Brian, as we all know, is a very nice man, but he's a coward. He wanted a divorce, but he was afraid to death of Claudia and too scared to do anything about it.

"Brian and Lisa have an affair. It heats up. Brian's getting laid so often he can't see straight." Burr looked at Lisa. "You were husband hunting." She didn't flinch.

"Your little plan was going perfectly ... except Claudia refused to give Brian a divorce, and he was too much of a coward to file.

"Then you turn up pregnant. So there you were. Pregnant and no husband to show for it. And no prospect of one because Brian won't file for divorce. Who wants to have a baby and no husband?"

Eve shook her head.

"The baby was going to be born too soon. That's why you moved away. It wasn't that there were no patients. It was the baby. Because the birth certificate says Becky was born in August, but you've always said it was the following June. Jacob found out when he went to Detroit. I thought Becky might be a bit big for her age. But she's not big for her age ... she's older than you claim she is. It just wouldn't work, would it, Lisa? Pregnant, with no husband."

"I'm not going to hear another word of this," Lisa said.

She stood.

"Sit down."

She sat.

"It all went so terribly wrong. Brian, Claudia and Chad were supposed to get their Christmas tree on Sunday because Claudia and Chad were supposed to be at the church on Saturday. Lisa, you came over on Saturday to have it out with Brian because you knew he'd be the only one home. But the plans got changed and they got their tree on Saturday instead. You got caught waiting for Brian and hid downstairs. The two of you had been careful never to be seen in public together, and you were careful to stay away from Brian's house. But you'd finally had enough.

"You saw Brian's rifle on the workbench. He'd made sure it was empty, but you put a shell in the chamber. How could you be so stupid?

"Brian came down to the basement and saw you there. He had no idea what to do. Then Claudia came down and saw you. She started screaming.

"I'm not sure how it happened. Either Brian picked up the rifle or you handed it to him. Which was it?"

Lisa didn't say a word.

"Brian screamed back at Claudia. He knew the gun was empty so he pointed it at Claudia. He took the safety off and pulled the trigger. He was sure it was empty, but it went off and killed her.

"Brian was in shock. You were scared to death. Brian called the police. You hid in the coal room until they left. No one thought to look for anyone down there. Why would they?"

"This is all lies," Lisa said.

"Or were you the one who shot Claudia?"

"I didn't. I swear I didn't."

"You were pregnant. You were desperate, and you were stupid."

"This is a horrible, horrible lie," Lisa screamed at him.

"Mrs. Larson saw you there that night." Burr picked up the locket. "When did you miss this?"

"You can't prove any of it," Lisa said.

"You were wearing the locket on a chain around your neck. Somehow, when Claudia was shot, the chain broke and the locket fell to the floor. You should have looked in the drain. Brian's real estate agent did."

"It's a lie and you know it," Lisa screamed at him again, louder this time.

"I might have some of it wrong, but I think I'm close," Burr said. "Which one of you set the fire? I'd like to think it was an accident, but after all this, I know better. Were you trying to destroy evidence, scare me, or kill me? Was I too close to the truth?

"I don't think you wanted Claudia dead. It just all went so wrong."

"You're lying. You made all this up." Lisa was still screaming but she was close to tears, too.

Burr put the locket back on the table and looked at Suzanne. "I don't know what you knew or when you knew it. I'd like to think it was after the fact, but I really don't know. You should have known better. You're a loyal sister, and I'm a true sucker."

"How can you let this happen to Brian? You've got to do something," Lisa said.

Burr looked at her. "Brian doesn't know what really happened. You never told him, did you," Burr said, not asking. He looked at Suzanne. "And you didn't either." He looked back at Lisa. "All you have to do is tell the truth. That's all. Tell Truax you put the shell in the gun. Then Brian is off."

Lisa looked down.

"But you can't do that, can you? Because then you're the one who's guilty of murder. And there's your daughter to think of. You must think it's better for Brian to take the heat. You already thought that through, didn't you?"

***

They were all in their places.

"Have you reached a verdict?" Gillis said.

"We have," the forewoman said.

"Defendant, please rise," Gillis said.

Brian stood, head down.

"On the charge of first-degree murder, how do you find the defendant?" Gillis said.

"Not guilty, Your Honor," the forewoman said.

"On the charge of second-degree murder."

"Not guilty, Your Honor."

"On the charge of involuntary manslaughter with a firearm."

"Guilty, Your Honor."

Brian looked up at the jury, then to Lisa. His chest heaved and he sat down.

"Stand up, Mr. Dunn," Gillis said.

Brian started to cry. Burr helped him to his feet.

Gillis turned back to the jury: "So say you one, so say you all?"

It sounds like a nursery rhyme.

"Yes," they said.

"Thank you." Gillis looked at Brian. "The court finds Brian R. Dunn guilty of involuntary manslaughter with a firearm. Mr. Dunn, you will be held in the county jail until," Gillis flipped through his papers, "until January 14, 1985, at which time you will be sentenced." He banged his gavel and stood.

"Your Honor," Burr said.

"What is it, Mr. Lafayette."

"May I address the court?"

"What is it this time?"

"Your Honor, the statute of limitations for involuntary manslaughter with a firearm is six years."

"I am aware of that," Gillis said.

"Your Honor, Mr. Dunn was charged after the statute had run."

Truax jumped to his feet. "That's not true, Your Honor. He was charged before the statute ran."

"Your Honor," Burr said, "As you may recall, the first arraignment was defective. Mr. Dunn was not properly charged until December 27th, 1983, ten days after the statute ran."

"That's not true, Your Honor," Truax said.

Gillis sat down and rifled through his papers. Then he looked over his glasses at the prosecutor.

"Mr. Truax, Claudia Dunn was killed on December 17, 1977. You first charged Brian R. Dunn with open murder on December 14, 1983. While that charge was within the statute of limitations, the Court of Appeals ruled that the charge was defective and dismissed the case. Brian R. Dunn was properly charged December 27, 1983, ten days after the statute ran."

"Your Honor," Truax said, "If that was the case, the defense had a duty to object to the jury instructions. He could not knowingly allow a charge that could not be carried out."

"Your Honor, the jury can convict my client of a crime," Burr said, "but there can be no sentence because the statute of limitations has run."

"Mr. Truax, I am afraid Mr. Lafayette is correct," Gillis looked at Brian. "Mr. Dunn, you either have a very fine lawyer or you are very, very lucky." Gillis shook his head. "Mr. Dunn, you are free to go." Gillis pointed at Truax, then Burr. "Approach the bench, both of you." The two lawyers stood in front of Gillis. He leaned forward and spoke quietly. "Calvin, do not, I repeat, do not ever, ever bring anything like this to my courtroom again."

"Your Honor, as county prosecutor, I have the responsibility ..."

"Stop right there. I said don't ever do this again. Is that clear?"

"Yes, Your Honor." Truax turned red.

Gillis turned to Burr. "As to you, Mr. Lafayette."

"Yes, Your Honor," Burr said.

"While I have come to appreciate your skills as a litigator, I would take it as a personal favor if you never appeared before me again."

"I'm sure that can be arranged, Your Honor."

Gillis looked out at the courtroom. "We are adjourned." He slammed down his gavel and left.

Truax stood at the prosecutor's table, his Adam's apple bobbing. He marched over to Burr and shook his hand. "My condolences, Mr. Lafayette."

"I beg your pardon."

"Your client was convicted."

"My client is a free man."

"On a technicality," Truax said, smiling. "On a technicality."

"You're an ass. An ambitious, manipulative, self-absorbed ass."

I know something about being self-absorbed.

Truax's Adam's apple bobbed.

"You were the one who ran me off the road. It's your white Riviera in the parking lot."

"My wife's, actually," Truax said. "My car wouldn't start."

Burr smiled.

The sugar worked.

"Why did you run me off the road?"

"I didn't know it was you," Truax said. "Until later. I just wanted to get by, and you were being stubborn about it. I had no idea you crashed until later."

"Why didn't you tell me?"

Truax shifted his weight from one foot to the other. "What good would that have done?"

"Your Oldsmobile may need a new engine."

"What?"

Burr ignored him. "I suspect that you got exactly what you wanted out of all this."

"I suspect I did." Truax went back to his table, picked up his papers and left the courtroom.

Brian wiped his tears with a sleeve. "I thought I was guilty."

"You are," Burr said.

"What happened," Jacob said, "is that your lawyer is half a step short of brilliant."

Lisa ran up and hugged her husband.

"What just happened?" Brian said again.

Jacob looked at Brian. "The law says that for certain crimes the defendant must be charged by a certain date. In the case of involuntary manslaughter with a firearm, within six years after the crime occurs."

"What does that mean?"

"It means that after all the delay back in December, after all the arguing and fighting, by the time Truax finally got you charged, it was too late for involuntary manslaughter," Jacob said. "But not for first- or second-degree murder. Those crimes don't have a statute of limitations."

Brian looked at Burr. "Did you know that all along?"

Burr took the locket out of his jacket pocket. He opened Brian's hand. "Ask Lisa about this." He dropped it in Brian's palm.

"You played with his life," Lisa said.

"You, madam, played with his life. Not me." He turned to go.

"Burr Lafayette," Suzanne said, "you're a liar and an arrogant fool."

He looked back at Suzanne. "And you're no angel."

Burr walked out of the courtroom, climbed into his Jeep and drove back to Crooked Lake with Zeke. He put his waders on over his suit and threw out the decoys.

THE END

Acknowledgements

To Ellen Jones for her copy editing, sage advice, encouragement and deciphering the scratchings on the yellow-pads that were my first draft.

To Mark Lewison for his copy editing, story editing, unflagging attention to detail, and especially for his enthusiasm.

To Nancy Anisfield, Jesse Melcher, Ellen Jones, Julie Spencer and Steve Spencer for reading the manuscript. They found countless factual, contextual and typographical errors.

To John Wickham for his cover design.

To Bob Deck at Mission Point Press for the book's interior design.

To Hart Cauchy at Mission Point Press for his enthusiasm, encouragement and all of his help with Amazon, Facebook and Instagram.

To Heather Shaw at Mission Point Press for her help with the cover design.

To Heather Shaw and Tricia Frey for all their help with publicity and marketing.

To Anne Stanton at Mission Point Press for her light-but-firm editing touch and for keeping me on schedule.

To Doug Weaver at Mission Point Press for his help with the cover and for his steady hand.

About the Author

Mr. Cutter is a recovering attorney. He lives with his wife, two dogs and four cats in East Lansing. He has a leaky sailboat in Harbor Springs and a leakier duck boat on Saginaw Bay. In addition to the Burr Lafayette series, Mr. Cutter has written screenplays and literary fiction. He is at work on the next Burr Lafayette mystery.

His books are available on Amazon and at your local bookstore.

For additional information, please go to www.CharlesCutter.com.

Also by Charles Cutter

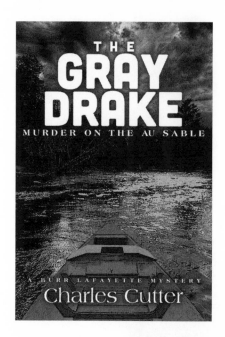

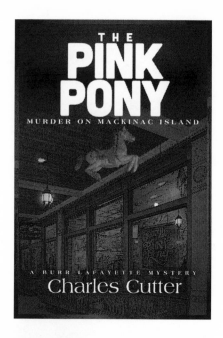

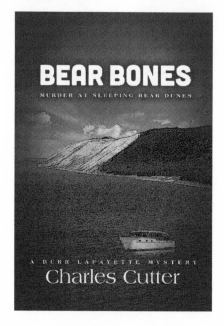

Made in the USA
Monee, IL
12 July 2021